PRAISE FOR
THE GREEK ISLANDS MYSTERIES

WHEN THE DEVIL'S IDLE

(Starred Review) "This classic fair-play whodunit, the excellent sequel to 2014's *The Devil Takes Half* (Serafim's first Greek Island mystery), takes Yiannis Patronas, the endearing chief police officer on the island of Chios, to Patmos, where someone has bashed in the skull of Walter Bechtel, a 90-year-old German, in the garden of his foster son Gunther's holiday residence—and carved a swastika on the victim's forehead. When Patronas asks Gunther about his foster father's past, Gunther becomes defensive and claims that his papa was 'just an ordinary man' and did not commit any atrocities during WWII. Serafim does an especially good job of integrating Greece's current financial struggles into the story line, and Patronas's colleagues, especially an eccentric priest with a taste for seafood, lighten what otherwise could have been a very grim tale without minimizing the underlying horror of the background to the crime."
—*Publishers Weekly*

4 Stars: "The pairing of cynical Patronas and optimistic Michalis injects some humor in an otherwise moderately paced procedural. Serafim expertly creates the beauty of Greece. However, the real draws of this book are the fully developed, complex characters, and the facts on Greek culture and history. Book two in the Greek Islands Mystery series is sure to satisfy."
—RT Magazine

"*When The Devil's Idle* is loaded with twists and turns and red herrings that will leave you guessing all the while you are flipping pages to find out what happens next. Ms. Serafim has provided us with a marvelous whodunit and I am already looking forward to the next book in the series."
—Vic's Media Room

THE DEVIL TAKES HALF

(Starred Review–Featured as a Best Sum~ prose is perfect for lovers of literary and sch~

is methodical and traditional, with subtle nods to Sherlock Holmes, Greek mythology, and historical events."
—Library Journal

"[An] impressive debut.... Serafim has a good eye for people and places, and sheds light on the centuries of violent passion that have created an oppressive atmosphere hanging over the sunny Greek landscape."
—Publishers Weekly

"The Greeks have a word for it, and in this fast-paced, delightful mystery, that word is murder.... The real buried treasure is pure pleasure in Serafim's debut novel."
—Mary Daheim, *New York Times* and *USA Today* bestselling author of the Alpine and Bed & Breakfast mystery series

"Whether it's police procedural genre convention, the exotic island landscape, or the passionate Greek character, Serafim knows the lay of the land, and she confidently guides the reader. Armchair adventurers will get a solid grounding in Greece's violent and tumultuous past. The quirky pairing of Patronas and Michalis has the makings of an unorthodox investigative team and the beginnings of a beautiful friendship. This immersive escapist mystery should put Serafim on the map."
—Kirkus Indie Reviews

"The Greek setting gives this book not only an exotic locale but also characters that have a different way of looking at life and often, motives that wouldn't exist if this happened in... Cleveland. Take a literary visit to Greece. You won't regret it!"
—Jodi Webb

WHEN THE DEVIL'S IDLE

WHEN THE DEVIL'S IDLE

A GREEK ISLANDS MYSTERY

LETA SERAFIM

coffeetownpress

Seattle, WA

coffeetownpress

Coffeetown Press
PO Box 70515
Seattle, WA 98127

For more information go to: www.coffeetownpress.com
www.letaserafim.com

Cover design by Sabrina Sun

ISBN: 978-1-60381-998-5 (Trade Paper)
ISBN: 978-1-60381-999-2 (eBook)

Library of Congress Control Number: 2015938969

Printed in the United States of America

For Philip

Also by the Author

The Devil Takes Half

Coming Soon

To Look on Death No More

Acknowledgments

———◆———

THE FOLLOWING PEOPLE were instrumental in the writing of this book. First and foremost, my husband, Philip Evangelos Serafim. Also my friends Dawn Lefakis, Stephanie Merakos, and Thalia Papageorgiou, my daughters and their husbands: Amalia Serafim and David Hartnagel, Annie and Yiannis Baltopoulos. I would also like to thank my precious grandchildren, Zoe and Grace Hartnagel and George Baltopoulos.

My thanks to all the people who have encouraged me to continue with the Greek Island Mystery series: my agent, Jeanie Loiacano, Jennifer McCord and Catherine Treadgold at Coffeetown Press, and my late parents, John and Ethel Naugle.

CHAPTER ONE

———◆———

An old enemy cannot become a friend.
—Greek Proverb

NIGHT WAS FAST approaching and the garden was half-hidden in shadows. The gardener unlocked the gate and quickly set about his evening's work, watering the roses first before moving on to the cypress trees at the periphery of the estate. The air was very still; the only sound, a flock of birds chattering by the fountain. The estate, cloistered on a hilltop and located in the village of Chora on the Greek island of Patmos, was well off the tourist trail. People rarely ventured there uninvited.

The gardener lingered by the fountain, enjoying the sound of the cascading water and the coolness it brought to the hot, late-summer air. He dipped his hand in the water and wiped his face.

Distracted, he didn't notice the wounded man at first, lying in a congealing pool of blood on the far side of the fountain. It was the birds that drew him. Crows, from the sound of them, far too many for this time of night.

His eyes open, the man lay sprawled on the ground, barely breathing. His hair was matted with blood and his forehead was carved with a swastika.

The gardener fell to his knees and screamed and screamed. He was far from the house, so no one heard his cries. Growing more and more desperate, he ran to the door and began pounding on it, crying for help. Eventually a woman answered. Pushing his way into the house, he demanded her cellphone and called the police. The station was located in the port of Skala, four kilometers away, the village of Chora being far too small to warrant its own station.

There was much shouting back and forth, given the poor connection, before the gardener finally yelled, "*Dolofonia!*" Murder.

At first the police dispatcher was skeptical and doubted the man's story, but the hysteria in the Albanian's voice finally convinced him to send someone, if only to lock him up in a padded cell.

A policeman named Evangelos Demos duly arrived on the scene.

It was, as he later told his former supervisor, Yiannis Patronas, exactly as the gardener described.

"Bloody?"

"Yes. One of the worst crime scenes I've ever seen." This was hardly significant. Evangelos Demos was no expert, having seen only one other crime scene in his life, a bloody mess on a beach. On that occasion he had fainted dead away, going down like a sequoia tree and vomiting as he went, contaminating every scrap of evidence. He was notorious among law enforcement officials in Greece, a legend almost.

"There was an old woman who pulled me aside as I was leaving the house. '*Prosehe*,' she said." Be careful.

Patronas had been at a taverna on the Greek island of Chios when the call came in, eating dinner with an elderly priest named Papa Michalis. The two were old friends and it was an idyllic evening. Far to the east, the moon was rising and he could see the dusky hills of Turkey across the narrow channel that divided the two countries, along with headlights of cars in the streets of Chesme.

Between them, the two had drunk nearly a liter of ouzo and were discussing the nature of evil, whether it was generated by humans or an independent entity. The priest, being a religious man, favored the latter view, quoting the Bible to bolster his case. " 'I saw Satan fall like lightning from heaven,' it says in the New Testament. 'For God spared not the angels that sinned, but cast them down to hell and delivered them into chains.' "

Patronas snorted. "So our troubles are caused by fallen angels?" As the Chief Officer of the Chios police, he'd seen plenty of the fallen and arrested more than a few of them, but he'd never encountered an angel. Not a single one in all his years on the force or in his tumultuous married life. Just the opposite in fact.

But the priest was not to be put off. "Fallen angels, the devil, call it what you will. There's too much evil in the world to be the work of man alone."

Patronas was later to recall that conversation. Papa Michalis had spoken the truth that night. Evil was indeed an entity and certain human beings embodied it, wore it like skin. He just hadn't realized it at the time.

When his phone rang, he hesitated, not wanting the evening to end.

"Chief Officer Patronas?" a man asked.

Patronas cursed, recognizing the tremulous whine of his former associate, Evangelos Demos. Fat and incompetent, he'd been forced out of the Chios Police Directorate after panicking during a stakeout and shooting up a herd of goats. It had been one of the worst nights of Patronas' career, Evangelos firing away with his service revolver and the goats falling, writhing, and shitting themselves as they bled to death. "Get rid of him," Patronas had told his superior at the time. "No living creature is safe while Evangelos Demos is on the job. He does harm just by breathing."

As usually happened, his superior in Athens, a self-serving bureaucrat named Haralambos Stathis, had ignored his warning and reassigned Evangelos Demos to Patmos. His duties there were few: overseeing the cruise ships that docked there and the hundreds of foreign tourists on holiday who inevitably drank too much and got into trouble.

"It's as far away as we can send him and still be on dry land," Stathis had told Patronas at the time. "Any farther east and he'll be policing fishes."

Pity the fishes.

"Why don't you just fire him?"

"His uncle is a representative from Sparta." This being Greece, it was a sufficient reason.

Ever the parade horse, his old colleague Evangelos Demos had become insufferable since being posted to Patmos, bragging about the celebrities he knew—Aga Khan and the like—who summered there. Although he'd been totally disgraced and his uncle had been forced to call in favors to save his career, Evangelos always spoke as if he expected to be listened to, prefacing every remark with '*na sou po'*—let me tell you—and pontificating as if he were king. This time was no exception.

Irritated, Patronas reached for his cigarettes. Just thinking about Evangelos made his blood boil. He wanted to hang up, but didn't dare. He was already considered a troublemaker, an outlaw, a rogue. No reason to make matters worse.

"There's a dead German here," Evangelos' voice dropped dramatically, "murdered."

Patronas puffed furiously on his cigarette. He needed to get a new phone, one with a screen that showed who was calling.

Homicide was rare in Greece, the murder of a foreigner, rarer still. After solving a case on Chios, he had become a celebrity of sorts among policemen and was often consulted by colleagues like Evangelos on difficult cases. Patronas didn't welcome the attention and wished they'd leave him alone. It had hardly been an achievement, that case on Chios, botched as it was from start to finish. Yes, he'd caught the killer, but it had been more by accident than design and only after the perpetrator had murdered three people and sliced him to ribbons. A rank amateur, he recognized his limitations. He only wished others did.

"I don't know where to start," Evangelos went on in an uncharacteristic burst of modesty.

"You said the victim was German?"

"That's right. Someone carved a swastika on his forehead."

"One of those skinheads? A tourist?"

Evangelos knew what Patronas was asking. Sometimes foreigners got into things, strange things better left alone. "No, the victim was an old man."

"How old?"

"Eight-nine, ninety. Old, old."

Patronas gave a low whistle. "Was it a robbery?"

"I don't think so. He was staying in Chora with his family, guests of an industrialist in Munich. A very powerful man. There's a bunch of them here now. Unlike us, they've got money to burn and bought up a bunch of old villas. Spend July and August there …."

The priest, who'd been listening, chuckled softly. "Summer, autumn, war." It was an old saying, dating from the time of the Spartans, on the inevitability of war, the enduring presence of one's enemies.

"Germans haven't made it to Chios," said Patronas.

"You're lucky," Evangelos said. "They're all over Patmos now. Couldn't get here with Hitler, so they bought their way in this time. Their weapon of choice, the Euro." His voice was bitter.

Patronas had heard similar complaints—Germans making themselves at home in places where they didn't belong. Ieropetra in Crete, for example, a village which suffered one of the bloodiest massacres of the war. The newcomers had no compunction about it, apparently, no sense that it was hallowed ground and they shouldn't trespass. Idly, he wondered what the Israelis would do if Germans turned up en masse in Tel Aviv, beach towels in hand, eager to buy property. Be interesting to see.

Hospitality was a Greek virtue and had been since ancient times. Guests were to be honored, given the best food, the last drop of wine. But what if they never left, those guests? Stayed on and bought houses and lived there beside you? What was the difference between a guest and the advance guard of an invading army? Patronas didn't know the answer. Wasn't sure there was one.

"You have to help me," Evangelos said. "I can't do this alone." There was something in his voice as he said this. Fear maybe.

"What about my job?" Patronas asked.

"I cleared it with Athens."

"I don't know if you know this, Evangelos, but I got a second job since you left Chios, overseeing the security on an archeological dig."

In addition to his police work, Patronas and a friend of his from the force, Giorgos Tembelos, worked part-time as guards on an excavation run by Harvard University. The job was easy and the pay was good. He'd be a fool to abandon it. Times were tough now in Greece. In spite of his twenty-two years on the force, he could be laid off at any time.

"Ask the Americans for a leave of absence," Evangelos said. "They'll give it to you."

A dead German, a man of uncertain vintage with varicose veins and a cane—not a case that stirred Patronas or cried out to him for justice.

"I don't know," he said. "Patmos is pretty far away."

"I'm afraid there might be more," Evangelos blurted out. Again, that note in his voice. "There are a lot of Germans here. I'm afraid this is only the beginning."

Patronas sat there, thinking. His country was hanging by a thread. Unsolved, a case like this could generate panic, keep tourists away. "All right," he said wearily. "I'll come."

Digging into his briefcase, he got out a notebook and pen. "Give me the details. Who found him?"

"The gardener. He said the old man was lying outside in a bathrobe and slippers."

"So he wasn't meeting someone?"

"No. He kept to himself. Liked to sit outside in the sun and listen to German music. Sometimes slept there in the afternoon."

Evangelos hesitated. "I thought it might be political," he said in a low voice.

Patronas smiled to himself. A Greek perspective, that one. Sooner or later, everything led back to politics.

"Our politics or theirs?" he asked.

"Theirs. Judging by the house, these people have a lot of money. Maybe it was someone from Germany, one of those leftists from the Baader-Meinhof gang or the Red Brigades."

"First, that was a long time ago and second, the Red Brigades weren't even German. They were Italian."

The priest continued to play, humming a few bars of the *Horst Wessel* song, the Nazi anthem, and breaking into song now and then, bellowing, "Millions are looking upon the swastika full of hope." A moment later, he shifted and began yodeling the words of *Deutschland Erwache*—another anthem from the war. He was very drunk.

To the swastika, devoted are we!
Hail our leader, hail Hitler to thee!

"What did the coroner say?" Patronas asked, motioning the priest to be quiet.

"We don't have a coroner on Patmos," Evangelos said. "A local doctor saw him."

"What did the doctor say?"

"That he was dead."

Patronas closed his eyes. He'd forgotten what Evangelos was like. A mosquito could outthink him.

"How long will it take you to get here?" Evangelos asked.

"I don't know. I'll have to fly to Athens first, then to Samos and from there catch a boat to Patmos. Twelve hours at least."

"Stathis doesn't want you to fly. By boat, he said, you and your men. Third class."

"More than twenty-four hours then. Midnight tomorrow at the earliest."

"I'll keep everything in place until you come."

With a sigh, Patronas closed his phone. A corpse in August, a day and a half gone. It wouldn't be pretty. Not to mention that the case was sure to have political repercussions, given the current antipathy between Greece and Germany, the sense among his fellow citizens that the Germans were bleeding them dry and finally achieving what they'd been denied during the war—the utter destruction of their country. He most fervently hoped the victim hadn't been attacked for that reason—that some crazed public employee, upset about the cuts to his salary, hadn't decided to avenge himself on an old man in pajamas.

The priest had heard every word. "I fear Satan is afoot in Greece once more," he mumbled, pouring out the last of the ouzo and drinking it down. "This killing is his handiwork, his calling card." He rambled on a bit. Something about how the devil had gotten loose in Greece once before, and that time he had been speaking German. Now it was the Germans themselves who were being killed.

"Some people would call that karma," Patronas said.

"Not me. I call it evil." Papa Michalis slammed his glass down. "Pure evil." He leaned across the table and clutched Patronas' arm. "Let me come with you. I studied on Patmos. I know people there."

"The people you know are priests, Father. It is unlikely one of them did this."

"The killer could be a priest. Who knows what a man of the cloth is capable of? Just look at America."

PACKING WAS NO problem. What Patronas needed, he stowed in a plastic shopping bag: underwear, a toothbrush, a comb he liked because it folded up.

After he left his wife, he'd taken to going to the Turkish baths when he needed a good cleaning, carrying his dirty clothes with him and laying them out on the stone bench and steaming them alongside his naked body. Ironing, however, remained a problem. He didn't dare discuss it with his ex-wife, Dimitra, since their leave-taking had been acrimonious. Scissors in hand, she'd been sewing when he'd told her he was moving out. Never one to hesitate, she had reached over and jabbed him in the calf, had threatened to castrate him if he didn't get out of her sight. In retrospect, he should have waited until she'd put the scissors down before telling her he'd had enough and was on his way. At least he'd escaped with his manhood intact and his intestines—no small thing, that. She was a praying mantis, his wife, an evil insect. If he'd let her, she would have drained him of his bodily fluids, bared her teeth, and chewed his legs off.

As it was, she'd gouged a gash in his calf that required eighteen stitches to close. He'd been on crutches for a month.

'Better to live with the devil than a mean woman,' the Greeks said, and it was true.

They'd separated after his last case, reconciled for a time, although Patronas' heart wasn't in it, and finally called it quits the previous winter. Their divorce had just come through and now he was free. The very thought of no more Dimitra made him feel lightheaded, and he danced around the room as he got ready, singing that paean to freedom, the national anthem of Greece, as he reached for his socks.

> Hail, oh hail, freedom.
> We know thee of old
> Oh, divinely restored
> By the lights of thine eyes
> And the swiftness of thy sword

He waved a sock around his head and slapped the dresser with it. He'd never fought the Turks. No, his war had been only with her, but by God he'd won it.

Before leaving for the house, Patronas called his second-in-command, Giorgos Tembelos, told him to pack up Papa Michalis, pour some coffee in him, and meet him at the harbor with a suitcase. "The three of us are going to Patmos. We'll be there for a while, so come prepared."

It was probably a mistake bringing Papa Michalis along, but he couldn't leave him in Chios, not drunk as he was and singing about Horst Wessel, a dead SS man. The bishop had been seeking to defrock the old man for ages. This would give him the ammunition he needed. He'd allege the priest was a Nazi and that would be that, when in fact Papa Michalis was just the opposite—a genuine war hero. He'd hidden people from the Gestapo and spirited them to safety—courageous deeds he rarely spoke of. He was a good man, a little flawed maybe—he couldn't hold his liquor, for one—but insightful and occasionally brilliant. Patronas trusted him with his life. It was an odd pairing, he knew, a priest and a cop, an atheist and a man of God, but somehow their partnership worked.

The year before, Patronas had hired him to work part-time in the department, counseling victims of domestic abuse, the drug-addled and an old fool who kept exposing himself, whipping it out and yelling 'hee haw' like a cowboy on a cattle drive. Papa Michalis wasn't very effective with the latter, who persisted in spite of the uproar it caused and the horror on the tourists' faces, but he worked hard and brought a level of decorum to the station. Tembelos and the other cops were less likely to pass around pornography and comment on it while he was present.

Addicted to television crime shows, the priest fancied himself a great detective and was always citing Miss Marple or worse, Hercule Poirot, whenever he and Patronas worked a case, even going so far as to refer to Inspector Clouseau on occasion, apparently unaware that the character from *The Pink Panther* was an incompetent buffoon. In addition, he had memorized *The Adventures of Sherlock Holmes* in its entirety, which he quoted almost as often as the Bible, the omniscience of God and the British detective having somehow gotten tangled up in his elderly mind.

"Holmes is a fictional character," Patronas kept telling him. "A figment of the author's imagination."

All to no avail. The priest's brain was a locked vault. Nothing got in.

Arterioskilrotikos. Thick-headed in the extreme.

Truth was, Patronas was fond of the old windbag. Papa Michalis might have mastered the basic vocabulary and techniques of police work, but he had absolutely no understanding of the forces that drove the darker side of human nature. Greed, lust, and anger were abstract concepts for him. Holy fool that he was, he believed everyone was good simply because he was.

Patronas had survived the last case in part because of Papa Michalis and his abiding faith in the goodness of people. If there was indeed an old man dead on Patmos, he'd be in need of his services again, crimes against the helpless being the hardest part of the job. Thankfully, he'd not seen much of it on Chios. But what he had seen had stayed with him, eaten into his soul like acid.

As THERE WERE no boats that connected Chios directly to Patmos, the journey necessitated going first by ferry to the port of Piraeus near Athens, then catching a second boat to Patmos for a lengthy ride across vast stretches of dark water. The boat was old and smelled of fresh paint. Judging by the sounds of the engine, it hadn't been overhauled in years. Another victim of the decaying Greek economy.

The inside of the cabin was hot and stuffy, dense with diesel fumes, and the boat creaked ominously as the crew lifted the anchor. Indifferent to the sound, Tembelos, a large shambling man with white hair, quickly settled down, closed his eyes and went to sleep while the priest, who was still a little drunk, continued to sing off-key. Eventually, he fell asleep, too, his wooly head on Tembelos' shoulder.

Patronas looked out the window. Soon he'd be back in the thick of it, examining a dead body and collecting evidence. The thought made him tired.

Restless, he got up and walked out onto the deck. The Aegean was a wondrous thing in the moonlight, the roiling water dark except where the light played across it. Not wine-dark, as Homer claimed, more the color of a summer sky at twilight.

A faint mist hung over the sea, magnifying the moonlight, and Patronas saw a school of fish close to the surface, tiny flecks of silver against the blue-black water. After the cabin, it felt good to be outside. He leaned over the railing and inhaled the briny air, droplets of spray stinging his face.

The strange thing about Patmos was the lights, he remembered. That shimmering crown of lights, so high they seemed to be part of the night sky, which appeared long before the actual island came into view. Patronas had never approached Patmos by day—the boat from Piraeus always docked after midnight—but the memory of those lights had stayed with him for years.

It was almost one a.m. when he caught the first glimpse of the lights.

As he'd expected, they disappeared for a time, only to reappear a few minutes later. Although he knew they were from a village high on a mountain and the mysterious lights that came and went were only streetlamps, they made him think of stars, a constellation of stars almost within reach.

He'd been to Patmos once before—on his honeymoon nearly twenty years ago. His new bride had been a pious woman and wanted to see the Monastery of St. John and its holy relics.

That boded ill for his marriage, although he'd not understood it at the time, had not understood that piety had little to do with kindness or compassion or love, that his wife, who'd kiss the bones of dead saints by the hundreds, would be more than a little reluctant when it came to kissing him. He didn't fault himself. He'd been twenty-two at the time, a policeman for less than six weeks, and under pressure from his widowed mother, who'd thought Dimitra would be their ticket out of poverty. There'd been other clues, but he hadn't read those either. Her voice, for one, which went off like a siren whenever he displeased her, or the way her jaw jutted out like a boar's when she was angry. Yes, there'd been plenty of signs. He should have seen it coming, but he hadn't.

He shook his head sadly. Who reads the cautionary notes the Almighty leaves for you at twenty-two, the modest hints that you might want to rethink your choices? Had Napoleon felt a chill as he was plotting the assault on Moscow? The German army as it approached Stalingrad? *We'd all be better off if God quit His hinting and used a bullhorn*, he thought. *Better yet, if He took up skywriting, spelled it out with flashing arrows: "Retreat! Retreat!"* Maybe Moses could decipher the message in the burning bush, but Patronas was sure if it had been up to him, he would have grabbed a bucket and thrown water on it.

St. John had written the Book of Revelation on Patmos, a vision of misery and doom if ever there was one, which just about described his honeymoon and the ensuing years of his marriage. *Ach*, what a fool he'd been.

A moment later the boat slowed to a standstill, shuddering as it turned toward Skala, the commercial port of Patmos. The wind gusted suddenly and the crew fought to secure the ropes on the quay. As far as the eye could see, the surface of the water was frothy, white in the moonlight.

As soon as the crew locked the gangplank into place, Patronas roused Tembelos and the priest, and the three of them exited the boat.

"Careful, Father." Patronas placed his hand on the priest's arm to steady him as they walked down the metal gangplank.

The propellers were still turning and the water beneath the ramp was a whirling vortex, swirling and eddying at their feet.

Evangelos Demos was waiting for them under a streetlight. He hadn't changed much since Patronas last saw him—a little grayer at the temples now, stouter and more walrus-like. He'd grown a mustache, too, a big one like Stalin's.

What is he thinking? Patronas wondered. *No one in his right mind wants to look like Stalin.* Perhaps Evangelos' politics had taken an ominous turn, Perhaps it was 'Comrade Demos' now.

"I appreciate your coming," Evangelos told him, reaching for his bag. "As a general rule, Patmos is very peaceful. A little shoplifting or public drunkenness, but little else of note. I must say this murder took us by surprise."

"Where's the body?" Patronas asked.

"Still at the scene. In Chora."

Patronas picked up his pace as he followed Evangelos Demos through the streets of Skala. The sun would be rising in less than three hours. They'd have to hurry if they wanted to bring out the body before the island awoke.

"Let's get started," he said.

CHAPTER TWO

———◆———

It has reached the ears of the gods.
—Greek Proverb

Aʟʟ ᴡᴀs ǫᴜɪᴇᴛ in the port of Skala. A lone Pakistani, hosing down the cement pavement in front of a shuttered coffeehouse, watched them approach with studied nonchalance, seemingly intent on his work. *Illegal*, Patronas judged, taking in the man's demeanor, his sweat-stained shirt, and cheap plastic flip flops. He greeted him in Greek and the man answered in kind, his tone friendly but careful. *"Hairetai, kyrie astifilaka."* Hello, Mr. Policeman.

Interesting, Patronas thought. *He knows the word for cop.*

He was struck by the man's presence on Patmos, an island in the farthest reaches of the Aegean and one of Christianity's holiest places. No doubt there were others like him here, all Muslim, all illegal, seeking work in a country that was almost bankrupt. It had taken him, a Greek policeman, nearly twenty-four hours to travel here, two lengthy boat rides and a significant wait in Piraeus, so how had this man come? Judging by his threadbare clothes, he had no money. So who'd smuggled him here and why? Some right-wing politicians alleged the recent influx of immigrants was a plot by Turkey to destabilize Greece. The Turks had been burning down Greek forests for years—every August, millions of trees went up—so why not this? Each immigrant who washed ashore, just another stick on the pyre.

He looked back at the immigrant. The man had put the hose aside and was talking to a young boy, dark-skinned like himself. The child waved at Patronas and called out *'Yeia sou.'* Hello.

Patronas called back with more enthusiasm than he felt. *"Yeia sou, paidi mou."* Hello, my child. Sometimes he didn't recognize his own country.

Evangelos Demos pointedly ignored the pair. "If the government doesn't do something, and do it quick, we're going to be overrun by these people, outnumbered in our own country."

Not 'Comrade' Demos, Patronas decided, one of those fascists in the political party, the Golden Dawn, who had declared war on the immigrants and were always beating them up.

"Most of them Pakistani?" Patronas asked.

"They're from all over—Albania, Africa—you name it, they're here."

"How many?

"Who keeps track? This is a way station, a stop on the way to somewhere else. People come, people go."

On a side street, the Pantelis Taverna was exactly as Patronas remembered it, as was the ocher-colored façade of the Arion Bar with its large portico and paneled interior. The blue cement fountain still stood at the center of the cobbled square, dry now as it had been on his honeymoon. But for the most part, Patmos wore a different face. The stores that had once sold duty-free umbrellas and liquor were all gone, replaced by upscale dress shops. A group of sleepy looking tourists were standing at the taxi stand, waiting to be ferried to their hotels, their suitcases piled up next to them.

Seeing the cellphones the tourists were consulting, the iPads and God knows what else, Patronas shook his head.

Once people had only needed food and water when they went on vacation, a towel to dry themselves after they swam. Now it was every kind of electronic device, as if sand and sunlight weren't enough, as if the sea itself, mother to us all, held no glory.

The police station was located on the top floor of a castle-like building overlooking the harbor. Its tower with its sculpted frieze was one of the abiding symbols of Patmos. The exterior of the building was outlined in brightly lit bulbs, giving it a fairytale aspect, a sense of playfulness at odds with its mission. Three police motorcycles were parked in front. A small force, but larger than Patronas had expected.

In spite of the hour, a pretty young woman in a uniform was sitting behind the front desk. Two Pakistani men were arguing with her in broken Greek, gesturing with their hands in an effort to be understood.

"You have to rent a room or leave the island," she told them. "You can't just flop down on the beach like a pair of dogs and sleep." She made no effort to hide her contempt.

Patronas had been surprised to see her—the force on Chios was resoundingly male—and he listened to the exchange with a sinking heart. The young female officer was nothing special. Just one more recruit for the Golden Dawn. She wanted the immigrants gone from her country. Women, men, it was all the same now in Greece.

Evangelos picked up the Tyvek suits and booties he'd set aside for them and a box of forensic supplies, an ancient fingerprinting kit and two spray cans of the blood-detector, Luminol, the labels yellow with age.

Idly, Patronas wondered what kind of murder book Evangelos was keeping, if he was using a quill pen to make his entries. Modern technology like so much else, had simply passed him by.

Well-acquainted with their colleague's methods, Patronas and Tembelos had brought their own gear from Chios, and seeing the rusting cans of Luminol, Patronas was glad now they had.

The police car was located in a back alley. An elderly Jeep Cherokee, it was a veritable tank compared to the other cars on the road, the Suzukis and tiny Fiats.

Patronas had assumed Evangelos would speed up once they got underway, but he continued on at the same steady pace, peering over the steering wheel and taking each turn with great deliberation. Less than ten kilometers an hour they were traveling. It was embarrassing. A bicyclist could pass them.

Growing more and more impatient, he drummed his fingers on the armrest. It wasn't a tank he was in, it was a boat, and Evangelos was rowing it. The corpse would be decomposed by the time they got there.

As part of his master plan, he'd insisted the priest sit in the front with Evangelos, saying it would be more comfortable for him.

Excited by the case, Papa Michalis was all wound up and ready to go. Let Evangelos deal with him now. Death by talking.

As expected, Papa Michalis started right in, discussing the victim's German origins and that country's tortured political history. Then he moved on to the strange and varied cuisine of that land, which according to him was based largely on pig in all its unholy manifestations—head cheese being a prime example.

"A terrine of jellied meat. It's easy to make. First you remove the whiskers from the jowls of the pig; then you split its skull and remove the eyeballs. It's probably a good idea to remove the wax from the ears, too, before you get down to boiling it ...."

Patronas rolled his eyes. He'd sampled Papa Michalis' cooking, a lengthy meal he still regretted. From what he'd seen, pig jowls were right up his alley.

Next the priest spoke eloquently of Martin Luther and the problems he'd had with his bowels and how they led to the Protestant Reformation—Germans as a rule suffering greatly from constipation.

It was easy to follow his train of thought. First a man eats and then a man ... or in Martin Luther's case at least, a man tries to.

"What about World War II?" Patronas asked, deciding enough was enough. "Was constipation the cause of that, too? Not enough prunes in Berlin, you're saying?"

The priest laughed good-naturedly, going along with the joke. "No, the Nazis had much more serious problems than that."

"Such as?"

"Well, for one thing, they were all psychopaths."

The size of the car necessitated taking a roundabout route out of Skala—a bumpy, unpaved road used by construction vehicles. They entered the main road a few minutes later and slowly wound their way up the mountain, passing the Patmian School, a Greek Orthodox seminary, and the Cave of the Apocalypse, a World Heritage Site where St. John had heard the trumpet of the Lord and written the Book of Revelation. The air smelled of pine, a thin forest covering the land above and below the cave.

A second World Heritage Site, the Monastery of St. John the Theologian, dominated the landscape. From the very top of the mountain, it resembled a storybook castle, its crenellated towers and walls so vast, they could be seen far out to sea.

The village of Chora, where the German had been murdered, lay at the base of the monastery.

Patronas was surprised to see two flags flying in front of the city hall where they parked the car, the yellow and black banner of the Orthodox Church with its two-headed eagle and the blue and white flag of the modern Greek state. The pairing was unusual and indicated that areas of the village were under the direction of the Patriarch in Constantinople. Not quite like Vatican City, but similar. Patronas hoped the duality would not impede his investigation. Dealing with the government in Athens was hard enough. Petitioning the holy fathers in Constantinople for anything would be a nightmare.

The wind was fierce and it thrashed the leaves of the eucalyptus trees along the road. A flock of black and white swallows, *xelidoni*, were circling high overhead, their cries faint against the wind.

Initially, Patronas had wanted to stop for coffee, but he decided against it. *Victim's been dead a while*, he told himself. *We'd best keep moving.*

He and Tembelos quickly unloaded their equipment and followed Evangelos Demos through the village—Patronas lugging a forensic kit of his own devising and Tembelos, the camera and plastic body bag. Evangelos said he'd already done the preliminary work at the crime scene, stringing up yellow police tape and hanging a tarp over the victim

"You need anything else," he told Patronas, "we can bring it from Skala."

A cloistered labyrinth, Chora reminded Patronas of the medieval towns on his native Chios. There was little visible evidence of the wealth its inhabitants supposedly possessed, only an impenetrable maze of stone walls and arched passageways. Here and there, he caught a glimpse of a courtyard or old-fashioned television antenna, but for the most part all was hidden. Unlike the other Greek villages he'd seen, there was no laundry hanging from the balconies, no plastic jugs under the eaves to collect rain water. All was quiet, the only sound, the relentless drone of the wind. Maybe it was the hour, but the village felt deserted.

Evangelos Demos confided that since the rich Europeans had come and bought up most of the houses, the actual Greek town had withered away. Seeing their opportunity, most of the residents had sold out; the ones who lingered now were isolated and alone, elderly people with no place else to go. "You should see it in winter. It's a ghost town."

The monastery was omnipresent, its gray bulk like a man-made massif towering over the houses of the village.

Although it was still very early, a waiter was setting up tables in the square. Music could be heard seeping from a nearby bar—something in English with a driving metallic beat. Someone was already inside, a maid perhaps, readying the place for the day's onslaught of tourists.

Few places played Greek music anymore, Patronas thought glumly. His culture was vanishing; the young wanted no part of it.

The owner of a taverna, in an apron, was sitting outside. He rose to his feet when he saw them and began questioning Evangelos Demos about the murder, the specifics of what had been done to the German. Two old men playing a game of *tavli*, backgammon, nearby stopped their game to listen.

Patronas wondered how the taverna owner had learned the news so quickly, who might have told him. Not the family of the dead man, that was for sure. No, the language difference would have precluded that. Perhaps Evangelos Demos had said something; he'd have to check.

Mentally, he made a list of things to do. As soon as he was done inspecting the crime scene and the victim, he'd come back to interview the two *tavli* players. Pensioners, they'd be only too happy to put their game aside and gossip. Perhaps they'd seen something, someone passing through Chora the previous night, or overheard an argument in one of the houses. Could be this was a domestic matter—the old man killed by a relative as sometimes happened. Fights sound the same in any language. Even if the *tavli* players didn't understand German, they'd know a fight if they heard one. At the very least, they could tell him who belonged in this sequestered world and who'd spread the news about the killing.

"The crime scene is southwest of the village," Evangelos Demos said, "just below the church of Profitis Elias, the highest point of land on the island."

As with many of the estates on Chora, the garden where the victim had been found was enclosed by thick stone walls. There appeared to be only one entrance, a metal door with a tiny, barred window.

The wind increased in intensity as they approached the door, ruffling their clothes and threatening to pull them off the hill. They were at the highest point of land in Patmos, walking along the curving spine of rock that defined the island like the skeletal underpinnings of a great fish.

The sun had risen and the sky was already white with heat. The priest was exhausted and had to be helped along by Tembelos. His black robe dragged in the dust.

Pulling out a handkerchief, Patronas mopped his brow. He wished he'd thought to bring water.

He looked back the way they'd come. Reaching as far as the eye could see, the Aegean Sea dominated the view, its surface gleaming in the sunlight. A Greek fishing boat was making its way into the harbor, its red hull bright against the water. He counted off the islands in the distance—Lipsoi, Arkoi, Marathi. No wonder the Germans had chosen this site. He was so high, he felt as if he could see the very curve of the earth.

The area around the estate appeared to be deserted, an arid wasteland used mainly to graze animals. Save for Profitas Elias and a few buildings along the road, there was nothing. A herd of goats was standing in the shadow of a withered olive tree, their bells tinkling softly in the wind.

An old woman in black opened the metal door, bowing slightly when she saw them, her face grim. Taking a step back, she gestured for them to enter.

The grounds of the estate were extensive—more than four *stremata*, or acres, Patronas estimated—and densely planted with trees. After the glare of the sun, it took him a few minutes to adjust to the gloom, the sense of being in a forest, albeit man-made. Although he could hear the wind outside, inside everything was peaceful and smelled faintly of flowers, although another odor kept breaking through, a far uglier scent. There was a fountain at the center of the garden, decorated by a life-sized statue of a child playing a flute. The corpse was on the the pavement beneath it. The statue seemed grotesque, given the circumstances, as if it were serenading the dead man.

The victim was lying on his back in a puddle of pink, scummy water, his sightless blue eyes staring into space. Flies were crawling all over his body, their buzzing loud in the quiet, and there was water everywhere. It had mixed in with the blood, thin rivulets of it running down and soaking the stones of the terrace.

Seeking to evaluate the scene, Patronas studied the fountain and the garden beyond. The exterior walls were at least two and a half, maybe even three meters high, certainly higher than a man could reach. He wondered how the killer got in, if he'd used a ladder. Could be this was an inside job.

Evangelos told him everything he knew, which wasn't much. Usually the gardener came in the evening to water the flowers and had duly arrived on the night in question. He'd seen the man lying there, hurried to investigate and slipped on the blood.

Patronas could see his footprints now, circling around the body.

"What time was this?" he asked.

"Eight, eight thirty p.m. The victim was still alive then. He died immediately after."

Contrary to what Evangelos had originally told him, there'd been a significant time lapse between the phone call to the station and his arrival on the scene.

"The man who reported it, the gardener, is foreign. '*Nekros ilikiomenos anthropos*,' he kept saying." Old dead man. "Also, there was a lot of yelling in the background, which made it hard to hear. To make a long story short, the dispatcher misunderstood him. He assumed the victim had died of natural causes and that the family wanted a hearse. It took me some time to get things straightened out."

"When did you realize he'd been murdered?"

"Around nine thirty, maybe ten. I called you right after."

Here, there, everywhere … incompetence. Even if the man had died of natural causes, Evangelos should have come to the house the minute he heard, coroner in tow, inspected the body and signed off on it.

"As far as I know, no one has been murdered on Patmos since the war," Evangelos went on, his tone defensive. "My staff is inexperienced. Aside from this incident, Patmos is a pretty safe place."

"Oh, yeah," Giorgos Tembelos said sarcastically, "aside from *this*."

He'd been there the night of the shoot-out on Chios and helped Patronas gather up the dead goats and bury them. "*Axthos epi gis*," he'd called Evangelos Demos forever after. A burden to the earth.

As Evangelos had said, tape was strung up around the crime scene, and there was a tarp suspended from the trees high above the body. Although the garden was shady, the victim was out in the open on the paved terrace. The square of canvas had been a good idea, offering a measure of protection against the sun.

Evangelos assured Patronas the victim was just as the gardener had found him. "It being August, we did our best to keep him cool."

That explained where the water had come from. The idiot had packed the body in ice—so much for forensics.

"It kept melting and I had to get more and dump it on him. I must have unloaded fifty kilos." The whine was back in his voice.

Patronas waved him off. "Where's the family?"

"Inside."

Getting out his notebook, Patronas scribbled some notes. After suiting up in his Tyvek gear, he knelt down next to the corpse and studied it closely. He noticed a tawny residue near the victim's feet and dug up a piece of it with his scalpel and placed it in an evidence bag.

Curious, he sniffed the open bag and passed it over to Tembelos.

"What do you think?"

"Tallow," Tembelos said.

Patronas nodded. Someone had been burning candles.

Every church in Greece had tallow candles in the narthex; the pious lit them when they entered as part of the ritual. Perhaps a Greek had indeed been involved.

Also, what looked like flower petals were scattered along the length of the body, a mixture of carnations and purple blossoms, lilacs maybe, although it wasn't the season. Not many, but enough.

Spooked, he looked back at the house. "You interview the family?"

"Not yet," Evangelos Demos said. "I was waiting for you."

"What did the coroner say?"

"I told you, we don't have a coroner. A local doctor fills in, a recent graduate of medical school doing his *agrotiko*, two-year service in the countryside. He was here earlier, said whoever did it shattered his skull."

Patronas didn't like where this was going. "Did he have any idea what was used?"

"No. We searched the area, but we didn't find anything."

"You're sure nobody touched the body?"

"Only the doctor. I swear, and me with the ice. It's just the way the gardener found it."

Patronas and his team quickly went to work. Tembelos marked off the crime scene with chalk and took photographs, while Patronas sketched the location of the body and noted its proximity to the house, calling out measurements to the priest, who entered everything in a large spiral notebook.

"The murder book," the priest called it, saying the words with reverence; homicide in all its various manifestations was a serious business.

"I know it seems unlikely," he'd once told Patronas, "but the Bible was the first murder book. Cain and Abel. Humanity hasn't changed much since it was written. Brother against brother, man against man. According to biologists, the species we are most closely related to—share ninety-nine percent of our DNA with—is the chimpanzee, the only other creature on earth that wars needlessly against its own kind, that kills for pleasure, for sport."

Evangelos was standing off to one side, watching Patronas work.

A large man, he was packed tightly into his Tyvek suit and booties. An astronaut with elephantitis.

"The pattern of the blood splatter is intriguing," Patronas said, looking over at him. "It ran down the back of his neck first, and then it went everywhere. I think we can assume the killer hit him in the back of the head, the blow weakening his skull until it shattered like a piece of glass. If you look carefully, you'll see where brain matter leaked out onto the pavement." He pointed to a smeary area on the ground.

Raising his hands over his head, he demonstrated how the killer had gone after the old man. "The first blow probably killed him. But the murderer just kept going, as if trying to obliterate him, erase him from the face of the earth. Man must have hated him."

Tembelos was still taking pictures. "Might have been a woman," he said.

Patronas raised his eyebrows. "Equal opportunity for murderers, Giorgos? Since when did you become such a feminist?"

"I'm just saying we need to keep an open mind." Tembelos mopped his face with his sleeve. "You about done? Sun's up. We should get the body out of here."

"Give me fifteen more minutes."

Patronas tested the limbs for rigor and took the victim's temperature, then gathered up the petals and bagged them. Given the copious amounts of watery liquid, he thought at first the victim might have been stabbed too, but on closer inspection he saw the damage to the skull was extensive; the river of blood had begun and ended there.

Seizing the victim's chin, he turned the man's head toward him. In addition to the swastika, the German had other scars. There were three of them, orderly and nearly uniform in depth. The biggest, five to six centimeters long, ran the length of the jaw bone. A much smaller one marked the bridge of the nose, and the third extended from the victim's mouth almost to his ear, making him look cartoonish, as if smiling even in the rictus of death. They looked to be very old—the scar tissue faded with age—unlike the sticky wound on his forehead.

Patronas asked Tembelos to take a close-up photograph of the victim's face and wrote a note to himself about the location of the three scars, thinking he'd send the information to police headquarters in Athens, see what the forensics people could tell him. Perhaps the German had been hurt during the war and medics had botched the surgery. The scars had that kind of look, as if someone had sought to repair his face and hadn't fitted the damaged parts back together properly.

He'd been a heavy-set man, and in spite of his advanced age, exuded strength. Although he'd been dead for over thirty hours, putrefaction had only just begun, the swelling in the abdominal region barely visible.

Opening the victim's robe, Patronas was startled to see he was naked, his scrotum distended in death, the thick gray hair around his genitals like the fur of a wolf.

Patronas got to his feet, thinking there were too many mysteries here. He should send the body to forensic specialists and let them deal with it.

"Why bother killing someone this old?" Tembelos asked, stepping around the corpse. "Why not wait a couple of years and let God take him?"

That, of course, was the question.

CHAPTER THREE

———— ◆ ————

Let us all get organized, so that you can go.
—Greek Proverb

THE DRIVER OF the hearse said the estate was too remote, that he'd never be able to bring his vehicle close enough to wheel a gurney in. "If you get the body down to the road, I can take over."

Patronas had been afraid the hearse would attract too much attention and was relieved they'd be removing the body themselves. Greek hearse drivers, in an uproar over increased road taxes, had held a recent protest drive in Athens, claiming the extra tolls would put them out of business. The photos in the newspapers had been chilling—hundreds of empty hearses parked in front of Parliament—death and taxes, all in one place. The driver on Patmos was sure to have an opinion and he didn't want to hear it, not today, not with a corpse lying outside in the heat.

Initially, he'd wanted to interview the family before transporting the victim, but it had taken him over thirty odd hours to get to Patmos and they'd had plenty of time to get their stories straight. Another hour or two wouldn't make any difference. The day was already hot and would only get hotter. The body had to be dealt with.

The family had emerged from the house at one point, a man and woman, a teenage girl, and a boy of about seven. The boy had a bandage over one eye. The children were visibly distraught, the girl especially, leaning against her mother and sobbing.

"The victim, who was he related to?" Patronas asked Evangelos.

"Him." Evangelos pointed at the man.

Approaching the family, Patronas introduced himself. "I'm Chief Officer Yiannis Patronas of the Chios police," he told them. "This is my second-in-command, Giorgos Tembelos, and my associate, Papa Michalis. You've already met Evangelos Demos."

He said this in English, doubting a summer visitor would understand Greek. His was a complicated tongue, and in his experience, few foreigners ever mastered it.

"Gunther Bechtel," the man said, introducing himself in turn. "How do you wish to proceed?"

"I will need to talk to each of you."

Bechtel frowned. "Everyone? The children, too?"

"That is correct."

Since his last case, Patronas had been working to improve his English. Overseeing security on the archeological dig on Chios had helped—for the most part, the crew was American—as did watching television with Papa Michalis, who tuned in regularly to British and American detective shows. Patronas understood most of what was being said now, but he still felt self-conscious when he spoke, painfully aware of his poor pronounciation and grade school vocabulary.

Bechtel walked over to where they'd been working and stood, looking down at the body. "What about my ...." He made a helpless gesture in the direction of the corpse. "What about my papa?" Overcome, he started to cry.

He reached for his wife and held onto her as if his legs could no longer support him. *"Papa!"* he sobbed. *"Papa!"* He said something else in German, his voice ragged with grief.

Bechtel wept for a long time, his wife comforting him. It was a pitiful sound, a meowing almost, and Patronas longed for him to stop.

He didn't try to console him, knowing if the circumstances had been reversed, he would not have welcomed the sympathy of a policeman. No, he'd have been irritated. The loss of a parent is a grievous wound. The murder of one? The pain had to be insurmountable.

Gunther Bechtel eventually pulled himself together and took a deep breath. "With your permission," he said quietly, returning to English. "I would like to take the body back to Germany and bury him beside my father and mother."

"Unfortunately we must send him to Athens first. I'm sorry, but it's customary in a case like this. After that, you can arrange to transport him back to Germany."

The man gave a curt nod. "Very well, then. We will remain here and wait."

And with that, he excused himself by saying he had to send some emails, and went back inside the house. The rest of his family trailed after him. The woman kept looking back at them. Unlike her children and husband, she appeared to be dry-eyed.

Being a Greek, Patronas found their behavior unsettling. *Maybe that's how they grieve in Germany*, he told himself. *They cry themselves out and return to their computers.* Maybe it was all the wars that had made them that way. It didn't matter that they'd caused it all; they'd still suffered. He recalled how Dresden had looked after the bombing, the mountains of burning ash. Maybe when a person's country becomes a vast cemetery and death is all around, it doesn't affect you as much. Maybe that's how you survive—unlike his people, the Greeks, with their black clothes and theatrical mourning.

After his father died, his mother had worn mourning the rest of her life, held memorial services every year on the date as was the custom, crying always when she spoke of it as if her heart would break, as if it had just happened. It had been hard growing up in her house, a child in that world of sorrow.

Still, Patronas questioned the Germans' reaction. The man and his wife were too young to have any memory of the war. Judging by the house in Chora, they were rich, had suffered no deprivation. So what was he seeing? Surely the man would miss his father, regret his passing, his violent end? After all, he'd lived with them. But Patronas had seen little evidence of that other than Bechtel's initial tears. This was a murder, after all. Yet there'd been no demand for justice, no crazed talk of vengeance. Though obviously anguished, Gunther Bechtel had also seemed resigned, almost as if he'd been expecting this.

The woman who'd let them into the garden stood in the doorway, watching them furtively. Not a member of the family, Patronas judged, noting the shabby clothes, the apron. A servant, perhaps.

"Who's that?" he asked Evangelos Demos, nodding in her direction.

"The housekeeper."

"She from around here?"

"No, northern Greece. Epirus, I think."

"Epirus? How did she end up here?"

"I don't know. Maybe she met them in Germany and they brought her here."

In the old days, Greeks from rural villages had immigrated to Germany—the men to work in the automobile factories, the women as maids, any job they could find. Patronas wondered if this woman had been part of that migration or if her move to northern Europe had been more recent. His cousin's daughter had just left for Hamburg, and others he knew would soon follow. His people were on the move again, leaving their homeland in search of work.

"I think this is her first summer working in Chora," Evangelos said. "You'll have to ask her. Her name's Maria Georgiou, *Kyria Maria*. She keeps to herself."

Patronas put a star next to her name. A Greek. He'd be able to converse with her in his native tongue, not have to struggle in German, mispronouncing the word for 'murder victim,' *Mordopfer* and the word for 'killed,' *getötet*.

Or God forbid, spend hours speaking English stuttering like poor King George in the movie, who'd had to be coached before he could declare war on Germany. Patronas had about fifteen minutes of solid English in him. Any longer and it came apart.

After he and Tembelos finished gathering evidence, they shed their Tyvek gear, lifted the dead man up and placed him in a black body bag, zipped it and carried it back down the hill on their shoulders to the waiting Jeep. An official in Chora had told them the cruise ship was due at midday and Patronas was determined to leave the village before it arrived. He didn't want tourists to take pictures of the deceased with their cellphones and post them on the Internet, didn't want the island to be tainted by the killing. He had the priest lead the way, hoping his robed presence would fool any people they encountered into thinking their sad little procession was a makeshift funeral.

He found it strange that the family hadn't wanted to accompany the body, to see the old man off as it were. Usually, grieving relatives behaved differently, refused to let go. They'd cry until they could cry no more, as if their tears could restore the dead to life. These people were different, and it wasn't just because they were from somewhere else. No, something was going on here.

He looked back at the house. Could be they simply couldn't bear it. Watching the body of a loved one being trundled off was hard. He recalled when his mother's body was taken, how he felt like he'd been struck by a tree. Could be the man and his wife wanted to spare themselves that, spare their children.

THEY LOADED THE body without incident. Evangelos Demos started the car and they drove off, the plan being to transport the body by boat to Leros, where there was an airport. From there it would be flown on to Athens.

Not wanting to put the body in the trunk of the Jeep, they'd put it in the backseat, laying it partially in Patronas' lap.

A fine metaphor for the case, he thought sourly, looking down at the shrouded form.

The murder of a foreign national, it would be the case from hell, no doubt about it. The language barrier alone would be a formidable obstacle. Patronas didn't speak much German, and he didn't know anyone who did. The German language had gone out of fashion, students in Greece preferring now to study English.

And Evangelos Demos would be no help. No, Comrade Stalin up there in the front seat would only get in the way.

Also, once the media got wind of the crime, politicians from both countries might well get involved. Right-wing or left, it wouldn't matter, they'd all have plenty to say, their voices rising in a self-serving chorus and impeding his investigation. Vigilantes had begun attacking foreign immigrants all over Europe in recent months, even killed a few. God help Greece if that were the case here.

Egine hamos, this was. Utter chaos.

Worse would be if there was a second murder, if someone decided to take it upon himself to cleanse his country of outsiders … a home-grown Hitler.

Patronas closed his eyes. He was too old to deal with such horrors, his homeland too broken. *Please Jesus, let that not be the case here.*

"Let's hope this is not what I think it is," he told the others. "That this man was not singled out because of his nationality.

The priest nodded. " 'To kill without pity or mercy,' that's what Hitler said. 'Who still talks nowadays about the Armenians?' Let us pray no one in Greece has succumbed to such madness."

THE CREW ON the police cruiser rushed to help when Patronas and Tembelos carried the body bag up the gangplank of the boat. "What happened to them? Was it an accident?" one of the men asked.

"No," Patronas said. "He was murdered."

He had called ahead and told them to clear a place in the hold and pack it with ice. A morbid kind of cooler, it would have to do until they reached Leros and the plane. The ice Evangelos had poured on the victim had already doomed a proper forensic examination. A little more wouldn't do any harm.

"Get there as fast as you can," he instructed the captain. "I've alerted the airport on Leros and they'll fly him out on the next plane. See that he gets to the proper authorities in Athens."

Before leaving the crime scene, Patronas had called the Forensic Sciences Division of the Hellenic Police in Athens on his cellphone and told the man in charge to red-flag the case, stating the deceased was a foreign national and that the lab needed to work the case and work it fast. There could well be international repercussions once word got out. No one in law enforcement wanted that kind of trouble.

"Of course," the man said. "I'll make sure the technicians start immediately."

"Make sure they ink his fingers and run them for prints," Patronas added. "I tried, but the facilities are limited here on Patmos and you people are the experts. Also check the tallow in the evidence bag—it's labeled, 'wax, body'— and compare it with the envelope, marked 'wax, church.' See if there's a match."

His colleague read the request back to him. "I'll check with the general police divisions on the islands and see if there's been any other attacks on foreigners," he said. "Could be this was a simple break-in and he surprised them."

"Check the mainland, too. All of Greece. Also run those scars on the victim's face through the international databases. Maybe you'll get a hit."

"Will do."

"And keep it quiet. No media, no loose talk."

Patronas checked his notes to see if he'd missed anything. The list in his head kept growing. "One of my men is escorting the body to Athens. His name is Giorgos Tembelos. He should be there in nine or ten hours. He'll hand over the evidence: the bags I told you about, everything else we found."

As a precaution, Tembelos was going along to make sure the victim got where he needed to go. Patronas doubted there'd be a problem with the pick-up and delivery, but he was taking no chances.

"By the book, Giorgos," he cautioned. "No fooling around. No 'I'm in Athens, I might as well go and visit my mother,' bullshit. If the hearse isn't there to meet you when the boat docks—drivers might still be on strike—call headquarters and ask them to send a van. Don't try to flag a taxi, Giorgos. You hear me? Don't leave the body lying on the curb and run off looking for a cab. You've got the address of the lab. Go directly there and deposit the body, make sure the coroner signs the release form, then turn around and come right back. We can't afford to screw this up."

"Okay," Tembelos said gruffly, miffed at the lengthy instructions.

"What did you say?"

"I said, 'okay.' "

'Okay' had become increasingly popular in Greek along with *chillaroume*—the Americanism, 'chill out,' reworked in Greek. Patronas, for one, didn't approve of the trend. His homeland was disappearing right before his eyes—his music, his language, everything was going. Socrates would have wept.

"Greek, Giorgos, Greek. That's who we are, that's what we speak. The word you should use to signal your assent is *entaxei*."

Tembelos was now thoroughly aggravated. "Whatever, you asshole," he said. "Need me to translate? It's where you shit."

PAPA MICHALIS HAD insisted on accompanying the body to Athens. "I'll go, not as a policeman, but as a priest and pray for the victim," he told Patronas.

He'd been deeply moved at the sight of the dead man, even wept a little as they loaded him into the cooler. "To meet such a fate so far from home. It's like something out of Exodus," he said. " 'He called his name Gershom: for he said I have been a stranger in a strange land.' "

He touched the cooler with his hand. "I'll accompany him on his sad journey and guide him to his rest."

"Father, he's not going to his rest," Patronas said. "He's going to a forensic laboratory."

"There, then."

With great reverence, the priest touched the large cross he wore around his neck, a mannerism Patronas found extremely irritating. Roughly translated, it meant, 'Don't trouble me with your earthly concerns, my friend. I am a man of God. I answer to a higher authority.'

In other words, Patronas could go to hell. The priest was simply too polite to say so.

"I think you should stay here," Patronas insisted.

A mulish expression on his face, Papa Michalis sat down on the floor next to the cooler and set about arranging his robe, "I will go wherever he goes. To a forensic laboratory, if that's where he's bound."

He looked up at Patronas. "I am not unfamiliar with forensic laboratories, Yiannis. I have seen such places on television." This was said as if watching television conferred an advanced degree in forensics, a PhD.

Patronas wanted to throttle him. "You won't like it, Father. Place reeks of death."

"Bah, I'm an old man. I've seen my share of death." He patted the cooler again. "He shouldn't be alone, especially now. He might not be one of us, Yiannis, but he's still a child of God."

And that was that.

Which left Patronas in the front seat of the car with Evangelos Demos. So much for his master plan.

CHAPTER FOUR

———◆———

In the house of the hanged, one does not mention
rope.
—Greek Proverb

After the midday heat, the air inside the house felt glacial to Patronas. The victim's family was there, the woman and two children sitting at a pine table in the kitchen, the man standing behind them.

A fireplace took up most of one wall. A pair of armchairs were positioned in front of it. Patronas took one when he came in, thinking to dominate the proceedings, and motioned for Evangelos Demos to sit in the other.

A woodcut of a dead hare hung above the fireplace. A compelling work, it seemed out of place in the kitchen.

"Albrecht Dürer," Bechtel said, nodding to the print. "My papa loved it and insisted we bring it with us and hang it where he could see it. 'Even in Greece,' he said, 'we must pay homage to our heritage.'"

It was as true a depiction of death as Patronas had ever seen. "Shouldn't it be in a museum?"

"Dürer was a printmaker, Chief Officer," Bechtel said, drily. "This is a print."

The German had shaved his head; and his glistening scalp only served to emphasize the sharp angularity of his features, the hollowed out cheeks and beaked nose, the thin, angry line of his mouth.

Thin and wiry, he was built like a long-distance runner. He was dressed in jeans and a polo shirt, worn cloth espadrilles on his feet. Aside from his coloring, he bore no resemblance to the victim.

He and Patronas had gotten off to a bad start. After returning to the house, Patronas announced he needed to search the grounds one last time before interviewing the family. The murder weapon had yet to be found and he was determined to look for it.

Gunther Bechtel was very unhappy about the delay. "Nearly thirty-six hours and no one from the Greek police has seen fit to interview us. By all means, see to the garden, Chief Officer. Take your time."

It didn't help that although they searched the garden high and low, neither Patronas nor Evangelos Demos discovered anything of consequence.

They then gathered in the icy room and at Bechtel's suggestion began discussing the killing in English, which was the only language they all understood. Bechtel sent the children away, insisting they not be present during the initial interview. Patronas agreed, thinking he could find out what he needed from them later.

He would have preferred to get a translator in order not to miss anything, but given the man's hostility, he didn't want to risk a further delay. "Well, then," he stammered. "Let us commerce."

"I believe the word you are seeking is 'commence,' Chief Officer," Bechtel said, moving swiftly to correct him. " 'Commerce,' the word you used, does not mean 'start.' It means 'business.' "

The interview crept along at a snail's pace, Patronas painstakingly licking his pencil and entering every word said in his notebook. When he asked the wife to repeat the word, 'blood,' not understanding her accent, Gunter Bechtel lost all patience. "One would think that police in a country with over twenty-five million tourists would know rudimentary English—would know the words for 'victim' and 'killed' and 'dead.' " His voice was venomous.

Patronas let it go. He knew his English sounded bad. As it had for King George, it deteriorated when he got nervous, and he was nervous now. "All my other victims were Greeks," he said. "This is my first foreign murder."

Bechtel examined him. "How many other cases have you solved?"

"I am Chief Officer of the Chios Police Force."

"I repeat: How many cases have you solved?"

Patronas concentrated on his writing. "One," he said in a low voice.

The German and his wife exchanged glances. "But how can that be?" Bechtel said. "When I called and asked about the delay, they told me they were bringing in an expert."

He shrugged. "By Greek standards, I am an expert. Such crimes are rare here. We are not a violent people."

Unlike you and your kind, he longed to say, hell-bent on genocide a generation ago. The Greeks might be lazy and disorganized, corrupt, too— he'd give him that—but at least they'd never gassed children.

Gunter Bechtel left the room and returned with an MP3 player. "Use this," he said, slapping the machine in the palm of his hand. "It will speed things up."

Patronas fiddled with the MP3 player, not knowing how to operate it and too proud to ask. Noticing his hesitation, the German stepped forward and started it.

"It has a button, Chief Officer. See? You push it."

Reddening, Patronas stated the date, time, and location of the interview, then set the machine down on the table and angled it toward the German couple. He had his own tape recorder—standard police issue—but had forgotten to bring it with him from Chios.

"Spell your name please," he said to the woman.

"Gerta Bechtel," she said in heavily accented English. "G-E-R-T-A B-E-C-H-T-E-L."

"And the children?"

Gunther Bechtel quickly answered. "They are Hannelore and Walter."

"And the dead man?"

"Walter Bechtel. My son is named for him."

"Describe your father to me,"

"He was not my father, not in the biological sense. My actual father was killed in a car accident when I was sixteen and in the *Gymnasium*. Walter took over for him after he died, caring for my mother and me and helping us financially. He supervised my education and has been my closest adviser, my dearest relative, for as long as I can remember."

Bechtel paused. "*Was*," he said, his face stricken. "He *was* my dearest relative, my one true friend."

Gerta Bechtel stirred restlessly beside him.

"You called him 'Papa,' " Patronas said.

"Yes. That's how I saw him. He might have entered my life late, but his influence on me was profound. He had no children of his own and he legally adopted me after my father died so you see, he was in truth my papa. I owe everything I am to him."

"You said something else in German? What was it?"

"I asked, 'Who did this to you'? It was a rhetorical question."

"He came with you to Patmos?"

"Yes, I didn't want to leave him alone in Germany. We only had each other, he and I. He served as a grandfather for my children. As I told you, he was part of the family."

"You say he was not your father."

"That's right. He was my uncle, my father's brother."

"Tell me about him. What kind of person he was."

"What do you want me to say, Chief Officer? He was a dutiful family man. He worked hard to support us after the car accident. He was an engineer and a Lutheran. He studied in Heidelberg."

Patronas continued entering information. He was very tired and didn't want to stay up all night transcribing the tape. His notes would give him what he needed.

"And you, what do you do?" he asked.

"I am an aid worker in Africa," Bechtel responded.

"Where?"

The man made no effort to hide his annoyance. "Darfur, Sudan, Congo, Burundi, wherever I'm sent. I don't see what relevance this has to my uncle's death."

Patronas interrupted. "In Africa, what do you do?"

"Nutrition. I work for the UN."

Back and forth it went, Patronas asking questions, the German making disparaging remarks and humiliating him, volunteering as little information as possible.

Patronas paused to regroup. Talking to Gunther Bechtel was like playing tennis with a broken racquet.

"Is this your house?"

"No, no, how could it be? I just told you. I am an aid worker. I cannot afford a place like this."

"Whose house is it?"

"A friend of mine, Joseph Bauer. I will spell it for you, B-A-U-E-R. Did you get that, Chief Officer? Or do you want me to spell it again? B-A-U-E-R. He bought the land and drew up the design. Greece being the way it is, it took him more than a year and a half just to get the permits; then there was a strike in Piraeus and a delay in customs. That's why it seems unfinished."

There was implied criticism in everything he said.

"Where is your friend now?" Patronas asked.

"He and his wife are in Turkey."

"When did they leave? Were they here when your father was killed?"

"No, they'd left some time before. Ten days, I think."

"I will need to talk to them. How long have you been in Patmos?"

"My wife came the beginning of July—the third, I think it was." Bechtel looked at his wife for confirmation.

"Yes, it was the third," she said, nodding.

"So you've been here about five weeks?" Patronas asked her.

"That is correct, yes," she said. "I go to the beach in Campos, sunbathe and read books there. See to the children. The days pass. Until yesterday, it was pleasant."

"And you, when did you come?" Patronas asked, returning to her husband.

"The day before yesterday. I had work to finish in Darfur."

Patronas wrote the date down and circled it. "I noticed there's no security system here. Who has keys to the house?"

"The housekeeper. As far as I know, she's the only one."

The wife jumped in. "The gardener has a key, too, Gunther. There are many keys to the house. Both the children have one. I have one, the Bauers."

Her husband didn't like being corrected. "So, how many keys?" he asked his wife sharply.

"Eight, I think. We have four, the Bauers have two and the gardener and the woman who cleans each have one."

Patronas cut off the discussion, thinking there were so many keys, they would be of no use in the investigation. "Does the housekeeper live here with you?"

"No," Gunther Bechtel said. "I believe she has an apartment in town."

The German hadn't referred to the woman by name, probably didn't know it. As with the keys, he did not appear to be aware of what went on in the house or care much.

"She works for our friends," Bechtel hastened to add. "They are the ones who deal with her."

"Does she speak German?"

"Only a few words."

Patronas frowned. "But this is a German household. How does she manage?"

The wife spoke up again. "Our friend's wife tells her *sauber,* clean, and hands her a mop and she mops. Tells her *schmutzige Wäsche,* dirty clothes, gives her the hamper and she does the laundry."

Patronas was liking them less and less. "Where is she now?"

"The housekeeper? I sent her home."

"Was she here on the day of the murder?"

"Yes," said Gerta Bechtel. "She came in the afternoon and stayed on to prepare our dinner."

"Let's go back to the deceased," Patronas said. "Did he have friends on Patmos? People he visited?"

"No, he rarely left the house." Gunther Bechtel was very emphatic on this point. "Once he got here, he remained, except for a few times when he joined us for the day at Campos. He loved the garden and liked to sit outside under the trees."

"So he came with you from Germany, and except for two or three trips to the beach, stayed within these walls?"

"That is correct."

Patronas felt a touch of pity for the old man. Confined to this hillside, he must have been very lonely. Maybe he'd been afraid to venture off the estate, afraid he'd fall and break his hip. After all, he'd been over ninety. Still, it seemed wrong. Everyone in the family had been occupied elsewhere: his nephew in Africa and his grandchildren and their mother at the beach, their hosts in Turkey. Aside from the housekeeper, he would have spent most of his time alone, and she didn't speak or understand German. If he'd wanted to communicate with her, he would have had to use sign language.

"He had everything he needed," Gunter Bechtel insisted stubbornly. "My friends arranged to import food, German beer, newspapers, books, and videos for him. It was just like at home, only warm and sunny. He thanked us many times for bringing him here. He was happy."

"How did he pass the time?" Patronas asked.

"He gardened a little. He was an old man, Chief Officer. Mostly, he napped."

"What was his relationship with the neighbors?"

"We are summer people living in a borrowed house. We have no relationship with the neighbors."

"What about the Germans who live on Patmos?"

"We do not know people on Patmos, German or otherwise." Again, Bechtel was emphatic.

"Did your father know the people who gave you the house?"

"Of course he knew the Bauers." His tone was hostile. "They are our friends. Surely you don't think they had a hand in this?"

"It appears unlikely, but we will still have to check." Patronas continued to write. "What was your father's relationship with his grandchildren?"

"His relationship with the children was good. They played cards. Especially my son, Walter. My daughter, as you saw, is a teenager, not so interested in adults."

"Was your father a veteran? Did he serve in the war?"

"What possible relevance does that have?"

"There was a swastika carved on his forehead. Why would someone do something like that?"

"I have no idea." Bechtel bit off the words.

"I'm sorry if I upset you. I'm just trying to get a sense of who he was."

"I'll tell you who he was. He was an old man with arthritis who liked to sleep in the sun, who liked to drink Lowenbrau in the afternoon and listen to the music of Mahler on an old-fashioned phonograph. He loved the smell of lilies because they reminded him of his mother. He especially loved pickles." For the first time, there was a hint of emotion in the man's voice. Sadness. "He never bothered anybody."

"Do you have any idea who might have killed him?" Evangelos asked.

He shook his head. "Perhaps it was a random event, someone attacking him because he was German. Germans are not so popular now in Greece."

Patronas drummed his pencil on his notebook. "What about the scars on his face? The old ones. Where did they come from?"

"Oh, you mean his *Mensur* scars," Bechtel said, visibly relaxing. "They are from dueling. The sport was very popular in the universities of my country when my papa was young. They called the participants *Paukanten* and a scar was a smite. To have one on your face was a badge of honor then, a mark of your class. It meant you were brave and had stood your ground and not flinched."

He smiled for the first time. "Otto Bismarck once remarked that a man's courage could be judged by the number of scars on his cheeks."

Again, everything was generic, nothing specific to the dead man.

"Your papa had three scars, so he must have been a very brave man."

"He was."

"Where in Germany was he from?"

"He lived with us in Stuttgart. It worked very well for everyone. My wife had company when I was away in Africa and he had someone to look after him."

Another evasion.

He'd have to enter the decedent's name and search the Internet. Maybe send his photograph to Interpol, see what came back.

He returned to the war. "Was he in the army?"

"Everyone in Germany served in the military during the war, the Wehrmacht predominantly. You know the word, Chief Officer. No need for me to translate."

"Where did he fight?"

"I don't know. We never spoke of that time."

"Surely you must have some idea."

"What are you asking? If he was a war criminal, my papa? If he killed Jews?" His voice grew shrill. "You think the agents of Mossad left their headquarters in Tel Aviv and came to Patmos, broke into this place and killed a ninety-year-old man in a garden?"

Said like that, it sounded preposterous.

Bechtel began pacing back and forth. "You people are all the same," he said angrily. "You assume if a man is a certain age and has a German accent, he was in Auschwitz running a crematorium. There were nearly seventy million of us at the beginning of the war. Not all of us were in the Gestapo, Chief Officer! Not all of us were SS men, no matter what you think, loading people onto trains and sending them off to be gassed. Most of us were ordinary people caught up in events beyond our control. Certainly my papa was that, just an ordinary man." There were tears in his eyes. Tears of anger, tears of grief, perhaps both.

"I meant no disrespect," Patronas said softly.

"Chief Inspector, you've been asking that question in one form or another for the last five minutes. As I told you, you are not alone in your prejudice. Everywhere, people see Germans—my papa in this instance, my murdered adopted father—and they wonder. You can see it on their faces. The more impolite among them, they ask."

Patronas nodded, recognizing the truth in what he said. He wondered how it worked in families, when a son asked a father, 'Where were you in the war?' If you were German and the answer was Poland, how did the conversation go?

CHAPTER FIVE

———— ◆ ————

He sows on barren soil.
—Greek Proverb

GERTA BECHTEL WEPT silently, twirling a strand of blonde hair around her finger. At least fifteen years younger than her husband, she carried herself like a dancer. Her face was lovely, reminiscent of Heidi Klum's, and her blue eyes were carefully made up, her hair tousled in an artful way. She was wearing jeans and an embroidered tunic, sandals with little tassels that jangled when she crossed her legs. Like the rest of her family, she was very tan, her hair streaked in places by the sun. Even now, with tears running down her cheeks, she was one of the most beautiful women Patronas had ever seen—gazelle-like in her movements, soft in the way women should be.

She was wearing a musky scent that seemed to envelop him as he sat there, make him forget why he'd come.

He and Gerta Bechtel were alone in a room at the back of the house. It was his friend Bauer's study, her husband had informed him, and Patronas and his colleagues on the police force were welcome to use it, the computer and Internet, whatever they needed.

Patronas had demurred. Thanking Bechtel, he said he'd prefer to work at the police station downtown, leave him and his family in peace when he was done speaking with them.

The windows in the room were large and faced the garden, and the room was full of sunlight. Although Gunther Bechtel had objected, Patronas had insisted on interviewing his wife separately.

"Let's start at the beginning," he said, seeking to put her at ease. "Where are you from?"

"Tübingen. There I meet my husband. I was in university and he was, how do you say, an instructor." She hesitated. "Have you a cigarette? Is hard, this."

He handed her a cigarette and took one for himself. They smoked in companionable silence for a few minutes.

"Gunther, he hates the smoking, but sometimes I must. Is hard, like I say. We were always together, Gunther's uncle and me, many years, always together."

Tears filled her eyes. "At first, I go with my husband, but later Gunther said it was too dangerous. Too much war in Africa, he said. Look at Rwanda. No good for me."

"Did the children go with you?"

"No, they stayed in Stuttgart. We had a woman and Gunther's uncle was there. I was never away for long, two weeks, three. No more. They were happy in Germany, our children, happy and safe."

Pushing her chair back, she got up and walked over to the window, cigarette in hand. Her tunic was heavily beaded and it shimmered when she moved.

"I always wanted to see Greece," she said with her back toward him. "When our friends invited us, I told Gunther we must go." She spoke in a very precise way, taking care to enunciate her words so that he could understand, nodding a little as she did so. "I am good. You understand my English, no?"

Patronas nodded. He couldn't take his eyes off her.

"I said, 'Gunther, is only two months. Let me have this.' "

Silhouetted against the window, she seemed to glow, her hair, her clothes, everything about her bathed in golden light. "Patmos, it is good. Every day I go to the beach with the children and we swim together. Eat lunch sometimes. Have fun. My son learns to wind-surf. It is good for him and Hannelore to be here and go to the beach. Fun in the sun."

He studied her, puzzled by what he was hearing. Her words didn't match the anguish he'd seen in her eyes; they sounded counterfeit somehow. She was holding something back, he was sure of it. Maybe out of fear of making a mistake, like the smoking, revealing something that satrap of a husband didn't want him to know. Or maybe that stolid cheerfulness was just another manifestation of grief, an effort to convince herself that the trip to Patmos hadn't been a tragic mistake.

"What was your relationship with the deceased?"

"I took care of him always." She struggled to find the right words. "I made sure he had the food he liked, the Schnitzel and *Mohnkuchen mit Streusel*. Clean clothes to wear. Supervised the woman, Maria, to make sure she did what he wanted, cooked the way he liked. I taught her how to make the *Mohnkuchen* for him."

"Excuse me," Patronas said, "but what is *Mohnkuchen*?"

"A cake of poppy seeds. It is very good, a favorite of us all."

After a pause, she continued. "Sometimes we two, we watch television together. He was my family, too."

There was little warmth in her voice as she said this. Duty had called and she'd answered.

"Did he ever express fear, the victim, or seem worried about anything?"

"No, no. He got up every morning, ate his breakfast and went outside. He loved the garden. He'd cut flowers and put them in a vase for me. He liked to surprise me with roses." Her voice caught.

"Your husband said he was often alone."

"Yes, we didn't take him to the beach with us. It was too difficult. His knees, they pained him, the stairs up and down."

Not quite the same version, but close enough.

"Gunther said you took him to Campos a few times?"

"Yes, but it didn't please him. Too hot, he said."

"What was his relationship with the children?"

Was it his imagination or had she flinched? "Like my husband said, it was good. The children, they loved him. Gunther's mother is dead, my parents also, so he was the only grandparent they had. Hannelore, she learned a violin solo for him, Mahler, and he used to ask her to play it. Many times he asked her."

"What about your son?"

"Walter, he is a little boy. All day long, computer games. Not so much time for *Opa*. Sometimes they make Legos together, little houses. In Germany, my son has a train and they play with it."

"I noticed your son has a bruise over his eye."

"Yes. He said someone pushed him, but maybe he said this because he broke his glasses and did not want us to know. Walter does this sometimes. He does not lie, but he does not tell the truth either."

She fell silent, lost in thought.

"Was the deceased there when it happened?" Patronas asked. Perhaps the killer was lurking in the garden and the boy encountered him.

"No. He was with me in the house. Walter was getting his bicycle. He wanted to go for a ride. Maybe Maria was there. She spends much time outside sweeping. Always sweeping is Maria, back and forth with the broom. All the day, she does this."

"Tell me about yesterday."

"We went to Campos and came back. I didn't have my watch, so I don't know what time. Seven-thirty, eight. A little dark, but not yet night. *Grobpapa* was sitting out in the garden and I called to him, 'Do you want anything?' *'Nein,'* he said. *'Nein.'* After this, I go inside."

"And that was the last time you spoke to him?"

"Yes. The gardener found him later that night. He was yelling and hitting the door and I opened it to see what he wanted. I screamed when I saw *Grobpapa* and I couldn't stop—screaming, screaming, screaming. Gunther woke up the children. *Grobpapa* was still alive then and Gunther thought we could save him. I gave the gardener my phone and he called the police. But there was a mix-up and by the time they got here, he was dead."

"Why didn't you or your husband call the police?"

"We were too upset. Also the gardener, his Greek, it is better."

She touched the pane of glass with her fingers. "We have air conditioning. The windows, they are sealed shut."

Gerta Bechtel looked back at him. "If an intruder came and *Grobpapa* called for help, we would not have heard him."

THE DAUGHTER, HANNELORE, a sullen sixteen-year-old, was less forthcoming than her mother, reluctantly volunteering that while Patmos was fine, she would have preferred to spend the summer in Stuttgart with her friends.

"I only have one friend here, Hilda. We go to the same school in Germany, but we're not friends there, only here. She's a lot older than I am, almost eighteen." Hannelore grew slightly more animated as she described her friend, saying Greek boys were always hanging around her. They just wouldn't leave her alone.

In the old days, Greek men who pursued foreign women were called *kamaki,* the instrument men use to spear fish—the fish dangling off their hook, the female tourists they'd snagged. A song had even been written about them. "*S'aresei i Ellada, Señorita?*"—"Do you like Greece?" The key word in the lyrics changing from 'Fräulein' to 'Mademoiselle,' to 'Miss.' Such men were enterprising and versatile, could speak a few words in nearly every European language.

Envious, Patronas had watched them work the beaches over the years, yearning for a little taste of Sweden himself, a bikini-clad piece of England. In those days, native girls had been reluctant, to say the least, more trouble than they were worth. Perhaps now that he was divorced, he'd give spear fishing a try. Find a lonely housewife like Shirley Valentine and show her a good time.

"Does Hilda like the boys' attention?" he asked the girl.

"She talks to them. She has a boyfriend in Germany, but she likes to flirt." *How unfair,* she was saying, *Hilda with many boyfriends and me with none.*

Unlike her mother, Hannelore Bechtel had a sturdy, somewhat masculine physique and an androgynous way about her—feminine and coy one minute, boyish and abrupt the next. Her arms were unusually well muscled, her biceps well defined.

"Do you play sports?" Patronas asked, wondering if she spent a lot of time roughhousing with boys—if that would explain her manner, what he was seeing.

"Oh, yes, yeah. All the time. I cycle and I ski. All winter I am out. But mostly I scull." Holding her arms out in front of her, she mimed rowing. "I like to be on the water and go fast. I am most happy then."

She'd made a clumsy effort to pretty herself up, he noticed, painting her nails a lurid orange and applying a chalky foundation and red lipstick so dark it made her mouth look bruised. The makeup looked off to Patronas, seemed to be at odds with her tomboy persona, but then what did he know of adolescent girls?

He wondered why her mother didn't take her in hand, pass on a little of that elegant fastidiousness.

Her shirt had a shiny Hello Kitty cartoon printed on it, its childish innocence clashing with the girl's Kabuki-like face. A child masquerading as a woman.

"When you're at the beach, do you and Hilda go off alone?"

"There's no place to go. That's the problem with Patmos." She gave him a long, assessing look. "Don't you want to ask about my grandfather? Isn't that why you're here?"

"Yes. How did you get along with him?"

"He was my grandfather and I loved him." End of story.

"Did he ever act afraid?"

"*Grobpapa*? No, not him. Nothing frightened *Grobpapa*." She kept fussing with her hair. Like her mother's, it was bleached by the sun, but hers was greasy and dirty looking.

"Your mother said you'd learned a piece on the violin for your grandfather."

She nodded. "The violin solo from Mahler's Fourth Symphony. It took me a long time to learn it. My mother made a CD of me playing. It was my Christmas present to him." Her voice was stiff.

"You must be very good violinist," he said.

"I have a good teacher, and I practice." Again, the same stilted politeness.

"How about your brother? Does he play an instrument?"

"Yes, the violin, the same as I do. We sometimes play together. What's the word?"

"Duets?"

"Yes, that's right. We play duets." Two of her nails were broken off and she kept chewing on the remnants, trying to even them out.

"Did your grandfather ever talk about the war?"

"The war?" She looked puzzled.

"Yes, about the time he was a soldier?"

She seemed surprised by the question. "I don't know. You'll have to ask my parents."

"How about you? Is there anything you're afraid of?"

Something passed over her face. "No, nothing. I am never afraid."

SEVEN OR EIGHT years old, the boy Walter couldn't sit still. He kept jerking his head this way and that and bobbing his knees up and down. He was wearing glasses and had a Band-Aid over his left eye.

Very polite, he'd shaken Patronas' hand as soon as he'd entered the room. "I am Walter Bechtel," he'd said. "How do you do?"

Patronas, in turn, had introduced himself. "I am Yiannis Patronas, Chief Officer of the Chios Police Force."

"I am very pleased to make your acquaintance, Chief Officer. I will endeavor to answer all your questions truthfully." He furrowed his brow. "Excuse me, but you said you were from Chios. This isn't Chios. This is Patmos."

"I know, son. I'm here about your grandfather."

"Grandfather," he said in a robotic voice. "My grandfather's dead."

His eyes kept darting around, looking at everything but Patronas.

Kid has some kind of handicap, Patronas thought, autism maybe.

"I know your grandfather's dead," he said gently. "Somebody hurt him and I'm trying to find out who it was."

The boy frowned. "Hurt him? Why?"

"I'm trying to find that out, too."

"How did they hurt him?" His voice went up a notch. "Was it like the cat?"

"What cat?"

"Bonzo. Someone killed it. It was a stray and Grandfather took it in and fed it, made it his pet. He is the one who called it Bonzo." The boy continued to fidget, tired of sitting in the chair, tired of the questions.

Patronas wrote the name of the cat in his notebook and underlined it. "What happened to it?"

"Someone strangled it. Whoever did it pushed me down. That's how I hurt my eye. My glasses broke and I got a piece of glass stuck here." He pointed to his eyebrow.

"Did you see who pushed you?"

"No. I was looking at Bonzo, wondering what was wrong with him, and then BOOM!" He clapped his hands together. "I was very upset about Bonzo, but my mother told me not to be sad, that we would get another cat when we got back to Germany."

"You said Bonzo was your grandfather's pet. Was he upset?"

"Yes. He was very angry and told my mother to fire Maria. I don't know why. My mother didn't pay attention. She just told the gardener to bury the cat outside and he did. She made us promise not to tell my father. She said he wouldn't like it."

The boy got up and skipped around for a moment before returning to his seat. "Grandfather never wanted us to be here. He said it would only bring us trouble, and it did. My mother cried when she found the cat … cried and cried."

BECHTEL TOLD PATRONAS to keep the MP3 player, saying the family had two others. Reluctantly, Patronas accepted, thinking he'd only use it until he could find a replacement. Bechtel was only trying to help; he knew that. Still, he resented the gift, well aware of the financial disparity between the German and himself. Even an aid worker in Africa was better off than a Greek policeman now.

The present German chancellor, Angela Merkel, had been forcing the Greek government to tighten its belt, and her actions had caused widespread suffering throughout his homeland, especially among the young, fifty-seven percent of whom were now unemployed. Patronas' salary had been cut repeatedly. He was poorer now than he'd ever been, and his father had been a *manavis*, a green grocer.

Looking down at the MP3 player in his hand, he sighed. "Fucking Merkel."

Before he left the estate, he searched the grounds a final time, accompanied by Bechtel. There were a lot of garden tools lined up against the wall, and he inspected each of them carefully, looking for evidence of blood, but saw nothing. He'd have to get the luminol and try again. He searched the outside walls, too, seeking a place where a rock might have been dislodged, but it was a hopeless task. The wall was high and went on forever. It would take an eternity to check it all. He'd have to wait for the autopsy in Athens. Maybe the coroner would be able to establish what had been used.

The victim had occupied a large guest suite on the far side of the house, well away from where the rest of the family slept. As with everything else related to the deceased, it was impersonal. There were no pictures on the walls or photographs in evidence, no books or papers anywhere, not even a discarded German newspaper. True, it wasn't the Bechtel's house, but usually when people occupied a space, they left some trace of themselves. Here there was nothing, almost as if it had been swept clean. The only item of note was an old-fashioned hearing aid lying on the nightstand.

Patronas picked up the hearing aid. It looked like it had never been used, the plastic unmarked and glossy. "Was your uncle deaf?" If so, that would explain why the old man hadn't cried out. He'd been taken by surprise.

The German nodded. "To a degree, depending on who was speaking and what they were saying. If you asked him what he wanted for dinner, he'd hear you perfectly. Other times, not so much. I insisted he get a hearing aid, but he didn't like to wear it. He said, 'If I get one now, what will I do when I'm old?' He was like that, my papa, always making jokes." Gunther Bechtel looked away.

Patronas opened the door of the closet and rummaged around. Everything was clean and relatively new. Pants with elastic waistbands, light-weight cotton shirts in a variety of colors. There was a row of shoes at the back of the closet, cloth slippers and a pair of white American sneakers still in their box. Wrapped in tissue paper, they had never been worn.

"You see," said Bechtel. "All is in order."

A chest of drawers held cotton boxer shorts and rolled-up compression socks for circulation. In addition, there was a wallet and a black and white photo of a man and a woman. It was very old, the photo, the style of the woman's hair dating from the 1940s.

"My parents." Gunther Bechtel reached over and shut the drawer.

Initially, Patronas had wanted to quiz him about the cat, but changed his mind after hearing the tremor in the man's voice. He'd discuss it with Gerta Bechtel when he got the chance, keep her husband in the dark in case he didn't know. The cat was a stray, and according to the little boy, save for the grandfather, no one had been overly attached to it. As Bechtel had pointed out, Germans weren't popular in Greece these days. The cat's death could have been an act of vandalism, the equivalent of someone spray painting 'Fuck Merkel' on a wall.

He felt like he'd trespassed enough. "Could this have been a robbery? Did you check the house after you found him? Was anything missing?"

"Not that I'm aware of. As my wife told you, they had just returned from the beach and were all inside, taking showers. I had recently come from Africa and was asleep in the bedroom. It is a long journey and very exhausting, hours and hours in airports and on planes, then the boat from Leros. Whoever did this might have been planning to rob the house and my uncle caught them. However, aside from the usual chair he sat in, nothing appeared disturbed in the garden and the outside lock had not been tampered with. Sometimes Walter is careless with the door, so it might even have been left open that night. I don't know. You must remember: we are guests here, so we do not know precisely what belongs. I've called my friends and asked them to return as soon as possible. They'll know better if something valuable in the house is missing. Also, they'll be able to tell you the names of the people who built the house. Perhaps one of them kept a key."

A long, complicated speech. Apparently, Bechtel had gone over things in his mind.

"I will let you know the results of the examination in Athens." Patronas took care not to say the word 'autopsy' out loud.

"Why does he need to be examined?" Bechtel asked angrily. "Any fool can see he was beaten to death."

"If we're lucky, forensics can establish the weapon."

"What difference does it make? Whatever it was, it killed him. He was a deaf old man who liked to sleep in the garden. Anyone could have surprised him. It would have been easy. No trouble at all."

"But how did they get in?" Patronas asked.

Bechtel continued to stare at him. "Finding that out is not my job, Chief Officer. It is yours."

Patronas thought about the interview as he walked down the path, going over Gunther Bechtel's words again and again in his mind. The German's remark about Mossad seemed strange, too emotional a response to what Patronas had been asking. It could have been a long-standing resentment—Bechtel saying he was a good man, that those had been different times, different people—but somehow Patronas didn't think so.

Also, the interaction between the couple felt off. Bechtel did all the talking, his wife remaining silent except when summoned to endorse his point of view. And why hadn't she told her husband about the cat? A stray, perhaps it hadn't seemed important to her, or maybe she'd wanted to preserve the illusion that all was going well for them on Patmos. The victim had been opposed to the trip, the little boy had said. Perhaps her husband had been opposed, too.

There was a puzzling formality about the whole family. Save for a few moments with Gunther Bechtel, they had all been deeply courteous, and in spite of their pain, endeavored to answer his questions. Their words had been thoughtful and precise. They hadn't wanted to discuss the war, but who could blame them?

How strange it all was.

CHAPTER SIX

———— ◆ ————

He who has no brains at twenty should not expect
them at thirty.
—Greek Proverb

Evangelos Demos was waiting for Patronas in the square, and they spoke briefly to the owner of the taverna. The man volunteered that the two *tavli* players had gone home earlier that day but would return the following morning. "They're my wife's cousins. They spend every day here."

A stout man with a mouthful of crooked teeth, he was cheerful and good natured. He and his wife were working behind the counter, ladling up food and handing it to the waiters while they talked to the two policemen. "Come back tomorrow, Chief Officer," the owner said. "I'll round up the men you want. We can all have breakfast together."

Patronas reluctantly agreed, and they arranged to meet the next day.

"Food's good here," Evangelos Demos said, eyeing the steaming dishes on the counter. "Let's take a break and eat."

They took a table in the corner. The taverna was bustling, full of foreigners. They were the only Greeks. The sun had gone down and the whitewashed buildings of Chora were luminous in the gathering darkness. A man was going from table to table with an accordion. Patronas recognized the tune he was playing. *Pame mia volta sto feggari,*"—Come Walk with Me in the Moonlight—by Hatzidakis. He had courted Dimitra to that song.

"Problem with songs like that is they lead you astray," he told Evangelos. "They never tell you what comes after those walks in the moonlight, when the sun rises and you and your beloved see each other in the light of day."

"You're right," Evangelos said. "In my experience, a woman acts one way before you get married and another way after. Worse, far worse."

A string of light bulbs were strung up overhead, lending the square a festive air. A group of boys were chasing each other in a nearby alley, full of bravado as they played a game of their own devising. From the looks of it, it was a war game, Patronas decided, watching them, full of shooting and falling down, dramatic dyings, the real Patmos showing itself in their laughing faces. Alive with people and noise, Chora felt like an island of light in the encroaching night.

The death of the old man, Walter Bechtel, seemed very far away.

Evangelos, a prodigious eater, rejoiced when he saw *kokoretsi* on the menu—intestines stuffed with offal—and ordered a plateful. His wife, Sophia, had forbidden him to eat *kokoretsi*, he told Patronas. "Says it's full of cholesterol and bad for me. Cheese, too. Everything I like."

In addition to the *kokoretsi*, he requested *loukaniko*—pork sausage—cheese pies, fried cheese, and cheese croquettes. Away from Sophia, he was having a free-for-all—a kilo of lamb and a mountain of fried potatoes.

"My wife wants me to lose weight," he said. "It's always salads with her. Six months now, only salads. Maybe a slice of watermelon or a fistful of grapes. She counts them, the grapes—only seventeen I get. I can't sleep at night, I'm so hungry."

Picking up a lamb chop, he chewed contentedly. "She made a graph and put it up on the refrigerator to chart my progress. She bought me a scale, too, so I could weigh everything that goes in my mouth."

Patronas watched him eat for a few minutes. Not a bad idea, the diet, as Evangelos was the size of a sofa and had been puffing like a locomotive most of the day.

"What did you think of the family?" Evangelos asked. "They hiding something?"

"I don't know. I've been thinking about it. Maybe Gunther Bechtel was right, what he said about the war—that we're prejudiced against Germans."

"Of course we're prejudiced. They killed a million of us."

"We can't let our personal feelings interfere with the case, Evangelos. We have to do our duty."

"Duty? You sound like one of them." In addition to all the food he'd consumed, Evangelos had drunk close to two liters of beer. Clowning around, he raised his arm and gave Patronas the Nazi salute, shouting, "*Sieg Heil, mein Führer!*" He tried to click his heels together, but was too fat and tipped the chair over.

The people at the surrounding tables turned and looked at them, aghast. Men in uniforms acting like Nazis. Patronas wanted to die.

It wasn't Stalin he was working with, it was Groucho Marx.

Laughing, Evangelos fought to right his chair. "Had a little trouble there. Good thing I didn't try goose stepping."

Patronas moved the beer out of his reach. "You said there weren't a lot of people here in Chora. If we separate, we should be able to interview most of them within the next twenty-four hours. See if anyone saw a stranger passing through, someone who didn't belong."

"They're foreigners. How are we going to talk to them if we don't speak their language?"

"You took a photo of the victim. Pass it around and gauge their reaction."

"We can't just go barging into people's houses."

"Sure we can, Evangelos. We're cops."

"I don't know, Yiannis. It seems a little intrusive."

"Intrusive? A man was murdered." Patronas fought to keep his voice down. People were still looking at them.

He counted out fifty euros and threw the money down on the table. "Come on, we need to speak to the man who found the body, establish a time line. It's important. After that, we'll call it a night."

"No fruit?" his colleague asked plaintively. "No coffee?"

"No, Evangelos. No fruit, no coffee. After we interview the gardener, I want you to go back to the police station, call the lab and get the results of the autopsy. We'll need every detail. Bring it with you when you pick me up in the morning."

Poor Evangelos. Instead of a slice of watermelon, he was going to get an earful of subcranial hemorrhage, followed by hypostasis, blood pooling in the lower extremities. It would go on for a while, the discussion. The coroner was nothing if not thorough.

Sieg Heil, yourself, *mein* Fatso.

THE GARDENER, a young Albanian with an earnest air, lived not far from the taverna with his wife and four-year-old son. He appeared relieved to see them and started talking immediately, saying he'd been picking oregano on the hillside and had arrived at the house later than usual. He'd seen the man lying on the ground and had run to help him. That's when he saw the blood and realized the man was dying.

"Old like my grandfather. I shook him a time or two, but I knew he wasn't going to wake up, that he was gone. I just hoped …." His face was stricken, his eyes damp.

"What time was this?"

"Eight, eight thirty. We were told to wait for the authorities to get there. They didn't come for a long time, over an hour. There was much confusion."

"Why did you come so late?"

"I always water after it cools off. Can't water during the day. Is too hot. Usually I am earlier, but I like I said, that day, I am getting the oregano."

"You said you pick it on the hillside. Do you go there often?" Patronas was hoping he'd seen someone, could provide them with a lead.

"Two or three times a week in the summer, we pick the oregano, my wife and I, and after I bring it and sell it to tourists. Also thyme and rosemary when I can find them. They're crazy for it, the tourists, especially the French. We get three euros for a handful, and it costs us nothing. They don't mind, the family, I do this. As long as the garden is done, I am free."

He spoke passable Greek and appeared to be what he said he was, a poor immigrant seeking a foothold in a new land. He had a kind of sweetness about him, a childish desire to please. He tended a herd of goats, too, he said, although they weren't his, looked after them for a man who lived in Athens. Anything to get by. He and his wife stayed on Patmos until November, when they left for Athens.

"What do you do in Athens?"

"Cleaning. Offices, houses."

Patronas continued to question him. "Do you ever see anyone else when you're picking oregano?"

"Tourists."

They inked his fingers with a kit they'd brought with them and wrote down everything he said. After they'd finished, they took a cast of his shoes, planning to compare it to the prints they'd found in the garden. Patronas wanted to chase the keys down, too, but doubted they would lead to anything. Like the gardener's shoes, just another dead end.

"You got a passport?" he asked the man.

The man retrieved it from a drawer and quickly handed it over. Patronas copied down the number, thinking he'd ask Evangelos Demos to run it and see what came up. Then he handed it back to him. "Don't leave Patmos without telling us. We might have to talk to you again."

"I am here," the man said. "My wife also. We are not going anywhere."

"You sure you don't want to stay with us?" Evangelos Demos asked when they got back to the car. "It's a big house. There's plenty of room."

Patronas shook his head. He'd spent time with Evangelos' wife, Sophia, on Chios and had no desire to repeat the experience. A country woman of the old school, she was built like a fire hydrant and was just about as malleable. Evangelos' mother-in-law, Stamatina, who'd been living with them at the time, had been even worse. She was a ferocious old battle-ax who was hard of hearing and consequently shouted everything, instructions mainly, from a chair in the kitchen, banging her cane on the floor.

"From Sparta, your wife?"

"Yes, her mother, too. The whole family. *Sparta bore you. Sparta you adorn.*"

An old saying meaning one was loyal to where one came from. The part about 'adorn' wouldn't apply to Sophia though. There'd be no dressing that one up. She'd stay as she came—stout and humorless—a warrior to the core. Everyone talked about how warlike Spartan men had been, but they were nothing compared to the women.

"*E tan e epi tas*," Spartan mothers were said to have told their sons as they headed into battle. Come back with your shield or on it. In other words, victory or death. They were a force of nature, those women, human tsunamis. Made his ex-wife look like Tinkerbell.

Evangelos turned the key and they started down the mountain, the gravel of the road gleaming in the headlights of the car.

Patronas patted the seat appreciatively, admiring the American workmanship. The Jeep might be two decades old, but it still ran better than his old Citroen with its pathetic two-horse-power engine. His car had given up the ghost during a rainstorm—it and his marriage within a week of each other—its canvas roof coming loose and flapping in the wind like a wet sheet on a clothesline. As a result, the car had filled with water and molded, speckles of mildew darkening its interior and scenting the air. Although he'd tried, Patronas had been unable to sell it. He'd been forced to pay an exorbitant fee to have it towed away. Now he rode a Vespa.

Not a step up in the world, he thought gloomily, more like a move sideways.

He lit a cigarette and watched the countryside, struck anew by how empty this side of Patmos was, just one bald hill after another. It suited him, the barren landscape, matched his mood.

"My wife is very unhappy on Patmos," Evangelos Demos confided. "She told me she was lonely and asked her mother to come for a visit. Eighteen months, it's been." His voice grew unsteady. "Eighteen months and she's still here."

Patronas nodded sympathetically. "A long time, eighteen months."

No wonder Evangelos Demos was so useless. Living with those two warrior women had wrecked him, taken his manhood and rendered him a steer.

"They said in Athens this case was a chance for me to redeem myself. Get my old job back."

"You said you cleared it with Stathis about me coming here."

"Oh, yes. He said and I quote, 'It was a stroke of genius summoning him.'"

"You're kidding."

"That's what he said."

"Let him say what he wants. I'm nothing, Evanglos. Just a broken-down old cop, waiting for his pension." He flicked his cigarette out the window. "You can't depend on me."

"You caught that killer on Chios, didn't you? You didn't give up even after you got hurt. You never give up."

"I give up sometimes." Patronas was thinking of his marriage as he said this, how he'd just taken his suitcase and left without a word of farewell.

"Not you. That's why I called you. You're a better cop than I am." His colleague's voice was wistful. "A better cop than I'll ever be. The best cop I know."

Poor Evangelos, putting his faith in him. It was the equivalent of boarding the Lusitania.

If things didn't work out, his colleague would be stuck on Patmos for the rest of his professional life, Sophia and his mother-in-law riding him day and night; his suffering would be like Job's.

Patronas looked out at the night. Maybe he should give Evangelos the name of his divorce lawyer.

Or better yet, solve the case.

THE HOTEL WAS in Hochlakas, the westernmost section of the port of Skala. The town bridged a narrow isthmus of land, and Patronas could hear the surf pounding in the distance, the coast here being far less protected than the area to the east where the harbor and tourist sites were located. There was a children's playground across the street from the hotel, the metal swings and slide sparkling in their newness.

The room was tidy, with three single beds and a rickety desk. The orange curtains and bedspreads had faded over time to a muddy yellow, as had the threadbare carpeting, making Patronas feel like he was trapped inside a bottle of mustard. The shower consisted of a handheld faucet over a hole in the floor, and the toilet was the old-fashioned kind, with a metal box high overhead and a length of rusty chain. It took forever to refill once flushed, which would pose a problem once Papa Michalis and Giorgos Tembelos arrived. The room's one saving grace was the small balcony that overlooked the children's playground and beyond it, the sea.

A woman named Antigone Balis owned the hotel and said she'd include breakfast in the price and prepare it for Patronas whenever he liked.

A handsome woman, she had a mane of unruly brown hair and was dressed in a red housedress, a robe thrown over her shoulders. She apologized for her appearance, saying she'd been just about to turn in when Patronas rang the bell at the front desk.

"You can have any room you want," she said. "The hotel is empty."

He told her he'd like a triple room on the top floor. "Something with a view if you got it."

Smiling, she handed him his key, said the room was up a flight of stairs on his left, and took her leave. "I'll see you in the morning. *Kalinyhta*." Good night.

Patronas watched her go. The air seemed warmer where she'd been, fresher somehow.

He told Evangelos Demos to pick him up at seven thirty and dragged himself up the stairs. He stowed his belongings in the closet and took off his shoes, then called Giorgos Tembelos on his cellphone.

"How'd it go in Athens?"

"Body got there without incident. Hearse was waiting and it bore the three of us away. Papa Michalis and I should be back tomorrow."

"Any clue as to the history of the deceased, who he really was?"

"Not yet. They're checking. It's hard. Staff's been cut. Might take some time."

"How's Papa Michalis bearing up?"

"Stubborn as ever. He drove the technicians crazy. 'What's in the liquid in your pipette? After you weigh the organs, do you put them in formaldehyde? If so, how long does it take before the flesh degrades?' He's a ghoul, that one. Could star in a zombie movie."

Patronas shook his head as he closed the phone. He could see the priest in his robes peering over the technicians' shoulders, poking his nose in their trays of gore and holding body parts up to the light. 'Putrefaction' was one of his favorite words. 'Cadaver' was another, and he could go on at length about 'adipocere,' the soapy foam that occasionally forms on corpses and 'saponification,' the process that produces it. He'd often discussed these things with Patronas—unfortunately, more often than not, during meals.

Patronas was too tired to undress and fell asleep on the bed with his clothes on. His sleep was restless, his dreams disturbed—there was something or someone crying out that he couldn't get to. He woke up at three a.m. and got up and drank a glass of water. There'd been a message somewhere in his dream, he was sure of it. Something he'd missed during the day or forgotten to ask. If only he could remember.

He fumbled around for cigarettes and stepped out on the balcony. Across the street, the children's playground shone in the darkness, the metal bright under the moon, the swings creaking in the wind. Music was coming from a taverna at the end of the street, a Greek cantata from the time of the war. He stood outside listening for a long time, smoking in the dark.

CHAPTER SEVEN

———◆———

Everyone is a physician, a musician, and a fool.
—Greek Proverb

P ATRONAS AND THE owner of the hotel had a friendly conversation over
breakfast the next morning. She'd fried potatoes, poured in beaten eggs,
and cooked it all in oil until a crust had formed, then slid it onto a plate and
handed it to him. A loaf of fresh bread was set out on the table, along with
butter and a clay pot full of homemade orange marmalade.

She set the long-handled pot, the *briki,* on the propane stove and lit the
flame. "How do you want your coffee?"

"*Metrio,*" Patronas said. Medium.

He cut off a piece of the omelet and ate it slowly, savoring the taste. "My
mother used to make eggs like this. It was one of my favorite dishes as a child."

She smiled. "Mine, too."

"It's delicious. Thank you."

When the coffee boiled, she poured it into a tiny cup and handed it to
him, then, unbidden, sat down at the table next to him. The room was warm
and she wiped her brow with the back of her hand, touched her hair with
her fingers. She was wearing a green dress of the thinnest cotton, so sheer
Patronas could see the stitching on her brassiere underneath, the line of her
panties. The latter appeared to be a thong, although he couldn't be sure, his
wife having favored far more substantial underwear. Like shorts, Dimitra's
panties had been, Bermuda shorts, reaching almost to the knee. Big and white
and hideous.

The woman's hair was pinned up today, a damp strand escaping and
curling at the nape of her neck. She was sitting so close he could smell the
soap on her skin.

Antigone Balis told him the hotel had been in her family for nearly twenty years. She'd inherited it after her father died. "I couldn't be bothered with it for a long time," she said. "I mean, who wants to be stuck on Patmos in the winter? Summer's fine, but the rest of the year, it's a graveyard. But then my husband died and I said to myself, 'Why not give it a try?' He was much older than I was and had been sick for a long time. I needed a change."

"How long have you been here?" Patronas pushed his notebook aside, not wanting to trouble her. She wasn't a suspect. They were just a man and a woman having a conversation.

"I opened it in June and renamed it the Sunrise Hotel. I had that big yellow sun painted on the side, hoping it would attract people. But so far it hasn't."

Patronas nodded. He'd seen the sun and remembered thinking how pathetic it was, the concrete beneath it riddled with cracks. He felt sorry for Antigone Balis being saddled with this place. The Sunset Hotel might have been a better name.

"It's been hard," she said. "I never rent more than three or four rooms a week, barely enough to get by."

"So you're not from Patmos?"

"No, no. I'm from the Peloponnese, a place you've never heard of. The hotel belonged to my grandfather, got passed down to my mother and then to me. It's a dump, I know. I tried to sell it, but no one wanted it. I was thinking of getting some money from the government to fix it up, but then things got bad and I gave up."

She leaned toward him, her dress falling open. "What about you? What do you do?"

He was fighting a losing battle to keep his eyes on her face. "I'm a cop. Yiannis Patronas, Chief Officer of the Chios Police." He gave a little bow when he finished, surprised at how much he wanted to impress her.

"*Hairo poli.*" Pleased to meet you. "Chief Officer, huh? I'll have to watch my step."

They both laughed.

A voluptuous morsel. Patronas noted the tasty way the fabric tugged at her breasts, her splendid knee caps, and trim little ankles. She was something, Antigone Balis, reminiscent of Gina Lollobrigida in her day, far too good for the likes of him. *Den einai ya ta dontia sou,* his mother always said when she thought he was reaching too high. Not for your teeth. Still, a man could dream.

"You have a wife, Mr. Chief Officer?" Antigone Balis asked.

"No, I'm divorced."

"Children?" She'd noticed his interest in her dress and it amused her.

"No, nobody."

She gave him a sympathetic look. "Hard to be alone."

"I have friends."

"It's not the same. Without family, you're nothing. Believe me, I know." She fanned her face with her hand. "It's going to be hot today. I hope you're working some place air-conditioned."

"Part of the day. The rest of the time I'll be outdoors." He took a sip of coffee. "Oh, I almost forgot. Two men will be checking in this afternoon. They'll be sharing the room with me. That's why I asked for a triple."

"All those beds ... I did wonder what you were up to." She shifted suggestively and gave him a knowing look. "Are they policemen, too?"

"One is. The other's a priest."

"A priest!" she exclaimed. "What happened? Did someone die?"

He didn't want to alarm her. "No, no, nothing like that."

A newcomer to the island, she might not learn of the murder for a day or two. Maybe when she bought her groceries, she'd hear the story. A place as small as Patmos, there'd be no way to hide such a crime. Still, he didn't want to taint their relationship from the onset with such darkness. Let her find out from others.

If she asked him later why he hadn't told her, he'd say he wanted to spare her. Men had done that in Greece in the old days, shielded their women. Yes, that would be the answer he'd give her. He'd been trying to be chivalrous, he'd say. Sir Galahad.

"It's just a routine police matter," he added, buttering a piece of bread. "The local officer used to work with us on Chios. He's here by himself. He called and asked for help on some cataloging for the department of culture. Someone found relics on a hill behind Chora and we need to log them in. Things were slow on Chios, so I came."

A lie, but a small one.

"If you think things are slow on Chios ...." Antigone Balis shook her head ruefully. "You said a priest would be checking in. There are plenty of priests on Patmos—too many, if you ask me. No need to import another one."

Patronas wiped his mouth with a napkin. "He's retired from the priesthood and works part-time for the department. He doesn't have much money, so I asked him to come along. I thought a trip to the island would be good for him, be a vacation of sorts." He knew he was talking too much, but couldn't seem to stop himself.

She smiled at him. "Paid for by the government?"

Patronas grinned back. "Of course."

They shared another laugh; then she gathered up the dishes and stood up. "What time will your friends be arriving?"

"I don't know. Whenever the police cruiser gets here from Leros."

"A police cruiser for a routine matter? You've been holding out on me, Chief Officer." Her laugh was low and musical. "You're here about the German, aren't you? The old man someone killed in Chora."

So much for chivalry.

PATRONAS CALLED GIORGOS Tembelos a few minutes later, making sure first that Antigone Balis was well out of range. Not much got by that woman, that was for sure. She'd let him go on and on before delivering the *skylovrisi*—the dog's curse. He should have been more circumspect over breakfast, not run his mouth like a schoolboy. It was the see-through dress that had done it, that glimpse of her nether regions.

He could hear the roar of the engine in the background. "You on the boat?"

"Yup," Tembelos said. "Just left Piraeus."

"I rented a room for you in a hotel, the Sunrise. It is on a backstreet in Skala. A woman named Antigone Balis owns it. Be careful with her. She's a wily creature."

"Is she pretty? You sound smitten."

Remembering the dress, Patronas reluctantly answered in the affirmative.

"Married?"

"Nope. A widow."

"A widow!" Tembelos chuckled. "Oh, Yiannis, here we go again."

Since the divorce, Tembelos had started treating Patronas like he was some kind of Don Juan, a man who bedded a different woman every night. Swedish, French, it didn't matter, they were all after him, according to Giorgos. Patronas was Casanova and then some. Books could be written about his sexual peccadillos. Tembelos actually called them that. The playboy Hugh Hefner could take lessons.

Truth was, Patronas hadn't been with a woman in the biblical sense for more than two years. Long before his divorce, he and his ex-wife had occupied different rooms in the house. A homely man, he knew he was nothing to look at. He had a mirror. Sometimes he wondered if he'd ever sleep with a woman again.

Tembelos knew this and was trying to build his confidence, to give him the courage to start over. Women were necessary evils in his view. Without them, a man weakened and lost his edge. They were sort of like vitamins.

"I'm here on a murder investigation," Patronas answered primly, playing along. "I'm not looking for romance."

"Got to be careful with women, Yiannis. Some are like spiders; they eat their mates."

"I'm not unfamiliar with them."

More laughter. "Oh, by the way, your ex-wife, the *vouvala*, is leaving

Chios." A vulgar term for a woman, *vouvala* meant 'water buffalo.' Tembelos hated Dimitra and always called her that.

"What do you mean, 'leaving'? Where is she going?"

"Italy. According to my wife, the *vouvala's* uncle in Bologna said he could find her a job there. No worries, Yiannis; your ex is out of your life. She's finally moving on."

The news that Dimitra was leaving for Italy took Patronas by surprise. They'd been to Italy once, years before, walked through the streets of Rome and visited the Sistine Chapel, drank expensive coffees on the Via Veneto and inspected the Michelangelos. His wife had been stunned by the handsomeness of the Italian men, and he'd bought himself a fedora and a cashmere scarf, in an effort to look like them. Foolish now, he realized, him thinking a hat could make a difference. Turn a dumpy, middle-aged detective into Marcello Mastroianni. He'd been trying to impress Dimitra in those days—Dimitra, who'd adored the Italian actor. Hard to believe that now.

He looked down at himself, buttons straining across his midriff, his splayed feet, and ran a hand through what was left of his hair. She'd laughed at the way he walked, rocking from side to side, said he reminded her of Charlie Chaplin. At one time or another, she'd laughed at most everything about him. His camel's nose and boxy mustache—the mustache he cherished because he thought it made him look like his father. His clumsy eagerness in bed. He closed his eyes. *Oh, God. Dimitra. My wasted life.*

Soon she would be well and truly gone. Somehow this news did not make him as happy as he thought it would.

"Anything else to report?" Patronas kept his voice light. No reason for Giorgos Tembelos to know his news had upset him.

"Not really. They finished the autopsy in Athens. I'm sure you'll hear more from Evangelos, who called last night and got the report. It was pretty much just like you said: someone split his skull open. Death wasn't instantaneous, the coroner said, but close to it. The blow rendered the victim unconscious, but he was still alive when the perpetrator cut the swastika on his forehead. Alive, but on his way out. Hard to tell what they hit him with. Could have been anything. The coroner found dirt in the wound, and he's going to test it against the sample of soil you took from the garden. Going to run a toxicology screen, too—see if there's anything unusual in the victim's blood. Nothing but beer would be my guess, but the lab still has to check. Also, they're testing the tallow from the crime scene, comparing it to the church candles from Patmos to see if there's a match."

"Let's hope not. I don't want a Greek involved in this, Giorgos. I want it to be a stranger passing through who beat the old man to death. Not one of us. I couldn't bear it if it was one of us."

"Sometimes we don't get what we want, Yiannis. Greece has crazy people, too, just like everyplace else."

"Not that crazy."

"Suit yourself."

"What about Interpol?"

"They're still checking. If there's anything about Bechtel in their database, they'll get in touch with us. Otherwise, not. Same thing in Athens. They might never get to the databases, they said, given the backlog of cases and the budgetary situation. Cut the staff in half, the government did, and turned off the air-conditioning. It was hell in that lab, I can tell you. You wouldn't believe the smell."

Patronas quickly filled Tembelos in on what he'd learned from the victim's family. "Someone killed the grandfather's cat, tortured it apparently. Could have been random, but I don't think so. Someone's been targeting the family for a reason."

"But why?"

"Damned if I know."

There was a long silence.

"I don't like this, Yiannis," Tembelos finally said.

Patronas sighed. "Nor I, Giorgos. Nor I."

CHAPTER EIGHT

———— ✦ ————

You can knock a long time on a deaf man's door.
—Greek Proverb

THE AUTOPSY REPORT was as Patronas had expected: death from a subcranial fracture and bleeding in the brain. No indication of what had been used. The coroner rarely speculated; this time had been no exception.

"I thought of something as I was driving the other day," Evangelos Demos said as he and Patronas walked toward the car.

Must have been quite an experience—driving and thinking. A wonder he didn't kill himself. Patronas had concluded long ago that his colleague was incapable of thought. The process simply eluded him, as did the concept of cause and effect, tit for tat, many other useful things. Zippers would give Evangelos trouble.

Edging closer, Evangelos Demos whispered in his ear. "It occurred to me that terrorists might be involved."

"Terrorists!" Patronas was astounded. Even for Evangelos, the idea was stupid.

"Yes. Remember that terrorist group, November Seventeeth? Their leader, the mathematician, resided on Lipsi. That's very close to Patmos. Less than an hour away by boat."

"So?"

"So one of them could have done it."

"November Seventeenth shot people, Evangelos. CIA agents, Greek politicians, and industrialists. They never went after Germans. And if they did, a rock would not have been their weapon of choice."

"You don't know it was a rock."

Patronas fought to keep his voice down. "Evangelos, they used *bazookas.*"

"Maybe they've changed their tactics."

Patronas had been trying to quit smoking, but the situation demanded nicotine and he pulled out his emergency pack of Karelias and lit up. "You share this 'thought' of yours with anyone else?" he asked.

"I told Stathis in Athens."

Patronas closed his eyes. That's what you get when you try to help someone. They ruin your career. How did the proverb go? I taught you to swim and now you try to drown me.

"And what did Stathis say?" He drew on his cigarette furiously. He would have eaten it if he could.

"He said, and I quote, 'November Seventeenth is no longer a threat.' "

"There you go."

"I still think we should check it out."

"Listen to me, Evangelos, we're going to interview the residents of Chora. That's what's on the schedule for today—not Lipsi, not terrorists. Understand?"

"But what if the killer doesn't live in the village? We'll be bothering a lot of innocent people."

It's a wonder he doesn't blow a fuse in his brain, overload that one, hard-working cell. "We're cops, Evangelos. Like I told you before, we don't care about bothering people."

"That's not true. I care. I care a lot. I live here."

"I have an idea. Why don't you go back to your office and wait there? Maybe the killer will come and find you."

"What if you're wrong? What if the crime was political?"

"You think someone's declared war on Germany?"

Evangelos nodded. "It wouldn't be the first time."

THEY DROVE IN silence through the backstreets of Skala, slowly making their way to Chora. It was a beautiful morning, the sunlight piercing. Patronas yearned for Chios, for the security of what he knew, to forget about the case and the mastodon sitting next to him.

He rolled down the window and inhaled deeply. Tembelos and the priest were due to arrive in a few hours; he could last until then. Hopefully, what was wrong with Evangelos wasn't contagious.

"What do we say to people?" Evangelos asked fretfully, a moment later. "You can't just ask, 'Did you do it?' I'd be insulted if someone asked me that."

"Oh, for God's sake, Evangelos!"

They continued in this manner for another ten minutes, Evangelos proposing and Patronas resisting.

Groucho Marx, no doubt about it.

Patronas remembered the way the comedian had talked in circles in the movies, answered questions no one had asked and derailed entire conversations.

Maybe I could get a harp and strum it like Groucho's brother, Harpo. Forget about police work; we could swing from the rafters, Evangelos and me, reenact A Night at the Opera.

They started with the two *tavli* players in the square, Themis Poulis and Philippos Zanaras.

"You see anything?" Patronas asked the men.

He had bought them breakfast earlier and the table was littered with crumbs. The man called Themis had offered to read his fortune in the coffee grinds—an old custom that involved dumping the grinds out on a plate and studying them, prophesying the way the ancients had once done with entrails—but Patronas had declined. He was here to work. Besides, he knew his fortune. A divorced policeman, he was destined to spend the rest of his life lonely and poor. First, his hair would go, after which he'd probably lose control of his bladder.

He opened his notebook. "Was someone hanging around the house?"

"I never saw anyone," Poulis said, "just the family and the people who worked for them, the gardener and the maid."

He'd been a farmer in the old days, he went on to say, had wrestled with the stony earth for over sixty years. "I grew tomatoes and raised a few sheep. It was a hard life, but a good one. I helped out at the monastery, too, on feast days."

In his eighties, he had skin like wrinkled brown paper.

"Did you ever speak to the Bechtels?" Patronas asked.

"Only the little boy, Walter."

The child had wanted to learn *tavli* and had watched them avidly for a morning or two when the family first came. "He couldn't get it," the farmer said. "Maybe it was the language …." His voice trailed off. "I know a little German," he added, embarrassed. "Nothing formal, only what I picked up during the war. The soldiers, they occupied my house. But I didn't want to use the German I knew on the boy. It was ugly, the German I knew, curses mostly. Hateful talk."

The taverna owner had nothing to add. Although the Bauers and their guests, the Bechtels, had eaten often in his tavern, aside from taking their orders, he'd never spoken to them directly. He, too, had seen nothing the night of the murder. Over and over he repeated that he couldn't believe something like this had happened on Patmos. "We're not the way we were," he said.

The two old men nodded.

"Greece has changed," Themis Poulis said.

THE HOUSEKEEPER LIVED in a rooming house in Skala, about four blocks away from the Sunrise Hotel. An abandoned water desalination plant had once occupied the site, Patronas remembered. Immense in its ugliness, it had been a vast graveyard of shattered glass and rusting metal frames. He saw no trace of it today.

Made of reinforced concrete, the housekeeper's building appeared to be relatively new, two stories high with a row of windows overlooking a small parking lot in front. Dumpsters were lined up along the left side of the building and pots of fake flowers adorned the entrance, their plastic leaves gray with dust.

"Tourists stay here?" Patronas asked.

"Some," Evangelos said. "Church groups, mostly. There are only sixteen rooms and the owner prefers to rent them by the month, so the majority of residents work in the tourist industry or for private families like the Bauers. It's not a bad place to stay. It's cheap and the rooms are clean."

"How does she get from here to Chora?"

"Bus probably. It drops you off at the top of the hill near the city hall, and then you walk the rest of the way."

Illuminated by fluorescent bulbs, the lobby was full of elderly Greek women, at least fifteen of them, chattering like magpies.

Some kind of religious tour, Patronas guessed, seeing the women had a priest with them. That had been the only kind of tourism permitted widows in the old days. They all had the same brochure in hand and were discussing the Cave of the Apocalypse, where trumpets had sounded and a saint had foreseen the end of the world.

Dimitra's kinfolk.

Listening to their excited voices, Patronas again remembered his honeymoon—not quite the end of the world, but close.

The owner of the hotel directed Patronas and Evangelos down a dimly lit hallway to Maria Georgiou's room.

Not wanting to alert the other residents of the rooming house of their presence, Patronas tapped softly on the door.

How did the saying go? It is better if a priest, a doctor, and a policeman not enter one's house.

He'd called the hotel the previous day and spoken to her to arrange the interview, so she was expecting them.

The housekeeper looked as if she were on her way to church, dressed in a blue rayon shirtwaist with a lace collar, stockings, and high-heeled shoes. A poor woman, she probably kept the outfit for special occasions—feast days, perhaps—an interview with the police evidently counting as one.

Patronas introduced himself. "I am Yiannis Patronas, Kyria Georgiou," he said, "Chief Officer of the Chios Police Force, and this is my colleague, Evangelos Demos, who's in charge of the police here."

"Maria Georgiou," the woman said shyly. "*Hairo poli.*"

Glad to meet you.

The room was clean and spare, light streaming in from a row of open windows. Patronas saw a pair of birds pecking at some seeds scattered along the sill. Swallows, they came and went, fluttering their wings as they landed. Their nest must be elsewhere.

The housekeeper nodded to the little birds. "I feed them." she explained. "I'm alone and they keep me company. It's a small reward for their songs."

Maria Georgiou was a handsome woman with perfectly symmetrical features, reminiscent of classic statuary. Her nose was long and straight and her lips were full. Her eyes were dark and her unplucked brows were as thick as a man's.

What Nefertiti might have looked like in old age, Patronas thought.

Her white hair was coiled in a bun at the nape of her neck.

There were two upholstered chairs in front of a bank of windows, a broken down coffee table positioned between them. A neatly made bed and a tiny kitchenette occupied the rest of the space. A pine chest, stained to look like mahogany, was pushed up against the back wall.

A small fan on top of the chest whirred softly as it rotated back and forth. In spite of it, the room was hot and stuffy.

Maria Georgiou had made an effort to make the space her own, he saw, setting out an icon of the Virgin Mary and a photograph of a man and woman in a silvery frame. Her mother and father, Patronas judged, noting the family resemblance. A piece of cloth was artfully draped across the top of the coffee table. Hand-embroidered in the style of the Epirus region in northern Greece, the fabric was dense with blue and ochre stitching, gold threadwork. It looked out of place amid the cheap furnishings.

Patronas fingered the cloth. It seemed an odd thing to travel with.

As was the custom in Greece, she had set out a tray of sweets for them.

"The *koulourakia* are fresh," she said, pushing the plate of cookies toward him. "I bought them this morning."

Patronas took one and ate it in awkward silence while she sat and watched him, having taken nothing herself. Evangelos was leaning against the wall by the door. He and Patronas had mapped out their strategy on the way there, and his colleague was doing as instructed, stepping aside and letting Patronas take the lead.

"You know why we're here?" Patronas asked her.

"Yes, the murder of Mr. Bechtel's father." Her Greek was heavily accented. Like the cloth on the table, she was from Epirus, Patronas judged, hearing the way she spoke, the distinct regional intonation. She might even be a Greek from Albania.

"May I see your identity card?"

Getting up, she walked over to the chest and opened a drawer. She removed a tired leather handbag, took out a square of plastic, and handed it to him.

Patronas compared the photo on the ID to the woman standing before him. They looked to be the same, although the photo did not do her justice. She was older than he'd originally thought, born in 1937.

As he'd done with the gardener, he wrote down the information and handed the card back to her.

"How long have you worked for the Bauers?" he asked.

"Since June. I came to Patmos on a holiday. The owner of the place where I was staying said a family was looking for a woman to do housework. They wanted a Greek, he said. It was important to them."

"And you volunteered?"

"Yes. It's hard to find Greek maids now and he said it wasn't hard work. Only a little cleaning, two or three hours a day, and the pay was good."

"Where did you have this conversation?"

"Campos. That's where I was staying. In a place that rents rooms, smaller than here. Pavlos, it's called."

"Is that the owner's name?"

"Yes, Antonis Pavlos."

Patronas entered the name in his notebook. "How did the owner know the Bauers were looking for someone?"

"He's married to a German woman, and she's friendly with them. There's a group of people from Stuttgart who come to Campos every summer and they know each other."

"Where are you from originally?" he asked, curious about her accent.

"A village near Ioannina. Aghios Stefanos."

"Do you still live there?"

"No, I left years ago. I'm in Athens now. Exarhia."

No wonder she'd wanted to linger on Patmos. Exarhia was a crime-ridden slum, one of the worst in Greece. A woman alone? She'd be afraid to step outside her door.

"You said you came to Patmos on a holiday? That's a long trip, over eight hours by boat. Wouldn't one of the islands near Athens, Poros or Aegina, have been more convenient?" *Cheaper, too.* Patmos was expensive by Greek standards.

She touched the gold cross around her neck. "My father was a priest and he studied at the seminary on Patmos. I am a religious woman and I wanted to see it and the other churches on the island—the Monastery of St. John and the Cave of the Apocalypse—have a *mnimosina* sung for my parents." A memorial service. "It was important to me."

"Do you work in Athens?"

"No, I'm retired."

"What did you do before you retired?"

"I was a beautician."

Strange, a beautician who didn't dye her hair or bother with makeup, whose whole persona seemed frozen in time. He decided to probe further.

"What was the name of the salon?"

"Electra. It was on Solomos Street."

"Do you remember the exact address?"

"It's gone now. It went out of business last winter. The building's been empty for months."

He underlined the name, thinking he'd have the police in Athens follow up. "Let's talk about your job here. How did you get along with the family? Not the ones who hired you, but their guests, the Bechtels."

"I got along good. Mrs. Gerta, she wanted to learn how to cook Greek sweets and I showed her how to make *baklava* and *kataifi*, other things she didn't know. The children were very well behaved and polite. And they always paid me on time. Overtime, too, if I worked late."

A serious woman, her gaze was steady, her voice unwavering.

"No offense, Kyria, but aren't you a little old to be working as a maid?"

Her smile was sad. "I am a poor woman, Chief Officer. What choice do I have?"

"What about Mr. Bechtel's father? How did you get along with him?"

He was watching her closely. It was the key question and they both knew it.

"We were not friendly." Raising her head, she gazed at him for a moment before continuing. "He was an old-fashioned man, used to getting his own way, and not very patient. But he didn't ask for much, only a cold beer in the afternoon and to keep his newspaper where he could find it. His daughter-in-law, she was the one who took care of him."

The old man was *her* problem, she was saying, not *mine*.

What she said was consistent with what Gerta Bechtel had told him. Due to the language barrier, Maria Georgiou's contact with the victim had been limited.

"And his son?"

"Mr. Gunther? The same. Mrs. Gerta was the one in charge. My job was to help her. They might be different from us, those people, but not in that. For them, too, the house belongs to the woman."

Patronas scribbled down what she said. "And the children?"

"Little Walter, we were together sometimes in the garden. The girl, Hannelore, no."

"Did you ever see anyone suspicious hanging around?"

"No. The house is isolated. No one goes there."

She spoke no more than necessary and always in the same steady voice.

"What about the entrance? The door in the stone wall, is it kept locked?" He'd meant to go back to the subject of the door and who had the keys to it with the Bechtels, but had forgotten. He made a note to discuss it with them again.

"The gardener is supposed to lock up after he's done watering, but sometimes he forgets and it stays open all night. Or the little boy leaves it open after he puts his bicycle in. The old man liked to stay in the garden, and I guess they believed no one would bother them as long as he was there. But he was deaf. You could walk right past him, and he wouldn't hear."

"So it wasn't your job to secure the outside door?"

"When I was there at night, I'd see to it, but usually I just cooked dinner for them and left it on the stove. I didn't like to stay on in their house after I finished my job."

"Who has keys to the door?"

"The one in the wall? I do, and the gardener. Also the family kept extra keys around the house, one on a nail by the outside entrance for Walter to use—a big skeleton key like in the old days. Little Walter would take it down, use it when he left with his bicycle, and slide it back under the door." She demonstrated, sliding her hand along the floor.

"How many extra keys?"

"Five, maybe more. You'll have to check with Mrs. Gerta. Anyway, you didn't need a key to get into the garden. Most of the time, the gate was open."

On his list, Patronas drew a line through the word, 'key.' He'd keep after them, but it wouldn't be the focus of his investigation.

Arthritic, the housekeeper's fingers were thick and reddened with work, her palms heavily callused. She rubbed the swollen joints as she talked, one hand going back and forth over the other.

Patronas' mother had made a similar gesture, and he wondered if her hands pained her the way his mother's had.

"What about the cat, the stray the grandfather befriended?"

"I told Mrs. Bechtel I didn't like cats, that they were dirty, and she told me not to worry, that she'd take care of it, feed it, and make sure it had water. She was very upset when it died. Walter, too. I stayed in the house. I didn't want to see." She shuddered, remembering. "The gardener got a shovel and buried it in the garden. A crow tried to peck at it after, but he chased it away."

"You don't know who killed it?"

She shrugged. "Kids in the village, maybe. Who knows?"

Unable to think of anything else to ask her, Patronas got up from his chair. "Thank you for your cooperation. We will verify everything you said and get back to you if we have any further questions."

"Of course," she said, bridling a little. "I am an honest woman. You will find everything is as I said it was. I have nothing to hide."

CHAPTER NINE

———◆———

Either the coast is crooked or our boat is going the
wrong way.
—Greek Proverb

AFTER LEAVING THE rooming house, Patronas and Evangelos Demos
worked their way through the rest of Chora, fanning out separately
and going from door to door. There weren't more than eight or nine streets.
Patronas drew a grid and checked off each one as he completed his interviews.
He and Evangelos Demos had agreed to meet at the car when they finished,
then drive back to Skala to meet Tembelos and the priest.

Morning, most of the residents were still at home, drinking coffee on their
terraces or eating breakfast inside. In spite of their wealth, most were dressed
casually, men and women alike. Similar to the Bechtels, they wore jeans and
t-shirts, espadrilles or leather flip-flops. A few had children running around,
overseen by bored-looking women from the Philippines. For the most part,
they welcomed Patronas and were eager to share what they knew. They had
all heard about the murder and wanted whoever had done it apprehended.

He'd been expecting grandeur, but found instead artful imitations of Greek
village life: clay water jugs and primitive furniture, hand-loomed tapestries
and rugs. One house even had an old spinning wheel on display, a spotlight
shining on it as if it were a work of art in a museum. Patronas had studied it
with amusement, wondering how much the owners had paid, thinking the
further away people got from their peasant origins, the more they celebrated
them. How little they actually knew of that life, the hardship and the struggle.
Again, he thought of his mother's hands.

He laboriously interviewed more than thirty people in a variety of tongues.

Before they'd started, Evangelos Demos had suggested Patronas use the
translation application on his phone and shown him how to use it. Painful
advice, given who it was coming from, but Patronas had tried it out and found

it useful. Most of the residents spoke passable English. He'd only needed it with the Russians.

The majority of the people admitted that while they might recognize the Bechtels on sight, they did not know them well. They were unwilling to speculate about what went on in their house. There'd been no incidents with the children, and they could think of no reasons anyone would bear them a grudge.

"How about strangers hanging around?" Patronas asked one elderly British man.

"Strangers disembark from the cruise ships all summer, Chief Officer, and come swarming through the streets of Chora. It's quite unsettling. I'll be sitting outside and look up and see some Chinese woman in a hat, peering over the wall at me." He gave a snigger of laughter. "I'm not a native. Truth is, I wouldn't know a stranger if I met one. As Casca said to Cassius in Julius Caesar, 'It's all Greek to me.' "

Patronas did not find the man nearly as entertaining as he thought he was. "So you never saw anyone suspicious?"

The Englishman paused for a moment. "I might have. It's hard to say. Personally, I loathe tattoos and think those who possess them must be criminals. Only jailbirds sported them in my time. However, my grandchildren inform me that such things are all the rage now, the height of fashion. I fear I am out of date, Chief Officer, a throwback to an earlier, and if I may say so, more genteel era. I don't trust my judgment with respect to people anymore. Nor should you."

"So no one suspicious?"

"None that I am aware of."

A French woman with a high-pitched voice claimed she'd seen Maria Georgiou coming away from the house on the night in question. However, her description was highly inaccurate, as eye witness accounts often were. For one thing, she considered the housekeeper to be a gypsy, 'une gitane,' or possibly a Moroccan, 'une habitante du Maroc' and said she had 'les cheveux gris,' gray hair, when her hair was white. Although the French woman was a pretty thing, stylish and petite, her voice began to grate on Patronas, the going back and forth between French and English.

Couldn't she have learned the word for maid, at least? Domestique, be damned.

Still, pencil in hand, he dutifully transcribed what she said and entered it in his notebook. Useless, every word of it.

Many people had seen the children, Walter and Hannelore, in the square or waiting for the bus on the road. Their parents, too, on occasion. Yet, no one could recall ever seeing the victim in Chora.

They recoiled when he told them about the cat. One woman—a matronly Greek-American with bleached hair—commented that torturing animals was what serial killers did. It was their defining characteristic, the only thing they all had in common. According to her, "As children such people wet the bed, set fires, and hurt animals." He must be vigilant, she warned, in case such an individual was now on Patmos.

All in all, quite tedious.

EVANGELOS HADN'T FARED much better. "It's worse than I imagined," he told Patronas when they met up later by the car. "Only fifteen Greeks in the whole village and most of them only work here during the day. Even if they were born in Chora, they can't afford to live there anymore. I ended up speaking English nearly the whole time."

"You learn anything?"

"Everyone I spoke to said that while they'd probably recognize Gunther and Gerta Bechtel, they had never had what amounted to a conversation with either one of them. As far as they knew, the victim, Walter Bechtel, didn't exist."

Patronas nodded. He'd heard much the same. "What about the kids?"

"Same thing. They said they knew the girl on sight, Walter, too, but that's it. They never talked to them."

"How about Hannelore's friend, Hilda? Did you speak to her or her family?"

"Yes. Nothing there."

Patronas made a note. They were ciphers, the Bechtels. It was almost as if they avoided people. Again, he wondered why.

He opened the door of the car and got in. A day lost and they'd come up empty handed. As the proverb went, *They spoke only of winds and water.*

THE POLICE CRUISER arrived later that day and Giorgos Tembelos and Papa Michalis disembarked, the priest inching down the ramp like a tortoise.

"I think the identity of the old man is the key," Papa Michalis announced when they'd all gathered in a taverna to review the case. "I analyzed it and that is my conclusion. It simply cannot be anything else. It has elements of an Agatha Christie story, one of her locked-room mysteries like *And Then There Was None*. Nobody else had access; *ergo*, one of the people inside the estate, a family member or a servant, must be the guilty party."

"Anyone could have gained access," Patronas pointed out. "The Bechtels were careless. They didn't keep the door locked and there were keys lying around everywhere."

"No matter. It's got to be one of them. We can interview other people forever, but it will eventually come back to them. Them and them alone."

"I think Father is right," Tembelos said. "The identity of the victim is the important thing here. There was nothing about him in any of the European databases I checked. I called our counterparts in Germany and asked them to run him through their system, but I doubt they'll find anything. It's like he never existed. We need to establish who he was. Could be he changed his name."

"Why would he change his name?" Patronas wondered.

"I don't know."

The four of them were sitting outside by the water, it being too hot to venture inside. A haze hung over the sea, and the air was very still. Suddenly, a soft breeze rose up and stirred the tamarisk trees that lined the shore, setting their feathery branches in motion. Patronas liked the rustling sound the trees made, the relief the wind brought. It was almost as if he could hear the earth breathe.

I'll go swimming tonight, he told himself, looking out at the harbor. Float on my back and look up at the stars. Frolic like a dolphin.

Maybe he'd ask Antigone Balis to join him. He pictured her dripping wet, that long hair of hers hanging down over one shoulder like Botticelli's Venus. Adrift in his vision, he subsequently lost track of the conversation.

"Hey, boss, you with us?" Tembelos nudged him with his elbow.

Patronas made a show of straightening his back, stretching. "Sorry, it's the heat. Always makes me sleepy."

"You were grinning."

"So what if I was? A man's allowed to grin."

"I don't know, Yiannis," the priest said. "I think when one is discussing a homicide, it might be better if one dispensed with grinning. At such a time, such behavior is unseemly. It makes one appear insensitive at the very least."

"Thank you for that, Father. In the future, I will dispense with grinning." He tapped his pencil on his notebook. "So, to sum up, we have nothing concrete in the case, no witnesses or physical evidence, nothing that will lead us to the killer."

"Gardener's clean," Tembelos reported. "I ran his fingerprints and there was nothing. There was a match on the shoes, too, exactly like he told us."

"What about the housekeeper, Maria Georgiou?"

"Same thing. The case is heating up. If we don't catch the killer, it could get ugly. Ministry's already clamoring for action."

"We need to turn the housekeeper, Maria Georgiou, inside out, also the members of the family," Patronas said. "Check their history. Something's going on here, but as of yet, I haven't established what it is."

"You can't rule out a random act of violence," the priest said, "directed at them because of their nationality."

"Worse would be if it were a case of mistaken identity," Patronas said, "the killer targeting the owners—the Bauers—and killing one of their guests by mistake."

He was thinking of Charlie Manson, who along with his disciples had wiped out six people without blinking an eye, not realizing his intended victim was a subletter. "Personally, I think someone targeted the family for reasons we don't know. The cat, the old man. It stands to reason."

"I'd start with the housekeeper," Tembelos said. "What she said doesn't add up. That bit about coming to Patmos on holiday and staying on as a maid."

"Unlikely, Giorgos. She's in her seventies."

Papa Michalis continued to promote the locked room concept. Citing a case in *The Adventures of Sherlock Holmes*, he described how the killer had released a cobra through a fake vent and activated its poisonous energy by whistling. " 'Oh, my God, it was the band,' the victim shouted, 'the speckled band.' "

"Fiction, Father, fiction," Patronas said impatiently. "Remember? We discussed it."

"My point is if you are determined to kill someone, a lock is no deterrent. Sometimes murderers are ingenious. Using a cobra as a murder weapon is brilliant when you think about it. Absolutely brilliant. No fingerprints involved, no way to trace it back to you. The snake does all the work."

"I repeat, Father, there is no snake involved here. A stone maybe, but no snake."

"A stone? What makes you think that?"

And around they went again, weighing the possibilities. The victim had been hit on the head, but with what? A hammer or a rock? A shovel or pickax? Rock, scissors, paper.

Forget swimming, Patronas told himself. I might as well drown myself.

At one point, Evangelos launched into a long, convoluted discourse on terrorism, which no one paid much attention to. "Christodoulos Xeros of November Seventeenth escaped in January and he's threatening to organize the Greeks to fight against the austerity measures. He might be making a move here against the Germans. We need to go to Lipsi and speak with the authorities there, see if there's been any movement in or out. Could be the Greek terrorists have liaised with Osama Bin Laden."

"Liaised?" Tembelos raised his eyebrows. "Such a big word, Evangelos, 'liaised.' "

"Evangelos, they are all in jail," Patronas snapped. "November Seventeenth is gone. They're history."

"I spoke to Athens again and they want us to explore the possibility. 'Leave no stone unturned,' they said."

And back they were to where they'd started. Rocks, scissors, paper.

"I think it all comes down to history," Patronas finally said. "We keep coming back to it. It's the operative word."

PATRONAS SWAM FOR a long time that night, rolling around like a seal in the shallows before paddling out into the harbor. He trailed after a departing ship, one of the Blue Star ferries, floating up and down on its massive wake, watching the single light of the boat move back and forth across the water like the fiery eye of the Cyclops. There was a warning buoy in the middle of the harbor, and he swam toward it.

According to a local legend, a sorcerer named Kynops had fought with St. John there, lost the battle and been turned into a rock, where he remained to this day, petrified and unmoving at the bottom of the sea. Hence the buoy. There were many such tales in Greece, describing how pagan forces had been defeated by the new order, Christianity. They dated from the time the two traditions had overlapped, the power of the saints gradually overtaking that of the gods on Mount Olympus—but then again, not quite. You could still find depictions of St. Dionysius with vine leaves in his hair, nearly identical to his ancient counterpart, the wine-sodden god Dionysus, and there was no question that Prophet Ilias, saint of the mountaintops, was a reincarnation of the Greek god, Apollo, both of them chasing across the sky in fiery chariots.

Antigone Balis had told him the story of Kynops that morning, saying many people on Patmos still believed it.

"The coast guard has tried to dynamite the rock many times," she'd said. "It's a hazard to ships. But they've never succeeded, and fish caught anywhere near it taste foul."

"What? Like sulfur?"

"Stop teasing," she'd said and swatted his hand.

Patronas smiled, remembering the exchange. It had felt like flirting. Maybe it was.

Sticking his head underwater, he searched for the rock, wanting to tell her that he'd seen it, but it was close to midnight; the water was dark and impenetrable and he saw nothing.

He grabbed onto the buoy and rested for a moment, fatigue washing over him. Made of metal, it rocked back and forth under his weight, clanging softly.

Releasing it, Patronas swam farther out into the harbor. He was a good swimmer and moved quickly through the water. A sailboat was anchored not far from him and he could hear people talking on board, the trill of a woman's laughter. The lights of Skala glimmered in the distance, but where he was, all was darkness.

The woman's laugh came again.

For a moment his solitude overwhelmed him.

"I'm so alone."

Everywhere people were enjoying the summer's night, but for him there was nothing. Antigone Balis or someone like her was a dream, a hopeless dream.

"So alone," he said again.

Dimitra, his dead parents, the only family he'd ever known, all of them lost or soon would be. Where had it all gone? His hopes for children, a house full of toys and laughter? He lifted up a handful of seawater and let it run through his fingers.

All my life I've been an onlooker, he thought. Maybe that's why I became a policeman, so I could peek through a keyhole because I'm unable to open the door. My only friends are a priest who talks too much and a cop who barely talks at all. He didn't count Evangelos Demos.

He lingered at the buoy a few more minutes before starting back, swimming at a leisurely pace. The stars were so near, he felt like he could reach up and grab them, cast them into the water and watch them explode like fireworks in its inky depths. He could see the entire length of the Milky Way, gauzy and bright with stars, follow it with his eyes as if it were a road across the heavens. He wondered what lay beyond it—if the universe went on forever, expanding, like people said.

Maybe, like his mother believed, there was a heaven and he'd find his way there one day. Somehow he doubted it. No, probably he'd be buried in the dirt when his time came and that would be that. Otherwise, his grave would be as it was tonight, dark and solitary, the sense of life being lived all around him, just beyond his reach.

PATRONAS WAS SOUND asleep when the priest barged in and shook him awake. He had taken Patronas' notebook the previous night, saying he wanted to study it downstairs before turning in, and had it open in his hands. He was very agitated, vibrating like a tuning fork.

"The maid, Maria Georgiou, is she really from Aghios Stefanos?"

Patronas nodded.

"Aghios Stefanos in northern Greece?" Papa Michalis' voice rose. "It's important. There are other villages with the same name."

"Judging by her accent, that would be my conclusion, Father. 'Tha si' instead of 'tha sou.' Epirus for sure."

The old man seemed strangely exhilarated. Holmes closing in on Moriarty.

"What is it, Father? Tell me."

"Aghios Stefanos has a terrible history. The Nazis …." His voice rose. "You must remember what happened there. You must have learned about it in school. It was one of the worst massacres of the war. Not as bad as Kalavryta and Distomo, but a tragedy, nonetheless. They killed whole families, women and children, and beat the village priest to death. That's how I came to know the story. They talked about it in the seminary when I was a student and held a memorial service for him on the anniversary of the day. August sixteenth, I still remember, it was—the day after the Assumption of the Virgin, if you can imagine. They said people were asleep in their beds when the soldiers came and that some of them tried to escape by wading across the river. The Nazis shot them, too. The water ran red for days."

"How many?"

"I don't know exactly. A hundred, maybe fifty or sixty more. All non-combatants."

"Maria Georgiou said her father was a priest."

"If that is indeed true, this might well have been an act of revenge, Yiannis." Patronas nodded. "As a motive, it's a good one."

"A tragedy if it was." The priest's voice was sorrowful. " 'Before you embark on a journey of revenge, dig two graves.' "

"That yours or did you read it somewhere?"

"It's Chinese, Confucius." He continued, "Nearly all religions counsel against revenge. It says in Romans, *Avenge not yourselves … for it is written, vengeance is mine; I will repay, saith the Lord.* The Lord, not you or me, Yiannis. The Lord. Maria Georgiou was the daughter of a priest. She should have known that."

"Seventy years is a long time to wait, Father. Maybe she got tired of waiting on the Lord."

CHAPTER TEN

———◆———

Time leads truth to the light.
—Greek Proverb

Patronas immediately telephoned Athens, thinking he'd better tread carefully. He had no proof that Maria Georgiou was responsible. It could be coincidence that the daughter of a victim of the Nazis was in the house with that family, but he doubted it. The murder of Walter Bechtel might well have been a revenge killing, a kind of geriatric score settling. Still, he needed hard evidence. The tragic history of one's birthplace is hardly admissible in a court of law, and as he'd told Papa Michalis, the war was a long time ago. It didn't help that his suspect was a seventy-eight-year-old woman, and as a general rule, women that age didn't beat people's brains in, no matter what the provocation. Also, there was no evidence that the victim had been anywhere near Aghios Stefanos during the war or taken part in the massacre of its inhabitants.

Maria Georgiou was a long shot, he knew, but at this point, she was all he had.

"Can you get me whatever you have on German reprisal operations in Epirus?" he asked the dispatcher, explaining what he was looking for and why.

"Our records don't go back that far. You'd be better off going to the village yourself and talking to the old timers. Take a photograph of the victim with you and pass it around, see if they recognize him. Her family, too. If her father was indeed the priest, they'll remember. Or you could speak to someone from the university. Some of those reprisal operations still have cases pending in court and they've been gathering evidence for years. They might be able to help you."

To complicate matters, his boss in Athens called later that morning and told him to follow up on Lipsi the next day. "I want to be able to tell the

German ambassador that we are pursuing every angle, and that includes a possible terrorist attack."

"Lipsi, sir?" he said politely. "A terrorist attack? It seems a little far-fetched, in my opinion."

"No more far-fetched than you and your revenge fantasy, Patronas, your female Count of Monte Cristo. The dispatcher told me your theory and I think it's crazy."

"I have a feeling about this, sir."

"A feeling? You plan on taking that into court? Have the prosecutor announce that you, Chief Officer Yiannis Patronas of the Chios Police Force, have a *feeling*? You have any proof that the victim, Walter Bechtel, was even in Greece in 1944? Anyone identify him as a member of the First Mountain Division, as one of Roser's men?"

His boss had researched the massacre, which made Patronas hopeful. All was not lost. He'd get a chance to look into it.

"I haven't got a positive ID yet. Give me a couple days in Epirus with my men, and if I don't find anything, I'll go to Lipsi."

"No. You'll go to Lipsi tomorrow. You hear me? Tomorrow. After that, we will discuss a trip to Epirus."

As INSTRUCTED, PATRONAS duly departed for Lipsi early the next morning, planning to return early and prepare for the trip to Epirus. Evangelos Demos had elected to stay on Patmos and research Aghios Stefanos, as had Giorgos Tembelos and Papa Michalis. They were all eager to see what they could discover on the Internet, believing as Patronas did that the massacre was the key to the case.

Lipsi was picturesque, the area around the harbor a study in blue and white like something generated by the National Tourist office, but Patronas discovered nothing relevant to the case while he was there.

He and a local policeman had examined the files on the terrorist organization and discussed it at length, the bulk of the crimes having been committed long before either of them entered the force.

"They were active for more than twenty-five years," the man said. "Launched one hundred and three attacks and assassinated twenty-three people. I was five years old when they killed their first victim in Athens—the American CIA station master, Robert Welch."

"Any actions you know of against Germans?"

"None that I'm aware of."

"Any acts of violence perpetrated by November Seventeenth on or near Patmos?"

"No. They wouldn't have risked it, not with their leader living so close by."

"He was a mathematician, wasn't he? A university professor in France. I saw photographs of his house on the news. How did he afford it?"

"That's one of the many mysteries concerning November Seventeenth, Chief Officer. No one knows."

Patronas left the police station around two o'clock, intent on making the three o'clock boat back to Patmos and picking up the investigation where he'd left off, the massacre in Aghios Stefanos. The wind had quieted down, the placid water of the harbor golden in the sun. A group of children were crouched down next to the sea, tossing chunks of stale bread into the water and catching the fish that gathered with a net.

The island reminded Patronas of the Chios of his boyhood, the slow idyllic summers he'd spent with friends before his father died and everything changed. He'd caught fish the same way, silvery little minnows.

Two men were sitting outside on kitchen chairs, mending yellow nets with long metal needles, and he paused to speak to them about the case.

"My boss in Athens thinks November Seventeenth might be involved," he said.

"Not a chance," one of the men said. "You said the victim was an elderly German. With November Seventeenth, there was a point to what they did. They wouldn't have wasted their bullets on an old man."

Patronas nodded, seeing logic in the man's words. Hadn't been a bullet, but he had a point. The terrorists had eluded capture by law enforcement for a quarter of a century. They'd never do something as stupid as killing Walter Bechtel. No, the German's murderer had been on another kind of mission.

He passed around his pack of cigarettes and bought them all coffees. "It must have been something, the day they arrested the head of November Seventeenth, Giotopoulos."

"*Hamos*," the same man said, chaos. "Lipsi is small, only six hundred people, and the government sent more than that here just to arrest him, over seven hundred. They couldn't afford to let him get away, you see, not after he'd made fools of them for all those years."

The fishermen smirked. It pleased them that the officials in Athens had been bested by the terrorist. Patronas could see it in their faces.

"They had frogmen in the water, gunboats. It was as if war had broken out."

"You ever talk to him? The terrorist?"

"Sometimes." The man hesitated before answering, began to shut down.

"He say anything against Germany?"

"Not that I can remember. Anyway, that was before things got really bad. Hell, now everyone's against the Germans."

"IT MUST BE distressing being there in that house with the grieving family," Papa Michalis said, "especially if, as you allege, Maria Georgiou is the guilty party. Having to wash dishes and put away the laundry as if nothing happened. It would require great presence of mind."

They were eating dinner at a taverna in Skala. Evangelos Demos and Giorgos Tembelos were still working at the police station researching Aghios Stefanos on their computers.

Patronas had already lost a day and when he returned from Lipsi had wanted to go back to the hotel and review his notes. The priest, however, was hungry and insisted they eat first. He chose a fish restaurant, saying he longed for some *barbounia*—little red mullets—which cost close to sixty euros a kilo. "Being on an island always makes me yearn for fish."

"You live on an island."

"Hence, my yearning is continuous." He took the largest of the fish and put it on his plate, looked at it reverently for a moment. "Such a lovely color, *barbounia*, such a sweet red."

Patronas wished with all his heart that just once Papa Michalis would long for something besides the most expensive food in Greece, red or otherwise—a pizza, maybe, or bottled water.

The order had depleted nearly all his cash reserves. The fried crawfish the priest also had a longing for, which rang up at eighteen euros, used up the rest. He'd have to find an ATM tomorrow.

Papa Michalis filleted a fish and took a bite. "You spent time with Maria Georgiou. What's your impression of her?"

"Steady. Not easily taken by surprise."

"Did she volunteer that she was from Aghios Stefanos? It seems unlikely that she would have been so forthcoming with that information if her purpose was indeed revenge. It would have made more sense for her to have disguised her origins."

A fair point, Patronas conceded, recalling the interview. Maria Georgiou had been absolutely straightforward with him, made no effort to disguise her background or family history. If she was indeed the killer, wouldn't she have pointed him in another direction? Instead, what she'd said had led him straight back to her. Without a moment's hesitation, she'd given him the classic three: means, motive, and opportunity.

Shit. He could feel his theory collapsing. Guilty people didn't behave that way. No, they lied and dissembled.

Papa Michalis was wasting no time, Patronas saw, forking up the smaller fish two at a time. "Don't feel bad, Yiannis. I know you were sure you had her—that she was the one—but I thought from the beginning it was highly unlikely a woman committed this crime. Female murderers are few and far between. That's why we remember them. Lucretia Borgia, the Roman empress, and Livia, who poisoned all who stood between her son, Tiberius, and the throne. A few more maybe, but not many. Cleopatra is far more typical, taking her own life rather than killing another. Also, like Cleopatra, women prefer poison. It's their weapon of choice. They also lack the musculature to beat a man to death."

Patronas snorted. Musculature? Where the hell did he get this stuff?

He moved to grab a fish. "So all the talk of revenge, that little speech you gave me earlier, you didn't mean it?"

"I have since reconsidered. As I said, I think it's highly unlikely. Being a woman, Yiannis, it trumps everything."

As if he knew.

AFTER DINNER PATRONAS returned to the hotel and told Antigone Balis that he and the others would be leaving for a few days, but would need the room back when they returned.

She was all business, chilly. "I'll have to charge you for the time you're away," she said, paging through her book. "When you registered, you said a week."

"That's fine."

Then she seemed to regret her coldness and went into the kitchen and packed him a parcel of food to take with him.

A promising sign, he told himself, packing him a meal. A woman doesn't make it her business to feed a man she doesn't like. First, she tends to one kind of hunger, food in this instance, and then she unzips her dress and addresses another.

Maybe all was not lost and he'd be clutching something besides a buoy or himself one of these nights.

He peered inside the bag. Praise the Lord, if there wasn't a little tub of *keftedakia*—meatballs—inside. They were fresh, judging by the smell. The bag also contained a dozen fresh figs and half a *karidopita*, walnut cake, wrapped up in foil. She'd even put in forks and napkins.

He looked around for Papa Michalis, and not seeing him, furtively ate one of the meatballs. They were delicious, delicately seasoned with onion and mint. So, in addition to possessing the torso of a goddess, the woman could cook. His cup runneth over, sort of like the contents of her brassiere.

'Not for your teeth,' his mother had said, but maybe Antigone Balis was. Maybe this time his luck would change and a beautiful woman would find her way into his bed. It had never happened to him before. Statistically, he was due. Thoughtfully, he ate another meatball.

Antigone Balis and him. *Sure, why not?*

But then she told him she'd charge him forty-five euros for the food—fifteen euros apiece—and add it to the bill.

He wasn't Romeo calling out to her Juliet. No, he was just a customer, a customer being ripped off. He felt like weeping, but he controlled himself, bade her *kalinyhta,* good night, and made a dignified exit.

Tembelos returned to the hotel late that night, so tired he could barely stand.

"How's the merry widow?" he asked, flopping down on a chair and taking his shoes off.

"Greedy," Patronas answered, still upset about the forty-five euros.

"Greedy is good. She wants you, Yiannis. I saw it in her eyes. So how are you going to go about it? You going to tackle her? Pull her down and have at it?"

"I think that's called 'rape,' Giorgos, and I'd get arrested." He wasn't in the mood for jokes, wished his friend would stop.

"Perhaps a dinner invitation?"

"With you and Evangelos hanging around? Not to mention a priest?" He nodded to where Papa Michalis was sleeping. "The presence of a priest is hardly conducive to romance."

"I could keep him away."

"No, you couldn't. I ate dinner with him last night. He's like a lion pouncing on a gazelle, Papa Michalis. He can smell a free meal from far away, track it for days across the savannahs of Africa and tear into it with his teeth." Patronas made a gnashing sound.

"No need to tell me. He's a shrewd one, our priest. All pious and full of cant—*Lay not up the treasures of this earth*—except when it comes to meals someone else is paying for. Then he's a fucking camel."

Patronas laughed. "A vacuum cleaner."

"A human Hoover."

"A whale. One of the big ones that eat plankton." He proceeded to suck the air, his head going from side to side, then attached his mouth to the fabric of his friend's shirt and pretended to inhale it.

It worked, the joking. Patronas was grateful. It eased his disappointment over Antigone Balis, about him not being Romeo. Maybe he should choose another role model. After all, Romeo had committed suicide. Things hadn't worked out so well for him.

CHAPTER ELEVEN

———◆———

Faithful earth, unfaithful sea.
—Greek Proverb

A FTER BREAKFAST, PATRONAS, Tembelos, and Papa Michalis walked to the police station together. Up two flights of stairs with no elevator, it was hidden away at the top of a tower and not easily accessible to the public.

There was an icon of Jesus in an arched alcove outside the station, a big one, nearly two meters high. In Patronas' mind the placement was inappropriate— police and Jesus, they didn't exactly go together—but Evangelos said such was the nature of Patmos. "The so-called 'holy island,'" he said. "Every third person is a priest. Criminals are rare here."

A row of potted plants and a filthy grill from some long ago Easter celebration took up the rest of the space.

In no hurry to go to work, Patronas lingered outside for a few minutes, smoking a cigarette and looking out over Skala.

The office of the Hellenic Coast Guard occupied the ground floor of the same building, and he could see men and women in blue uniforms walking briskly in and out, monitoring the traffic at the harbor with walkie-talkies. On a small hillside to his right was the seventeenth-century chapel of *Aghia Paraskevi*, said to possess a miraculous icon that restored sight. Another church, far older, stood almost directly below, virtually at his feet, its two domes glimmering dully in the sun.

He had tried to buy a Greek newspaper at a kiosk earlier but hadn't been able to find one. There'd been plenty of German ones, stacks of *Die Zeit* and the *Frankfurter Allgemeine Zeitung*, but no *Ekathimerini* or *To Bhma*. Apparently, Patmos wasn't Greek anymore; it had become an outpost of Berlin.

With a sigh, Patronas ground out his cigarette, pushed open the door and entered the station. Tembelos was already on the computer, typing feverishly on the keyboard. Papa Michalis was sitting next to him, doing a much slower version of the same.

Wearing headphones, Evangelos was listening to Bechtel's MP3 player, stopping and restarting it as he jotted down notes from the interviews with the family.

"You find anything?" he asked them.

"Maybe," Tembelos said.

He pointed to the computer screen. "I've been researching the Twelfth Company, the unit that butchered the people in the village of Aghios Stefanos, and I put in a request for pictures. One thing about Nazis: they kept good records, photographed what they did and who they did it to. There's a shot of a bunch of them riding donkeys in front of the Acropolis. About sums them up, if you ask me. Asses on top of asses; asses—if I may be so bold—squared. They even took photos of Kalavryta after they killed everybody."

He gestured at the screen. "A man named Böchner—two of those dots Germans use over the 'o'—was in charge. That's him there, see? Seems he was some kind of maniac. His own men called him 'Attila.' "

Patronas examined the picture. "No scars."

"No nothing. Partisans killed him in 1944."

"You find anyone who looks like the dead man?"

"Not yet, but if it's out there, I will find it. I've got people looking all over the world."

Patronas nodded. If Tembelos could place Walter Bechtel anywhere near Maria Georgiou's village, they might have a case.

He didn't hold out much hope. Unless she confessed to the crime, most probably all they would be able to establish was that she and her family were victims of a group of rogue foreign soldiers a long time ago. The police and the prosecutor would have nothing to go on but that … and even that was uncertain. She could deny she'd even been in Aghios Stefanos on the day in question, testify that she'd been living with relatives somewhere else. If what the priest said was true, the casualties had been many—nearly the whole village shot to death. There might be no one left alive to contradict her.

It was around four o'clock when the fax with the photograph came in. Tembelos retrieved it from the machine. Reaching for his magnifying glass, he studied the paper closely before handing it on to Patronas. "I'm pretty sure that's him. Take a look and see what you think."

Smudged and out of focus, the photograph showed a group of soldiers, rifles in hand, standing in front of a burning building. Judging by the uniforms, the distinct shape of the helmets, the soldiers were German.

"See those columns there, the frieze?" Tembelos pointed out details of the building. "That's the town hall of Aghios Stefanos. I recognize it."

Taking their time, the four of them took turns examining the fax, passing the magnifying glass back and forth over the image.

"It's him," Tembelos said with growing certainty. "See those scars on his face? That's Walter Bechtel. I'd stake my life on it."

Patronas hesitated. "You sure this is her village? Not Kalavryta or Distomo—one of those other places they annihilated?"

"Yup. It's Aghios Stefanos. The commission in Athens faxed it to me just now, the one seeking reparations for the massacres in Epirus during the war."

Taking the fax from Tembelos, Patronas looked at it again. There was no date or location on it, no identifying mark or list of names. Just a group of nameless jackals posing for a photograph.

"It's not enough," he said, handing the picture back. "So what if he was there? It doesn't prove he killed her father or that the two of them knew each another. She was a child. All the men that day would have looked the same to her—uniforms, guns."

Evangelos concurred. "There were soldiers in my village during the war, and I never heard anyone describe them physically or call them by name. Rank maybe, but not by name. They knew who the Gestapo agents were and did their best to avoid them, my grandmother said, but that was it."

"You researched the massacre," Patronas said, turning back to Tembelos. "How long did it last? How long did the soldiers stay in that village?"

"I don't know. All I know is it started early and they shot up everything. They might have been living there for all we know. There were German units stationed all over Epirus for the duration of the war, fighting the resistance. Two or three years in some places. If they were in Aghios Stefanos that long, she definitely would have known him."

He tapped the fax. "This photo gives us what we need, Yiannis. You'll see. It's going to unlock the case."

"What about the family? Do we show it to them? Get them to verify his identity?"

Tembelos considered the idea for a moment. "Not until we're sure, Yiannis. From what you said, Gunther Bechtel's pretty touchy on the subject. He might charge you with harassment if you imply his father was a war criminal."

"A Nazi on Patmos," Evangelos said in amazement. "Who would have thought? Sunning himself on our beaches, a man like that."

PATRONAS SCANNED THE photo and emailed it to his boss in Athens.

After he saw it, Stathis reluctantly authorized a trip to Epirus. The four of them were to take a boat to Piraeus that night—economy class, he was careful to specify—then take an unmarked car and drive to Maria Georgiou's village and question the inhabitants there. While they were in Epirus, they were not to discuss the murder of Walter Bechtel, but instead to gather as much information as they could on the Nazi atrocities in the region and work to determine the identities of the men who had committed them.

"Anyone asks, you're there on a pending reparations case."

"Didn't the German president say they were done with reparations—that they had a 'moral debt' and that was it?"

"People who lived through that time will be glad to talk to you, Patronas, no matter who you represent. They don't want these events forgotten. But be careful, this is strictly a fact-finding mission. We don't have solid evidence that the victim was involved in the massacre and we don't want to damage his reputation needlessly. For all we know, he might have spent the war working in the army canteen serving up stewed fruit or whatever slop those people ate."

A short man with a melodic voice and the build of a rooster, Stathis had risen swiftly through the ranks and was now in charge of both the northern and southern Aegean regions. Fiercely ambitious, he was quick to push his subordinates aside and take credit for their work and to punish those who displeased him. Patronas had suffered under Stathis' rule, even been fired and brought back once in the past. He despised him. A person would have to be a snake charmer to get along with his boss. Man was a cobra.

Taking no chances, Patronas carefully repeated Stathis' instructions back to him on the phone. "Tread lightly, you're saying."

"Yes, and leave no evidence of your stay. Sleep in another village if you have to and pay cash for everything. No paper trail. No photographs of you and Tembelos grinning at each other in front of some statue."

"Understood, sir."

"If the Bechtel family or anyone connected with the German embassy gets wind of this, I will personally strip you of your rank and court-martial you."

"We're the police, sir, not a military unit. I'm not sure you have the authority to court-martial people."

As usual, his boss had little use for his insubordination.

"*Tha se evnouchiso.*" In that case, I'll castrate you. Stathis paused before continuing, "I am authorizing an expenditure of ten euros a day per person plus an allotment for gas. Times are tough, Patronas. You're not going to be in Epirus long. You and your men can sleep in the car."

BEFORE THEY LEFT Patmos, Patronas phoned Maria Georgiou and told her she was to notify the department if she left the island for any reason. "We need to know your whereabouts at all times," he said.

She willingly acquiesced. "I will be here," she said, "With the Bechtels at their house or in my room in Skala."

"Do you have a cellphone?"

"No, but the man at the desk where I live can always find me. He has my contact information."

"Good."

The local police were going to monitor her movements while Patronas and the other three were away in Epirus, keep track of where she went and who she spoke to, in case someone else had been involved.

"I don't want her to know she's the object of your surveillance," Patronas had told them. "Tell her you're guarding the house to prevent further incidents. You're there to protect the Bechtels."

After Stathis approved the trip, Patronas and the others hurriedly returned to the hotel and packed their bags, intending to take the Blue Star Ferry at midnight. There being no money for cabins, they planned to sleep out on the deck.

"I'm no good on boats," Evangelos told Patronas while they were standing in line to buy tickets.

"What's the problem? Can't you swim?"

"Not very well."

Patronas tried to imagine resuscitating Evangelos as they boarded the boat, performing CPR if by some quirk of fate the man was swept overboard.

Wouldn't happen, he quickly decided. No matter what, he'd never put his mouth on his. He'd let him drown first.

His colleague continued to enumerate his fears. What if the boat capsized like that cruise ship in Italy, the *Costa Concordia*? Or the crew left the door open and water came flooding in like the ferry in the Baltic Sea? To hear him talk, anything connected with the sea undid him, caused panic attacks and palpitations.

Tuning him out, Patronas stretched out on a bench and tucked his bag under his head. It was a warm night. With any luck, he'd be able to sleep all the way to Athens. Tembelos and the priest quickly followed suit, each on a separate bench. Evangelos alone remained upright, watching the water of the harbor as if it was going to eat him.

Within minutes, the ferry got underway, gliding swiftly out of the harbor. It was a stormy night and the wind was fierce, the sea covered with whitecaps. With a groan, the boat began to mount the oncoming waves, teetering on the crest for a moment then crashing back down. To Patronas, it felt like a watery kind of earthquake—seven, maybe eight on the Richter Scale. The tourists quickly fled to the lounge below, and within minutes, the four of them had the deck to themselves.

Patronas and Papa Michalis were both from Chios and Tembelos was from

Crete—all islands with strong seafaring traditions—so they were untroubled by the *fourtuna,* the rough sea.

Not so Evangelos Demos, who hailed from the mountains of the Peloponnese.

"I don't feel so good," he said.

A few minutes later, he staggered over to the railing of the ship, gripped it hard with his hands and vomited. Although he'd turned his head away, he'd miscalculated the direction of the wind and everything had blown back onto Patronas.

"*Panagia mou,*" Patronas squealed. Holy Mother!

And him in his dress uniform, hoping to impress Stathis.

The situation brought to mind the old Greek saying, *I spit high, I spit on my face. I spit low, I spit on my chin.*

Patronas looked down at his uniform, picking off things he'd rather not think about.

God, how he wished it was spit.

"Ach, Evangelos Demos," Tembelos said, shaking his head, "a burden to the earth and now the sea."

THEY WERE ALL gathered in Stathis' office. Putting his arm around Patronas and calling him his 'trusted colleague,' Evangelos Demos spoke eloquently to Stathis, describing the flash of insight that had led him to summon his former colleague to Patmos. He hadn't brushed his teeth since the incident on the ferry and was breathing heavily in Patronas' direction.

"When I realized the complexity of the case, the possible international repercussions, I requested his assistance," Evangelos was saying. "I have many theories as to who might have committed this heinous act and anticipate an arrest forthwith."

"Forthwith?" Tembelos whispered to Patronas. "Heinous? Who does that *vlachos,* that imbecile, think he is? Demosthenes?"

Stathis doled out the money, all 160 euros of it, and handed the car keys over to Patronas. "Remember what I told you. Keep it quiet or else." He made a scissoring motion.

"Yes, sir. I will, sir."

"And keep me informed. I don't want this to be one of your rogue operations, Patronas. You're not Digenis Akritas, so don't try and act like him."

A Greek version of Superman, Digenis Akritas was the hero of the twelfth-century epic poems, the *Acritic Songs.* In a way, Stathis' words were a compliment.

Patronas grinned at his boss. "Understood, sir."

Evangelos, Stathis pointedly ignored.

He led them out to the parking lot and pointed to a sad-looking white car in the far corner. "Off you go," he said and turned on his heel and left.

The car was a ten-year-old Skoda that looked like it had been driven across a couple of continents—large continents, Asia or Africa maybe. It had a sense of angst about it—dents, a rusting underbelly, bald tires—which made Patronas wonder about its history, if it had run over someone in a former life and was being punished for it. Although the insignia of the department had been painted over and the light bar removed from the top, it still looked like a police car. When people saw it coming, they slowed down. What was it they said, *Once a soldier, always a soldier?* He prayed it would do its duty, the little car, and soldier on.

The car wasn't big enough for the four of them and their four suitcases and they had to repack, stowing what they needed in one and leaving the rest behind. It hadn't been pretty, the co-mingling of their pajamas, shaving gear and briefs, and had caused the priest acute distress. He'd balked at first, insisting he would hold his bag on his lap.

Apparently he'd been anticipating famine, for his suitcase proved to be full of food, food he hadn't wanted them to know about, food he hadn't planned to share—loaves and fishes and an entire round of cheese, three jars of Nutella, a bag of sugar, and an entire canned ham from America.

"Father, Father," Patronas said, "we're going to Epirus, not Somalia."

"Some of my relatives are from Epirus. The Pindus Mountains. They ate grass during the war. You never know what will befall you, what the day will bring."

Patronas weighed the bag of sugar in his hand. Two kilos, easy.

"Insurance," the priest said, reaching for the bag. "If need be, we can bargain with it, trade it for other things. I keep a stockpile in my room. If our history has taught us anything, it's to prepare for the worst."

Patronas handed the sugar back to him. "Keep it, Father, and the rest of the food. We'll find the space."

Before they left, he doled out the *keftedakia* Antigone Balis had given him, and they ate them in the parking lot. Then he assigned seats: Evangelos Demos and Papa Michalis in the front, in keeping with his death by talking formula, and he and Tembelos in the back. Evangelos would drive as far as the town of Arta, about halfway there; then they'd switch and Patronas would take over.

Although Patronas had changed his clothes after the meeting with Stathis and done his best to clean himself up in the bathroom of the station, he remained deeply disgruntled.

In a decent vehicle, the trip to Epirus would take six hours, but in a car like the Skoda, it could well take twice as long. Hopefully he'd get back to Chios someday and not end up wandering the earth like Ulysses. He might have been gone a long time, Ulysses, and had his share of shipwrecks, but at least his crew hadn't thrown up on him. Goddamn Evangelos Demos! He should have thrown him overboard when he had the chance, fed his carcass to the fishes. Maybe on the trip back.

Tembelos leaned over and whispered in his ear, "What was that business with the scissors?"

"Stathis said if I mess up, he'll castrate me," Patronas whispered back.

"Bah," Tembelos said. "Better than him have tried—your wife for one. And look where it got her? Yours are made of iron, Yiannis."

Patronas pondered what his friend had said. *Not necessarily a bad thing, iron,* he decided upon reflection. *Except that with lack of use, it's susceptible to rust.* Idly, he wondered if the same principle applied to a man's parts, if they locked up and ceased to function after a period of inactivity, creaking and groaning when a person started them up again.

CHAPTER TWELVE

———— • ————

He who becomes a sheep is eaten by wolves.
—Greek Proverb

THEY DROVE OUT of Athens and headed west, passing the petroleum
refineries of Elefsina. It had been the site of a shrine to Demeter, the
goddess of the earth in ancient times—one of the most sacred in the Greco-
Roman world. Now burning gas cast a yellowish pall over Elefsina, and the sea
along its coast was iridescent, a rainbow of colors like a vast pool of gasoline.

Supertankers were anchored in the gulf, and ahead lay Kakia Skala, the
Evil Passage, the mountainous cliffs that marked the entrance to Attica. In
mid-August there was a lot of traffic on the road, and it took them more than
five hours to reach the city of Patras, twice as long as it should have.

A few minutes later, they crossed the Rio-Antirrio Bridge. It was unlike
any bridge Patronas had seen, the white cables strung in a series of triangles
like sailboats linked together in space. It had been built for the 2004 Olympics,
Tembelos told him. It remained an impressive accomplishment, supposedly
the longest of its kind in the world.

They passed through a marshy lagoon and entered Messolonghi. Called
Iera Polis, the sacred city, Messolonghi had been the site of a terrible massacre
during the War of Independence, Patronas had learned in school. The Turks
had killed over nine thousand people—the English poet, Lord Byron among
them—and hung their severed heads on the city walls.

Although he searched, he saw no trace of its bloody past today. Just
modern cement apartment buildings and traffic. Evangelos eventually tired
of driving and Patronas took over for him, Tembelos riding shotgun next to
him. They continued to move steadily north.

Near the town of Preveza, Papa Michalis pointed to a sluggish river. "That's the Acheron," he said. "The Necromanteion was there, the oracle where the ancients spoke to the dead."

Patronas could see a scrim of mist rising from the distant water, wisps of it drifting across its surface like ragged strips of cloth. A vast flood plain surrounded the river, thick with myrtle trees, half-swathed now in fog.

"The dead ever talk back?" he asked.

"Supposedly, when summoned, the dead appeared and advised the living," the priest said. "I don't know if you know this, but the Acheron was one of the three portals of hell. It emptied into a lake where the souls of the dead began their journey to the underworld. It was guarded by the dog, Cerberus, who prevented those same souls from escaping. If you recall, he had three heads and his fur was made up of snakes. The ferryman would meet the dead on the shore and row them across the lake. The kingdom of Hades was at the bottom. The dead had to pay the ferryman a coin—a single coin; otherwise they would roam in torment for all eternity."

"Ulysses stopped here, didn't he?" Patronas asked.

"Yes, Orpheus, too. Hoping to catch a glimpse of the woman he loved, Eurydice. Poor Orpheus! For all his songs and gaiety, he was a prisoner of grief."

Patronas watched the river for a moment. Maybe it was what the priest had said, but it felt haunted to him, the mist rising endlessly from its depths and the pale leaves of the trees rippling in the wind. Perhaps the ghosts had retired after the coming of Christianity, but somehow he doubted it. He sensed their presence there in the gloom, believed he could hear them crying still.

Not far from the river, they came upon the ruins of an entire city.

"Nikopolis," Papa Michalis told them, reading outloud from a guidebook he'd brought with him. "It was built by the Roman emperor, Octavian, to celebrate his victory over Anthony and Cleopatra."

There was nothing left of it now. Just a handful of crumbling walls on top of a hill.

Ghosts and more ghosts.

"*Dust to dust,*" Patronas said out loud. "So it was and will always be."

He remembered when he'd disinterred his mother's bones five years after she died, as was the custom in Greece. He'd been seeking a sign that day in the cemetery, some evidence that she was still with him, but there'd been nothing as he'd boxed up her remains, only a strand of her hair still attached to her skull. He'd broken down when he saw it and sobbed like a child.

He continued to drive, following the signs to Ioannina, the city closest to Aghios Stefanos. The landscape grew more rugged and majestic as they approached the Pindus Mountains, the great range that defined northern Greece. The lower slopes were heavily forested, and even in August, there was water everywhere, trickling down and pooling in shadowy ravines.

"Our ancestors developed a breed of oxen, famous in ancient times," the priest announced, reading an entry from the guidebook. "King Pyrrhus, who lived here, was responsible for them. But something happened and they degenerated over time and became short and misshapen."

"Hear that, Giorgos?" Patronas called out. "Short and misshapen. Same as us."

"Same as *you*," Tembelos said. "I, myself, am a comely man."

"He was an unlucky man, Pyrrhus," the priest continued. "Suffered great losses in battle. He may have won over the Romans, but it cost him so much, his victory was tantamount to defeat."

They were now deep in the Pindus Mountains. It was late afternoon and the peaks were half-hidden by clouds, the rocky slopes below, the color of rain-soaked slate.

A woman was standing next to a stream by the road, watching a flock of sheep and knitting, swallows soaring and dipping around her. The shadows of the clouds were dark against the looming expanse behind her, the mountains framing the scene like a painting. Urging the sheep forward, she vanished into the forest a moment later. Patronas wondered where she was going, if there was a village nearby.

A river in the region had once been called the Vedis, the priest said, the word for water in the hymn of Orpheus, the father of music. "The area has been settled since Paleolithic times."

"You think that's the Vedis?" Patronas asked, nodding to the stream where the woman had been.

"Could be. Legend, history? Epirus has long combined the two."

Patronas nodded. It was easy to see where Orpheus had gotten his song. You could pull it out of the air here. Weave the birdsong and the rushing water together, the hushed murmurings of the trees.

"You see that up there?" Papa Michalis pointed to a distant peak. "That's where the Souli women fled to escape the army of Ali Pasha. Holding hands, they danced the traditional dance of their people and jumped off. There's a statue commemorating it carved out of the mountain. Looks a bit like Stonehenge."

"Got anything more recent, Father?" Tembelos asked. "World War II, say? The reason we've come?"

"Yes, yes, of course. Some of the worst fighting of the war took place in Epirus. In 1943, the Nazis and a rogue group of Albanian Cham Muslims massacred hundreds to the north of here. The crime was so terrible it was cited during the Nuremburg Trials, but the general in charge—Lanz, I think his name was—defended it, saying it was part of 'war regulations.' The judges didn't accept his explanation. The executions were 'plain murder,' they said."

Yet another tragedy. Patronas could feel the burden of the past weighing him down. All those slaughtered innocents rising up and demanding justice.

"What happened to Lanz?" he asked.

"Nothing. He got away with it. They all did. No one was ever found guilty."

"It's always like that," Evangelos Demos said, leaning over the front seat. "The Greeks die and their killers go unpunished. You wouldn't believe what the Germans did to my village, the carnage. That's why I became a policeman."

"You became a policeman to fight the Germans?" Patronas eyed him in the rearview mirror. "They've been gone a long time, Evangelos. You might have miscalculated."

"You know what I mean. To serve justice."

"We all did," Tembelos said. "That's why we became cops. To serve justice." After a lengthy pause, his friend went on. "I'm not sure that's what we're doing here."

"What do you mean?" Patronas asked.

"If this woman, Maria Georgiou, did in fact murder the man who killed her father, there's a kind of symmetry to it, a catharsis. I probably would have done the same thing, had it been me. Ancient or modern, that's who the Greeks are, people who fight for their families, who avenge the wrongs that are done to them."

Patronas frowned. "So you think this trip was a mistake?"

"Maybe. All I know is if she killed him, killed the man who murdered her father, what she did was just. Maybe not legal, but just. And maybe we shouldn't be up here, chasing our tails in Epirus, seeking evidence to convict her."

"There has to be an accounting," Patronas said. "Justice for the victims, no matter who they are."

"With respect to the war, the Nazis got off easy. Their victims—some six million of them, historians say—didn't get justice. There isn't enough justice in the world, in the whole fucking universe for them."

CHAPTER THIRTEEN

———◆———

Old age and poverty, incurable wounds.
—Greek Proverb

AGHIOS STEFANOS WAS located to the north of the city of Ioannina. Tembelos had printed out the directions and was reading them aloud to Patronas, using his cellphone for light. Night had fallen and it was very dark. They'd passed the village of Lingiades earlier and driven on, the road narrowing ominously and shifting from asphalt to gravel. The village was located on the western slope of Mount Mitsikeli, Tembelos said, well over 1800 meters high.

"Better for goats than people."

Patronas was inclined to agree. About a kilometer straight down, he could see the lights of Ioannina, so far below the road he was on, it was like the view from a satellite.

Lingiades had been the site of another massacre, Tembelos had said as they drove through the town. "The German president apologized for it, said it had been a 'brutal injustice' and that he was apologizing to the families of victims—as if saying 'we're sorry' would cover it."

"Anything about where we're headed?" Patronas asked.

"No, nothing. But from what I read, they burned their way across the whole region. More than a thousand villages were destroyed during the war and most of them were here."

They'd seen no signs of life since turning off the highway, no houses or livestock, and Patronas was getting worried. In addition to its other problems, the car apparently had cataracts; its headlights were so weak he could barely see. Worse, they kept going out, only to come on again a few seconds later as if the car was blinking its eyes. He was wiping the windshield with his hand, praying he wouldn't drive off a cliff in the dark and die like the Souli women.

"How much farther?"

"Two or three kilometers. I Googled the place before we left and I think you'll find what you're looking for. There were some pictures of the residents of Aghios Stefanos posted on the Internet by the tourist authority. Older than time, most of them. Could have been with Moses when he crossed the Red Sea."

"You see any advertisements for hotels?"

"There were a couple in Lingiades, but not up here."

"Shit."

It was going to be a long night. The priest had fallen asleep in Evangelos' arms and the two were snoring up a storm in the back seat. Patronas couldn't face the thought of sleeping in the Skoda, of staying in the car with the other men one minute longer than he had to. He'd camp out, he decided. Pull up one of the car mats and use it as a blanket.

They reached Aghios Stefanos half an hour later. Built on the summit of Mount Mitsikeli, it was partly hidden behind a scrubby forest of pine. The buildings were in such disrepair Patronas thought at first the village must be be abandoned, but then he heard a dog bark, saw yellow lights in a few of the windows.

Not wanting to disturb the residents, he turned the car around and parked in a field below the village. Starving, he and Tembelos rummaged through the suitcase, searching for the priest's canned ham.

"God bless America," Tembelos said. Holding the can, he inserted the metal key and opened it.

They'd eaten about half the ham when, alerted by some kind of digestive radar, Papa Michalis sat up.

"What's that you're doing?" he asked.

"Eating," Patronas said. He took another piece and wadded it in his mouth, determined to eat as much as he could before the priest took possession. By rights, the ham was his.

Worn out by his travails on the boat, Evangelos slept on in the backseat.

The night air was cold on top of the mountain, and they gathered up sticks and built a small fire in the field, using pine cones for kindling and setting them ablaze with Patronas' cigarette lighter. The priest had packed a small bottle of brandy, and they passed it around as they watched the fire burn, the crackling flames bright against the darkness. The pine cones exploded as they caught, shooting geysers of sparks high in the air.

Patronas gradually relaxed, enjoying the smell of the woodsmoke. Taking a swig from the bottle, he passed it on to Tembelos. "You said it was a mistake coming here. What do you think we should do? Go back?"

"Hell, I don't know," Tembelos said. "All I was saying is I probably would have done the same thing if I'd been her. You can't let it pass, not a thing like that."

Patronas nodded. Giorgos was from Crete, an island where revenge was part of the culture. The need for it buried deep in the Cretan DNA.

"Scorched earth," Tembelos said, waving the brandy bottle at Aghios Stefanos. "That's what they did here. Shot them all and burned the place down."

Damage from the war had been evident on the road to Aghios Stefanos. The sunken indentations in the land could only be bomb craters.

Patronas had seen a monument to the victims in the town. A simple white obelisk, it had been like a beacon in the darkness. He had made a note of it, planning to have Tembelos photograph it as soon as the sun came up. There were similar memorials all over Greece, listing the names and ages of the dead. Judging by the size of the one in Aghios Stefanos, it was a miracle Maria Georgiou had survived.

The priest reached for the bottle. "I, too, grew up during the war," he said, taking a demure sip. "And I saw people I love die—my sister of hunger in December of 1941, my little brother six months later. They shot my uncle during a round-up and the fathers of many of my friends. *Love thine enemies as thyself?* It's a hard thing to do, I can tell you. *Forgive those who trespass against us*, harder still. But then what would be the point if it was easy? What value would it have?"

"So we should forgive the Nazis?" Patronas asked. He wasn't in the mood for a theological conversation tonight—one of Papa Michalis' little sermonettes.

"You say that as if forgiveness is a passive act, Yiannis. It's not. Believe me, I know. Forgiveness has power, purpose." He went on like this for some time, as usual, insisting on having the last word. "You don't forgive them for *them*, Yiannis. You forgive them for *us*."

MORNING CAME TOO quickly. Getting out of the car, Patronas walked stiff legged down to the stream and washed his face. It had gotten too cold to stay out in the field the previous night, and around one a.m., he, Tembelos, and Papa Michalis had put out the fire and returned to the car.

Surrounded by trees, the glade was full of shadows and the water was very cold. Wondering if this was where the river had run red in 1943, Patronas searched for evidence of the massacre but found nothing. It was very quiet, the only sound, the birds stirring in the trees.

Tembelos and the priest were pawing through the food when he got back, eating Nutella out of the jar with their fingers. Rolling up his sleeves, Patronas pushed them aside and ate his share.

Now that it was light, Patronas was able to observe the village in greater detail. The shale roofs of many of the houses had caved in, their walls blackened by fire. A stream coursed through the town, pooling in the forested glade where he'd washed his face, but there was little else of note. Athens had been bad, full of empty storefronts and graffiti, but this was far worse. Here the decay was palpable.

"You need to talk to Christos Vouros," the owner of the *kafeneion,* the local coffee shop, told him, nodding to a grizzled old man in the corner. "He is in his eighties and his father was in the resistance, one of the *antartes.* He knows better than anyone else what went on here during the war."

Remembering Stathis' warning, Patronas had been deliberately vague about why they'd come to Aghios Stefanos. "We're investigating the massacre," was all he'd said.

The owner had approved of their mission, saying he'd help in any way he could, even put them up in his house if they needed a place to stay. "Start with Christos," he said again.

The old man watched them approach with interest. Bent nearly double, he was no bigger than a jockey and supported himself with a cane. He was dressed in a white oxford shirt and shabby topcoat, a handknit woolen vest.

Keeping a hand on the table to steady himself, he rose to greet them. "*Kalimera,*" he said, nodding to each of the men in turn. Good day.

They bought him coffee and sat with him for over an hour, questioning him about life in the village after the Germans came.

"Georgiou was the priest then," Patronas said.

"That's right. Young, he was, with four children and a wife. Only Maria, the youngest, survived." His face darkened as he remembered the massacre. "It was a miracle, her surviving that day. Not many did, I can tell you. I'd gone up in the mountains with my father to gather firewood. It's the only reason I'm alive today."

Patronas handed him the photograph. "Was this man in Aghios Stefanos?" He pointed to the figure at the center of the picture, the soldier with scars on his face.

The old man got out his glasses and studied the photo. "Bech," he said after a moment. "That was his name. Bech. He was in the Gestapo."

Patronas and the others exchanged glances. "Are you willing to swear to that?"

Vouros nodded. "I remember the war. Remember it better than yesterday."

"Who else was here in the village then?"

"Most of them are gone now. What can you do?" His voice was resigned. "*As is the generation of leaves, so is that of men.*"

The words were from Homer, *The Iliad.* Patronas realized he'd underestimated the old man, his level of education.

Vouros had noticed his reaction. "I read a lot when I was younger," he said by way of explanation. "I wanted to go to university. Would have, too, if the Germans hadn't come." His laugh was forced. "Only wanted to eat then. Put my books away."

He had married a woman from Ioannina and had six children. Two were in Chicago; the rest lived in Athens. "My daughter hired an Albanian woman to look after me. She's asked me to come live with her in Athens. She doesn't like me being up here all alone."

"Will you go?" Patronas asked.

"Never!" He made a dismissive gesture. "What would I do in Athens? I've lived here my whole life. Everything I know is here. Who would see to my land if I left? Care for my flocks of sheep, the lambs in springtime?"

He named five people who were still alive and had been in Aghios Stefanos during the war, saying they would verify what he'd said, that the man in question was named Bech and that he had served in the Gestapo during the war.

"How did you know he was in the Gestapo?" Patronas asked.

"I don't know how I knew. Maybe I overheard my parents talking. It wasn't his uniform, if that's what you're thinking. He usually wore a suit with a little swastika pin in the lapel. All I know is he scared you. It was like the air went cold when he was around."

He pointed to a stone house on the corner. "He worked out of there. He'd come for a few days and then go. I don't know where he went. All I know is death followed him." His voice was raspy and his hands shook a little. "Everyone was afraid of him."

Patronas was writing down everything, which pleased Vouros, who asked him to read it back to him, adding more details and correcting certain items as he went along.

"My neighbors will tell you the same thing," he said. "Knock on their doors and they'll tell you. They're here, the five I said. They don't travel anymore. The only trip any of us will make now is to the cemetery when we die."

Thanking him for his assistance, Patronas and the others left, eager to get started on the interviews. Five people weren't many. If they worked hard, they'd be able to finish by the end of the day, get in the car and leave.

"A cheerful man," Tembelos said. "Only place he's going is to the cemetery."

"I hadn't thought of being buried as a journey," the priest said, utterly missing the point, "but I suppose in a sense it is—a move from this world to the next, from the earthly to the divine, from the cares of this life to everlasting peace in heaven."

"Ach, faith, Father, faith," Tembelos said, shaking his head. "Don't you ever get tired of it?"

Patronas had prepared a packet for each of them with a blow-up of the deceased's face and a photocopy he'd made of Maria Georgious' ID. The priest headed toward the church, telling Patronas he'd see if the marriage and baptismal records had survived the war, and if they had, he'd find out what he could about the Georgiou family. Evangelos was to search out the school, if there was one, and do the same thing. They arranged to meet at the car at noon.

Three of the residents Vouros mentioned were being attended to by immigrant caretakers or family members; the other two were living alone in their houses. Like Vouros, they all remembered the war. The Germans had stayed in Aghios Stefanos for weeks, a woman named Eleni Noutsopoulos said, billeted themselves in villagers' houses.

"They ate better than we did," she added, laughing a toothless laugh. "They took everything, you see, and left us with nothing. We were hungry. *Panagia mou*, how hungry we were."

The Germans had chosen the village for its vantage point, she added. "The view from Aghios Stefanos was its misfortune."

Leaning on a cane, she walked outside to show them. "See there, to the south, you can see all the way to Ioannina and to the north, deep into Albania and the heartland of Greece. Also, there weren't many trees then—people had been burning them for fuel—so there was no place for resistance fighters to hide."

The story of the massacre gradually unfolded as the day went on. "They saw two *antartes* near here and that was the end of us," a man named Stavros Georgakis said. "They rounded up everyone in the village and killed them, then moved down the hill and murdered the people in Lingiades, too, women and children. They didn't care who they killed. It didn't matter to them."

Patronas showed him Bechtel's photo. "Was he here that day?"

Georgakis studied the photo carefully. "Yes," he said. "Yes, I believe he was."

"Do you remember anything about him? His name or what unit he served in?"

"The others called him *Scharführer*. I remember because it sounded like what they called Hitler on the newsreels. *Führer*. Most of the time he was dressed like a civilian. I only saw him in a uniform once. Gray, it was, with SD on the sleeve."

An SS man. Vouros had been right.

"He stayed in the house next door to us. They're still there, the family. They might remember more."

A middle-aged woman answered the door. "It was before my time," she told Patronas, "but my mother might be able to help you. She's in the back. I'll get her."

The woman she wheeled into the room was a twisted, wizened creature with a pronounced tremor. Dressed entirely in black, she kept seeking to right herself and control her shaking limbs. Her daughter was very solicitous. Helping her over to an upholstered chair, she settled her into it and covered her knees with an afghan. The room was nicely furnished and there was a television, a new one, in the corner. The chair the old woman was sitting in was part of a set, its arms covered by embroidered cloths similar to the one Patronas had seen in Maria Georgiou's room.

Nodding to the two policemen, the old woman introduced herself, saying her name was Fotini Chalkias. She had been born in 1923, eleven years after Ioannina had been liberated from the Turks. She was very frail and it cost her precious energy to speak, but her voice grew stronger as she reminisced.

"Of course I remember him," she said when she saw the picture. "Bech, his name was." She also verified that he'd been in the SS.

"Bech, not Bechtel? Are you sure?"

"Yes, yes. It was said he ran the Gestapo."

She grew more and more agitated as she talked and her eyes kept straying to the window. Patronas wondered what she was looking for there, if she was searching for Nazis, afraid they might still come and claim her. "He interrogated everyone, even children. He was always seizing them for questioning, pulling them off the street and taking them down to that cellar of his."

Locked up in a room with a man with a scarred face, a man whose language they didn't understand, the children of the village must have been terrified. Worse still, if Bech had been aided by a Greek in a mask, a collaborator, a *maskoforos*. Patronas remembered the fear in his mother's voice when she spoke of them, how they couldn't be trusted and would betray their own kind. Thousands of them had been shot in Athens after the war.

"Why would Bech interrogate children?"

She continued to watch the window, didn't answer for a long time.

"Who knows the devil's purpose?" she whispered, her voice barely audible. "Who knows why the devil does what he does?"

"Did he interrogate you?"

"No, but he dragged my brother, Nikos, down there. He was never the same afterward. He went all quiet and stayed that way. Wouldn't play, wouldn't talk."

"Does your brother still live in Aghios Stefanos? Can we speak to him?"

"No. He died in the massacre. They killed all the boys."

"What about her?" He showed her Maria Georgiou's photo.

"Ah, Maria. Of course, of course, little Maria." She thumped the picture with a gnarled finger. "I'd know her anywhere. She looks just like her mother."

The old woman paused for a moment before continuing, "Her father was the village priest and he lived behind the church. The house is gone now, but you can still see where it was. He had four children, and she was the youngest. They killed all of them that day, every one but her. She'd been down by the stream and escaped somehow. There are caves in the rocks and maybe she hid in one. She was young when it happened, not more than six or seven years old."

She sank back in her chair. "I can still see them, Maria's mother and father, her brothers. They were my friends, and I wanted to stop the Germans when they took them away, but my mother held me back. 'Run, child,' she said, 'run to the mountains,' and I did. I ran and ran. I was wearing a dress and I remember I tore it. I was worried she would be mad, but she was dead when I got back and everything was burning." Tears filled her eyes. "My mother was gone."

Next Patronas and Tembelos questioned a man named Dimitra Spanos. Although he was much younger than Fotini Chalkias, he verified her story.

He said he'd be willing to testify in court that a man named Gunther Bech had stayed in their village during the war and that he had been a Gestapo agent.

"Gunther? Are you sure?"

"Yes. My uncle knew all of them. I don't know how, but he did. I heard him call him that."

Patronas made a note, underlining the name, convinced now that the nephew and uncle had switched first names and lengthened their surname from Bech to Bechtel. They'd kept it as close to the original as possible.

Tembelos had brought a video camera with him from Athens, and after getting permission, taped the interviews. Given the age of the witnesses, it was a prudent thing to do. Who knew how long it would take to bring charges against Maria Georgiou and haul her into court? Spanos was in his late seventies. He could be dead before the case came to trial, his memories of Bech and the massacre irretrievably lost. They needed to close the case and close it fast.

A Gestapo operative, Bech had conducted sweeps in the area around Ioannina, Spanos said, picking people up and bringing them back to Aghios Stefanos for questioning.

"Someone said he interrogated children," Patronas said.

"That's right. He favored kids."

The last villager they interviewed was an elderly spinster named Daphne Kallis. "After the Germans saw the *antartes* outside the village, he took me down to the cellar and told me he'd kill me if I didn't cooperate," she said. "I was afraid. There was blood on the floor, blood everywhere."

"Did you cooperate?"

She looked down at her hands, unwilling to meet his eye. "Yes," she said faintly.

"What did he want to know?"

"Names. The names of the men in the village."

THE PRIEST REPORTED back that although the church had been set on fire, not everything inside had been burned. A few of its relics had been saved, among them nearly a century's worth of baptismal records.

"Maria Georgiou's name is there. Along with the name of her father, Petros Georgiou, and her mother, Anna."

They also found her parents' names on the war memorial, along with the names of her three brothers—Philippos, Nikos, and Constantinos—nine, ten, and thirteen years old. All five were listed as killed on October 1, 1943. Altogether, 123 people perished that day.

"Nine years old." Patronas touched the engraved name with his hand. "Jesus Christ."

Tembelos was crouching down with the camera, videotaping the names. Patronas had written them in his notebook, but had requested that they be recorded, too. The victims' names would serve no useful purpose, but he wanted them anyway, a way of paying tribute.

"They murdered more than three hundred in Kommeno," Tembelos said, shutting off the camera and standing up, "seventy-four of them under ten years old and close to one hundred in Lingiades. One was a baby, less than a year old."

"I know *what* they did, Giorgos. What I don't understand is *why*."

"Evil comes, evil goes. You're a cop. You should know that."

CHAPTER FOURTEEN

———◆———

A flood of evils.
—Greek Proverb

PATRONAS AND THE others regrouped in the field where they'd parked the
car. Early afternoon, a man was driving a herd of goats down the hill, the
bells around their necks clanging as they made their way home. The grass in
the field was golden, bleached by the sun, and the air smelled of summer, *xera
votana, chortaria*—dried herbs and leaves.

"The victim was here," Patronas said. "That's for sure. We've got six
witnesses who'll swear to it, but that's it—nothing that links him specifically
to Maria Georgiou. As far as we know, he didn't shoot her father or burn her
family out. He came and went, they said."

"Something's off," Tembelos said.

They reviewed their notes out loud, Patronas and Tembelos bringing
Evangelos Demos and Papa Michalis up to date.

"Why take the children down to the cellar?" Evangelos Demos asked after
they'd finished. "It doesn't make sense."

"Maybe he wanted privacy," Papa Michalis said. "He would have been
alone there. Nobody would have seen him."

They looked at one another.

"No witnesses," Evangelos said.

Patronas nodded. "Maybe it wasn't information he was after," he said,
puzzling it out. "I had the sense that Daphne Kallis was hiding something. I
thought at the time she was ashamed of what she'd done, that she'd given up
the men in her village, but maybe it was something else."

"She never married," Tembelos said.

"No, she didn't."

"I remember there was something sad about her, crippled almost. Like a bird whose wings had been broken. I thought at the time it was the war, but maybe it was this, the evil he visited upon her."

None of them dared say the word aloud, as if giving voice to it would poison the air.

"There might well have been others," Patronas said. "We'll have to speak to everyone again. And if it's true, any number of people might have killed him—family members, if they learned of it."

"A vendetta, you're thinking?" Tembelos said.

"People in Greece stalked collaborators for years after the war, followed them all the way to Australia and murdered them there. This could well be the same."

"Been a long time since the war, Yiannis. People who did that are mostly dead now."

"I know."

"Weird, this geriatric murder. Victim in his nineties; killer, too, most likely. Guess whoever did it wanted it finished before they died."

Papa Michalis again recited the words of Confucius. "*When you seek after revenge, dig two graves.* Literally, in this case. One for Bech, another for the old man or woman who killed him."

"What are you going to do?" Evangelos Demos asked.

You, not *we*, Patronas noticed. Evangelos didn't like where this was going and was distancing himself from the case.

"Talk to Daphne Kallis again."

"It won't be easy," the priest said. "Such things are held close to the hearts of children—a great secret, usually. It might be a secret still. She might never have said a word to anyone."

SHE'D SET OUT pots of basil to ward off mosquitoes, Patronas saw—a row of them on the front steps of her house—and strung a clothesline across her yard. A cheap cotton dress was hanging from it, black like his mother used to wear, and two pairs of black cotton stockings. All of it was deeply familiar to him, transporting him back to his childhood on Chios.

The feeling was so intense that for a second, he felt like he was knocking on his dead mother's door. Shaking it off, he knocked again. He could hear Daphne Kallis shuffling around inside, hesitating on the other side of the door.

Papa Michalis was standing next to him. Patronas had left the others at the coffee shop, not wanting to overwhelm the old woman with their presence.

"We need to talk to you," he said. "Gunther Bech is dead, murdered, and if you don't help us, Maria Georgiou will be charged with the crime. You remember her, little Maria, the daughter of the priest?"

The old woman unlocked the door and opened it slowly. Walking ahead, she led them into a dank room that smelled of mildew. A worn cushion on a chair marked where she sat and watched television; an unfinished crossword puzzle was laid out on the table next to it, a pair of reading glasses on top. Patronas could hear a canary singing somewhere in the back of the house.

"We need to talk to you about Gunther Bech," he said. "We need to know what happened in that cellar."

Grasping the arms of the chair, she let herself down. "I told you. He asked me questions and I answered them."

"What else?"

"It was a long time ago. I don't remember. "

Patronas blundered on brutally, thinking it was better to get it all out in the open, to have it said.

"Someone said that he 'favored' children. That can mean many things. Among them that he preferred children sexually, that he was a pedophile. Was this the case with Bech? Did he rape you in that cellar?"

Raising her arms, Daphne Kallis shielded her face as if to ward off a blow. "Stop," she cried feebly. "Please! I beg you."

The priest sat down next to her and took her hand. "We wouldn't be asking if it weren't important."

Her eyes filled with tears and she fumbled for a Kleenex, her thin body trembling. "Yes," she said, "he did what you say."

And then there was no stopping her.

She'd been six the first time and hadn't understood what the German officer wanted when he led her down the rickety wooden staircase into the room with the dirt floor and began unbuttoning his fly. The cellar was cold and damp and smelled like rotten vegetables. He'd forced her to lie down and pushed her dress up, then lain down on top of her. A moment later the pain had come, surprising in its intensity. It had terrified her and she'd begun to scream.

"He covered my mouth with his hand. I couldn't breathe. I was afraid I'd die, that he was killing me."

She remembered all of it, the animal sounds of the soldier and the rough way he'd handled her. The spiders, how the rafters of the cellar had been snowy with their webs. Most of all how he'd hurt her.

"He tore me open, tore my childhood away, and trampled it in the dirt of that place. All that I was changed that day and I became something else. Something broken. I'll never forget it, never. He smelled of hair tonic and talcum powder. And after he was finished, he wiped his hands on my dress as though I'd dirtied him. He said he'd kill my mother if I told anyone. He said I was to blame and called me *Fotze* and *Schlampe*. I didn't know what the words meant then. I only found out later. Cunt and slut." She was crying in earnest now. "I was six years old."

After he was finished with her, he'd thrown her out and told her to go home. She'd been bleeding and didn't know what to do and had gone to the stream to wash. "I was trying to hide it, so my mother wouldn't see and ask questions. I was afraid for her. Bech had said he'd kill her and I wanted to save her. It didn't matter. They shot her anyway two days later."

"Did Bech take other girls to the cellar?"

"Yes. Boys, sometimes, too. I'd watch them go with him and came back out again, trying not to cry." She wrapped her arms around herself, seemed to shrink up into the chair.

"He's dead now," Patronas said, hoping the news would bring some comfort. "He can't hurt you anymore. Someone murdered him. Whoever did it carved a swastika on his forehead."

"A ston diabolo," she hissed. The devil take him.

Patronas asked Daphne Kallis for the names of Gunther Bech's other victims. There were two she knew of still living in the village—Dimitra Spanos, whom they'd spoken to earlier, and a woman, Maria Papayiannis, who lived some distance beyond the town. For the most part, their words echoed those of Daphne Kallis.

"He ruined me," Maria Papayiannis said, tears streaming down her wrinkled face, a balled up handkerchief clutched in her hand. "I was dead inside, dead to my husband, dead to life."

It was harder for Spanos, who balked at first and refused to answer. *"Psemata,"* he kept saying. Lies. *"Psemata."*

Patronas eventually wore him down. Not only had Bech victimized him, Spanos said, but two of his cousins as well.

"Children, they were. I remember the way they stumbled home after, bleeding where they shouldn't have."

Both female victims, Maria Papayiannis and Daphne Kallis, refused to let this portion of the interview be videotaped, not wanting to be identified, even now in the twilight of their lives, with the rape, the abiding shame of what had been done to them.

"People wanted to kill him," Spanos said at one point.

"Who spoke of it?" Patronas asked, pressuring him. "I need their names."

"It was just talk. Anyway, most of them are dead now. It was a long time ago. After the Germans left, we took up arms against each other. Too much fighting, too much blood to worry for one man."

"Names," Patronas repeated impatiently.

"They were relatives of the kids. They are in their nineties now or over a hundred. They are not the people you seek."

BEFORE LEAVING AGHIOS Stefanos, Patronas approached Christos Vouros again. "You knew, didn't you?"

The old man nodded. "All of us did, all of the children."

"Why didn't you tell us?"

He squinted at him. "It was something we didn't speak of ... not then, not now."

"So you weren't a victim?"

"No, never. We knew, like I said, but we didn't, you understand? We watched when a kid went down to the cellar, saw how they acted after. We kept track."

His face was clouded, difficult to read.

"There's a saying: *Otan o diavolos vrisketai se adraneia dernei ta paidia tou.* Bech was the devil. Only difference was they were Greek children. They were us."

When the devil's idle, he fucks his children.

CHAPTER FIFTEEN

———◆———

What the wind gathers, the devil scatters.
—Greek Proverb

THE VILLAGERS GATHERED to watch Patronas and the others leave, waving goodbye as they got in the Skoda and started back down the mountain. "*Na pate sto kalo*," one of the women sang out. A blessing on you.

Patronas was driving and Papa Michalis was sitting in the front seat next to him. He welcomed the old man's presence, hoping the priest would help him put what he'd learned from Daphne Kallis out of his mind.

"The rest of the German soldiers didn't know, did they?" he said, looking over at Papa Michalis. "Bech's commanding officers?"

"Probably not."

The sun was setting, its lengthening rays bathing the landscape in soft light, the peaks in the distance like hammered bronze. The air was cooling and fog was rising from the stream by the road. The window was open and Patronas had his hand out, holding it up as if blocking the oncoming rush of air.

"Let's stop for a minute," the priest said.

Patronas pulled over and parked alongside the road. Pushing their way through the underbrush, they walked down to the stream, leaving Evangelos Demos and Tembelos back in the car. Cedar trees lined the banks of the stream, so tall they blocked out the light, and the air was heavy with damp. Patronas had expected the priest to urinate and had come along to steady him as he sometimes did, but then the old man surprised him.

Kneeling down by the water, he ran his hand through it. "She probably bathed in a stream like this, as if it would make her clean, would give her back what he took from her."

He picked up a stick and began to draw in the sand, his eyes still on the water. "In answer to your earlier question, Yiannis. No, I don't think the German authorities knew what Bech was doing. I know the first head of the Gestapo, Rudolf Diels, worried that his organization was attracting 'all the sadists in Germany and Austria' … also unconscious sadists, men who according to Diels did not know they were sadists until they'd begun torturing others. In other words, the Gestapo was creating them. He didn't know why and speculated that it was the nature of the work that rendered them thus, unleashing inclinations long buried, letting loose the dogs of hell, as it were. Himmler, of course, was a different story. He wanted to set those dogs loose. He wanted his people to be savages."

The priest continued to draw. "As for these acts directed against children, the systematic crimes we've uncovered here … there might have been a few instances. But as a general rule, no, not even in the Gestapo."

"That explains the cellar."

"Yes, Bech had to hide his proclivities."

"What would they have done if they'd caught him?"

"Shot him, probably. Order above all else."

"But he was one of them."

"It wouldn't have mattered. They would have considered him a disgrace or—what was that word the Nazis were so fond of?—a degenerate."

"You read a lot of books, Father. How do you explain a man like Bech?"

"You know as well as I do that pedophiles are like serial killers. There is no rational explanation for what they do. I believe some of them are born that way. Others are created by the abuse they themselves suffered as children."

"I do unto others because it was done unto me."

"Exactly. Who knows what drove Bech? Maybe he was like the men Diels spoke of: the tendency was always there and the war provided him with the opportunity to act on it. All I know is evil visited that place. Evil visited Aghios Stefanos."

"This is where we came in, Father, you and me. The nature of evil. If God exists, which I seriously doubt, he has a lot to answer for."

The priest paused, stick in hand, and looked up at Patronas. "It seems we worship at different altars," he said.

"Father, you know me. I don't worship at all."

"You're not alone." Returning to his drawing, the priest made a face with his stick. "There are those who argue God died in Auschwitz, that He went up the chimney with the millions put to death there, that there was no point in religious faith or prayer. Some even go so far as to say hope has no meaning either, that it's a plague on humanity and serves no useful purpose, stops us from acting on our own behalf. 'It will be water coming out of that showerhead. I know it will, I know it will. It has to be. I haven't done anything to these men. Why would they kill me?' "

He drew another stick figure, this one with a smile on its face. It seemed grotesque, given the nature of their conversation. Then he drew another and another and put a showerhead above them. Patronas understood what he was doing. Hope. He was showing him hope—malignant, pestilent hope.

"And where was God then?" Patronas said. "I ask you. Why was it gas, not water?"

The priest sighed, his face a mask of sadness. "I don't know. I think about these things, too, Yiannis. And the only answer I've come up with, given my unwavering belief that God is benevolent and just, is that evil, too, exists and that it works independently of Him. Point, counterpoint, as it were."

As if for emphasis, he threw the stick in the water.

Night was fast approaching, and it had become very dark by the river. Helping the priest to his feet, Patronas led him back to the car. "Come on, Father. The others are waiting for us. We need to go."

"I think sometimes God made a mistake," the priest whispered. "The older I get, the more convinced I am."

"What? Mankind?"

"Yes. Some of it."

"Ach, Father. We're not alone in nature. Other animals *eat* their young."

"Yes, but they don't defile them first."

THE FOUR OF them discussed the case as they drove to Ioannina. They planned to interview the two people Christos Vouros had named in person while they were there. Patronas had already spoken to them on the phone and knew it would be a waste of time. One was bedridden with Parkinson's disease and the other had suffered a stroke the previous month. As he'd expected, the two people in Ioannina were able to account for themselves at the time of the killing and had witnesses who would testify to that effect—caretakers and nurses, a daughter who never left the stroke victim's side.

A dead end.

"Maria Georgiou is our only suspect," Patronas said as they got back in the car.

"You going to arrest her?" Tembelos asked.

"I don't know. I'll interview her again and go from there. I never had a case like this. What did you call it, Giorgos? 'The geriatic killing?' Those two old people. Jesus, their combined ages must be over one hundred and seventy. You would think they'd be done with the war by now."

"You heard what happened," Tembelos said. "How could they be done?"

"If Bech had been in a wheelchair, would she still have killed him? If he'd been bedridden? Palsied or comatose? At some point you have to let it go. She was younger than him. With any luck, she would have outlived him. Why didn't she just wait?"

ALL THAT WAS left of the food the priest had brought was the bag of sugar, so they ate in Ioannina before starting back to Athens. The interviews had taken longer than they'd anticipated and Patronas figured they'd probably have to drive all night. They had money left from the stipend Stathis had given them and ordered freely at a *tsipouradika,* a taverna that specialized in *tsipouro,* a potent local drink.

Feeling adventurous, Tembelos ordered two of the local specialties, cabbage with sausages and peppers and a pie called *pepeki,* made with yogurt and cheese. Patronas was too hungry to experiment and stuck to food he knew, *pastitsio,* a casserole of pasta and meat and *horta,* stewed greens.

Papa Michalis, as expected, ordered half a kilo of mackerel, the only fish available, and did not offer to share.

The restaurant was lively, Greeks of all ages eating outside at tables next to the famed lake of Ioannina, Pamvotis. Patronas was glad they'd chosen a place without tourists, that there were no Germans nearby. He didn't want to hear that language tonight, didn't want those people anywhere near him.

The air was very still and the lights of the city were reflected in the waters of the lake, the image wavering in the current.

Patronas poured a shot of *tsipouro* and drank it down. He could feel it burning and welcomed the heat. After downing another shot, he passed the bottle over to Tembelos, who poured some out for Papa Michalis and himself. Evangelos Demos, who would be driving the rest of the way to Athens, was drinking Coke Zero.

Tembelos proposed a toast to the victims of the war in Aghios Stefanos, living and dead, and they drank.

"May their memory be eternal," the priest said.

They drank the rest of the *tsipouro* and Patronas signaled the waiter for more. Stathis wasn't expecting them until tomorrow; they could drink as much as they wanted, take their time and enjoy themselves. God knows, after Aghios Stefanos, they needed it.

"I like *tsipouro,*" Tembelos said. His face was starting to get rosy, his cheeks glowing like apples. "After my father died, we used to lead musicians to his grave whenever there was a celebration in the village and have them play for him, pour a glass of *raki* into the soil there so he could join the party. When my time comes, I hope someone will do that for me."

"I'll do it, Giorgos," Patronas said, tossing back more *tsipouro.* "I'll douse your grave in *tsipouro*, kick up my heels and dance *zebekiko* on your tombstone."

"I hope when I die there's *tsipouro* in heaven," Tembelos said. He'd begun to slur his words.

"What makes you think you're going to heaven?" Patronas asked.

Bleary eyed, Tembelos peered at him. "Being a cop has to count for something. If not in this life, then in the next."

They both laughed.

"Heaven's not that important," Tembelos continued, "just a bunch of pious old farts. But hell, now, hell's the thing in my mind. We mess up as cops, Satan will see to it that the evil doers get punished." He raised his glass in a symbolic toast. "Here's to hellfire and damnation."

Patronas nodded, a bad idea, as the movement made him dizzy. He clinked his glass against Tembelos'. "Here's to hellfire and damnation."

Ah, alcohol, it's like Calypso in The Odyssey, the goddess who cast a spell on Ulysses' crew and turned them all to pigs. Patronas smiled, pleased with himself. Calypso and pigs. Not a bad analogy for alcohol. He was more than a little drunk himself.

"Here's to Satan," Tembelos said.

The priest had a pained look on his face. "Blasphemy," he kept muttering. "Pure blasphemy."

"Tembelos says you need hell for the evil doers," Patronas said, suddenly becoming serious. "But what of the good? What of them? Will heaven be enough of a reward for what they suffered?"

PATRONAS PASSED THE six-hour journey to Athens in a drunken haze, sleeping and talking intermittently to Papa Michalis and Tembelos, who were in similar shape in the back seat. He vaguely remembered leaving Ioannina, but everything else was a blur. Road, bridge, road. At some point, he thought they'd stopped and Tembelos had endeavored to pee out the window, being too drunk to open the car door, but he couldn't be sure. His friend might not even have made it to the window. He vaguely remembered him aiming at the dashboard and Evangelos yelling at him.

Stathis was waiting for them in his office in Athens. "Gerta Bechtel was attacked last night," he said. "Only bruises, nothing serious. She says she didn't see the assailant."

"Maria Georgiou?" Patronas asked. He'd sobered up, but just barely, a worrisome position to find oneself in with Stathis.

His boss glared at him. "Obviously," he said.

Patronas quickly briefed him on what they'd discovered in Aghios Stefanos—Gunther Bech's ugly history. "Given what he did, I'm surprised he lived as long as he did, that nobody killed him sooner."

Stathis studied the four of them. "A Gestapo agent. You're sure about that?"

"A pedophile and a sadist," Patronas said. "I have witnesses who will testify to it in court."

"Good, good. If it goes to trial, the case will remind the world of what we suffered under the Germans. Give us some leverage with Merkel." He straightened his uniform as if readying himself for an invisible camera.

"As soon as you get back to Patmos, I want you to arrest Maria Georgiou and charge her with the murder of Gunther Bech," Stathis instructed. "I want this finished."

Patronas and the others boarded the boat to Patmos early that same afternoon, a Blue Star Ferry making a circuit around the Dodecanese Islands. Two coast guard officers were in the process of removing a group of gypsies traveling in the hold of the boat, ostensibly with a truckload of potatoes. The potatoes, upon inspection, had proven to be only one layer thick and the rest of the truck full of contraband—lace tablecloths and cigarettes—neither of which the gypsies had permits to sell and all of which had to be off-loaded. The gypsies refused to comply, and by the time the coast guard got the stand-off resolved and the truck moved, four hours had passed.

They eventually left, but by then the wind had picked up, waves pounding the boat like artillery. The tourists got sick first, then Patronas and the other three succumbed, clutching the plastic bags the crew had distributed and burying their heads in them. Sickest of all had been Patronas. Any sicker and he'd have found out firsthand if heaven existed. Hell, he was pretty sure, he was already experiencing.

It was a Greek version of the *Perfect Storm,* only with tourists.

They reached Patmos around five a.m. Had he been alone, Patronas would have kissed the ground.

CHAPTER SIXTEEN

———◆———

Listen to it all and believe what you will.
—Greek Proverb

TEMBELOS REPORTED THAT he had found documentation on the Internet verifying that Gunther Bech had indeed been a Gestapo agent in Epirus at the time of the massacre. "He was known for his thoroughness," he said wryly. "Apparently the Nazis had mixed feelings about the massacre after it was all over. One of them called it a *Schweinerei*, a disgrace, unbefitting the German army. Another officer complained that it had placed an unfair burden on the conscience of his men."

"An 'unfair burden'?" Patronas said.

They were in the police station and Patronas was leaning over his friend's shoulder, reading from the screen. "Interesting choice of words."

"Wait, there's more."

Tembelos had been on the computer all morning, seeking evidence before they arrested Maria Georgiou.

After a lengthy discussion, the four of them had decided that Patronas and the priest would first interview Gerta Bechtel about the assault in the garden, after which they would seize the Greek woman.

The same local policeman was keeping an eye on her, Evangelos reported. She wouldn't escape.

Tembelos continued to read aloud. "One man, interviewed by a German newspaper, said and I quote, 'I used to shoot at everything, not just military targets. Women pushing strollers. It was kind of a sport, really.' Another bastard boasted of burning people alive in a church. 'They barricaded themselves in, so what could we do? We had no choice but to burn them out.' "

"Any references to Aghios Stefanos?"

"None that I could find. They questioned some men in his unit about the massacre, but they denied all knowledge. 'Never heard of it.' 'Must have been another division.' "

"So Bech was there—we got proof of that—but no evidence that he killed people?"

"That's right."

"Keep looking. In the meantime, Papa Michalis and I are going to Chora."

"You going to tell the Bechtels about the old man?"

Patronas shook his head. "Stathis ordered me not to. '*Oi nekroi dikaionontai*,' he said." One must show respect for the dead.

"Respect, huh? Stathis is a bigger ass than I thought."

AFTER PARKING IN Chora, Patronas stood for a moment and looked out, astounded again by how far he could see. Far below were the white buildings and bell tower that marked the Cave of the Apocalypse. Lower still was the village of Skala.

The yellow crime scene tape was gone and all was peaceful in the garden. A pair of mourning doves were cooing in the trees. Patronas' mother had hated them—saying they were harbingers of death—and the sound of the birds chilled him.

Gunther Bechtel greeted Patronas and the priest wanly. "You brought us news?" he asked in a tired voice. His face was more lined than Patronas remembered, and there was something missing in his eyes, as if he couldn't quite bring them into focus. He hadn't combed his hair or shaved in some time and there was a greasy stain down the front of his shirt.

Grief, Patronas told himself, remembering how his mother had looked in the weeks following his father's death—how she'd been lost to him for days at a time, unable to see or hear.

"I'm here to interview your wife."

"She's in the back," Gunther Bechtel said. "The Bauers are here now, too. You said you wanted to speak to them."

"Were they here when she was attacked?"

"No. They arrived late last night."

Patronas started with the Bauers, a heavyset couple with an avuncular manner.

"Was anything stolen from the house?" he asked after he and Papa Michalis introduced themselves.

"Stolen? No, I don't think so," the husband said. "Everything was as it should be."

They had been acquainted with the gardener and Maria Georgiou for only a brief period of time, they said, and couldn't or wouldn't speak to either's character. As for the victim, Walter Bechtel, they hardly knew him.

A problematic house guest, the old man. He was hard of hearing and kept to himself; consequently, it was difficult to carry on a conversation.

"How long have you known the Bechtel family?" Patronas asked.

"More than twenty years," the woman answered. "Gunther was at school with our son."

Patronas had sent Maria Georgiou out of the kitchen while he talked to them. She returned when he gave the signal and began preparing the midday meal, peeling eggplants over the sink. Turning her head, she gave him a long, searching look.

"We will miss Maria when we leave," the husband said, smiling in the servant's direction. "She is a very good cook. We like the Greek food she prepares, the moussaka especially." He smacked his lips. "Very tasty."

"Are they all this obtuse?" Patronas asked Papa Michalis when they were back outside.

"Yes. They are known for it, the Germans."

GERTA BECHTEL WAS relaxing in a chair at the rear of the house, reading a German magazine. She had a bruised lip and a line of scratches down her left cheek, but otherwise appeared unharmed.

Putting her magazine aside, she stood up and greeted them. "Chief Officer, Father, good afternoon."

Although not as lush as the garden in front, the backyard was equally pleasant, encircled with banks of bougainvillea and jasmine. A wooden fence screened it from the service area behind the kitchen, the trash cans hidden by the slats of the fence.

"I couldn't be in the garden in front," Gerta Bechtel said with a shudder. "The cat and then Gunther's father ... it is dangerous there, I think."

Odd that she'd started with the cat.

"Is there another entrance?" Patronas asked, silently kicking himself. The estate was so large, they'd only searched the grounds near where the corpse had been found, hadn't taken the back of the house into consideration.

"Yes," she said. "There's a door in the wall behind that fence there. A small door. You have to bend down to go through it. Maria uses it sometimes when she takes the trash out. She can show you."

"Do you keep it locked?"

"Now, yes. We lock everything—the gate and the front door, even the small door in the back—but before, no."

Patronas opened his notebook. "Take your time," he said. "Tell me what happened the night you were attacked."

"I will show you. It is better." She smiled, embarrassed. "The English ... I'm not sure I know the words."

She led them around the house to a group of rose bushes. "I was cutting flowers here. I wanted to have a bouquet for the table to cheer us up. I was bending over and someone pushed me. I fell and they kicked me many, many times. I started crying, afraid I would die like *Grobvater*."

"What happened next?"

"I screamed and they ran away."

Patronas studied her, thinking how rehearsed it all sounded. The stilted English, the elaborate pantomime. But then she was German, and as Papa Michalis had said, Germans were nothing if not thorough.

"I did not see who did it," she said, anticipating his next question. "The light over the door burned out and Maria hasn't changed it." She sounded aggrieved, as if the attack had somehow been the maid's fault.

"Which direction did your attacker come from?"

"I am not sure. Behind me, I think."

Patronas entered the information in his notebook. "Who was here that night?"

"Gunther and me, the children. Also Maria, she was here. She was helping with the dinner."

"Was she in the house the whole time?"

"I cannot say. I was in the garden."

"Did you hear anything before the attack?"

"The trash, I think. Maria was in the back with the trash."

So Maria Georgiou was outside.

"How about after you were attacked?" He was hoping for the sound of footsteps running down the path, anything that would lead away from the Greek woman.

"No, no sounds. Nothing."

Pushing her hair back, Gerta Bechtel showed him her lacerated cheek, then pulled up her t-shirt and pointed out the bruises on her abdomen.

"Do you want us to post a guard here until you leave? A policeman to watch over you and your family?"

She gave him a wounded smile. "No, we will be all right. But if you have a cigarette, I would be grateful."

He gave her his pack of Karelias, after which he and Papa Michalis left. Patronas didn't buy her story. He wondered what had really happened in the garden that night. Maybe her husband or perhaps that sullen daughter of hers had beaten her up.

CHAPTER SEVENTEEN

———◆———

A clear sky has no fear of lightning.
—Greek Proverb

MARIA GEORGIOU ACTED as if she'd been expecting them. Perhaps someone from Aghios Stefanos had phoned her the previous day and told her the police had come to the village asking questions about her. She'd changed out of her work clothes and was wearing her blue dress again. As before, her hair was braided, pinned up neatly at the nape of her neck. She was also wearing makeup—powder and fresh lipstick.

"Come in, come in," she said.

She treated them to baklava this time and stood by the kitchenette while they ate. She'd insisted Patronas and Papa Michalis sit in the upholstered chairs, and when they'd finished eating, she took their dishes and pulled up a straight-backed chair for herself.

Patronas had called the police station in Skala after he'd finished the interview with Gerta Bechtel and told Evangelos Demos and Giorgos Tembelos to continue researching the dead man and let him know anything they found as soon as possible. He also told them to follow up on what Maria Georgiou had said about her time in Athens, the salon she'd worked for and the rest of it. Perhaps she'd had an accomplice. Given what Gerta Bechtel had told him, they might be able to charge Maria Georgiou with the assault, although the evidence, as with the murder, was thin and largely circumstantial.

Worried, Patronas had also called his boss, Stathis, and told him that he had reached a critical juncture in the investigation.

"Be careful," Stathis counseled when Patronas told him what Tembelos had found on the Internet. "Tiptoe through those databases online and the newspaper files and for God's sake, whatever you do, don't contact the German authorities."

"What about the Bechtels? Do we confront them with the victim's history and see what shakes out?"

"Not yet. Remember, even if the dead man was a Gestapo agent, he was still their father and grandfather and they loved him. Don't go blundering in, making accusations. They're grieving now. Respect their feelings."

AFTER BRIEFLY OUTLINING what they'd learned in Aghios Stefanos, Patronas started the interview with Maria Georgiou. "The victim, Gunther *Bech*," he said, laying stress on the last name, "*Bech*, not Bechtel, was in your village, Aghios Stefanos, during the war. He played an instrumental role in the destruction of your family, the deaths of your mother and father, Petros and Anna Georgiou, and your three brothers, Constantinos, Nikos, and Philippos Georgiou."

Her eyes filled with tears. "I'm sorry," she said, wiping her face with the back of her hand. "You took me by surprise. I haven't heard those names in over sixty years."

"I'd like to know what happened the day of the massacre. You were there. Can you describe it to me?"

She didn't speak for a long time, just sat there, crying. "It would have been better if I'd died that day, too," she finally said. "How I longed for that, to have died with them. You can't start over after something like that. There's no way to go forward. My aunt took me in, but times were hard in Epirus and she didn't have enough for her own children. I was like the ghost at the banquet, the one they talk about ... I don't recall his name. He keeps turning up and reminding the living of all they wished to forget."

"Banquo," the priest said quietly. "It's from Shakespeare. *Macbeth*."

"Banquo," she echoed. "Yes, that's who I was."

Feeling guilty, Patronas pushed on, seeking to close the case. Bech's unholy appetite was the key, he was sure of it. "Did he ever take you to the cellar?"

"Ah," she whispered, "you discovered our secret." Her initial bout of crying over, she was sitting there peacefully, hands folded in her lap.

A stone that never smiles. Patronas remembered his mother's words.

"I repeat," he said wearily. "Did he take you to the cellar?"

"No."

"But you knew?"

"Yes, Daphne was my friend and I saw her after it happened. I saw her walking to the river and I followed her. It was just us and the trees and water. She was wearing a pink dress and standing in the shallows, washing what looked like spots of saliva off the front of her skirt. I asked her what was the matter and she wouldn't tell me, but then I saw the blood on her thighs and her filthy underpants. I helped her clean herself up and held her while she cried. We never spoke of it, but yes, I knew. Everyone knew. I sometimes wonder if that's why he burned our village … to cover his tracks."

"Did Bech give the order?"

"I don't know. I was a child, Chief Officer. But I always thought the timing was curious."

"You say everyone knew. Why didn't someone report him to his commanding officer, go to the German authorities?"

"And tell them what?" Her laugh was unpleasant, mocking. "That one of their Gestapo agents was behaving badly? We were at war, Chief Officer. We were the enemy. Vermin, they called us, same as the Jews. Cockroaches, nits. They didn't care if we lived or died. They took our lives, for God's sake. What difference did it make if one of them took our innocence?"

"You recognized him on Patmos," Patronas said, making it clear he wasn't asking, but stating a fact.

"Yes, I recognized him. I would have known him anywhere. Those scars. His face was etched in my mind."

"But how could you be sure? You were only six years old at the time of the massacre."

"Seven," she said. "I was seven."

He'd found an old tape recorder at the station, which he pulled out of his briefcase, turned on and set down on the table in front of her. They were coming to it and he wanted to have a record. Normally he liked to enter his impressions in a notebook, to jot things down, but he didn't want to interrupt her now.

Let her talk, he told himself, get it off her chest.

"He lived next door to us," she said. "Our village was small, and he was there off and on for months. I saw him often. I was little and he sounded funny. Now I know he was speaking German."

She took a deep breath. "He used to stand outside and talk to the other soldiers sometimes. They were loud and I'd hear them. All day long, I'd hear them. But that was a long time ago, and you want to know what happened this summer on Patmos."

"Yes. When did you first see him again?"

"It was late in July and I was hanging laundry outside my room in Campos. I couldn't believe it. I couldn't believe he had dared to come back to Greece and I walked closer to make sure. It was him, all right. Same physique, same face. He even parted his hair the same way he had in Aghios Stefanos. He was standing next to a parked car, talking to his son. That's when I knew for sure, when I heard his voice. My heart stopped, and even after all these years, I was afraid again."

"If you were afraid, why did you agree to work for them? Did you see it as an opportunity? A chance to kill him and avenge your family?"

If so, he'd have to charge her with premeditation. She'd be in jail the rest of her life.

"I wanted to confront him, yes." She paused, searching for the right words. "But not then, not there in Campos. I had to gain entry to his house, which is why I took the job. I couldn't confront him in the middle of the road, could I? But maids, they are invisible. People wipe their feet on you. I could watch him without anyone knowing and learn what I needed to know."

"And then you killed him?"

"I killed him?" Shocked, her voice caught in her throat.

"You had cause. Gunther Bech was an evil man. He murdered your family. He raped your best friend."

"I would never kill him," she said, growing more and more agitated. "Never kill any of them. Oh, I might have thought about it over the years, when I was younger, but not now. What good would it do? Killing him wouldn't bring back my family, the childhood I'd lost."

"So why did you go there?"

"I wanted to see him up close, see what kind of man he was. I thought it would show on his face, the evil he'd done, that the devil would have branded him."

She started to cry again, tears running down her powdered cheeks. "In Aghios Stefanos, I'd watch him from inside the house, him and the others. I saw them as monsters and maybe they were. I don't know what I was expecting in that house in Chora. Horns? Eyes that burned? Something. But all I saw were dentures and a hearing aid, a cane hanging on the back of a chair. He was senile. I don't know if they told you that. He couldn't remember what day it was, let alone what he'd done to my people. I was too late. He'd outlived his evil. Maybe it had just departed. I don't know. All I know is I never saw it. For me, it was gone."

Maria Georgiou continued to weep. "I had it all planned what I'd say: 'I'm from Aghios Stefanos,' I was going to tell him. 'Remember that place? I hid in the river the day you killed my family, covered myself with blood so you'd think I was dead and wouldn't shoot me, too. The water was cold and my teeth were chattering and I was afraid you'd hear. You stood on the bank above us, above me and the other people from my village who'd fled to the river.'"

She paused a few seconds before resuming her conversation with the dead man.

"'You had a name for what you did to us. You called it *Sauberung*, a cleansing. I heard you talking about it. My father was the village priest ... and you shot him when you came that day and set fire to all the houses.'"

Maria Georgiou turned to Patronas. "You asked what I wanted, Chief

Officer. I wanted to say those things. But after I saw him in Chora, saw how he was, I gave up the idea of confronting him. Maybe he'd been tormented by the war like I was. I don't know. All I know is, the person he'd been—the man who'd held my people's lives in his hand and crushed them like paper—that man had vanished. He was still a *lycos*, a wolf. I was sure of it. But the wolf had grown old and lost his teeth." She smiled at this. "He would not have understood what I was saying. 'Aghios Stefanos?' " She imitated a German accent. " 'Vere is dat? Vat?' "

"What about the children?"

"Oh, his hunger was still there. You could see it when the gardener came with his boy, see it on his face, the way he watched him. I always stayed outside then. Took my broom and swept."

"Standing guard?"

"Yes. With Walter, too, sometimes." She paraphrased the old Greek saying, "*Even though he got old and his hair was white, he has not changed his disposition.* In this, like the wolf, Bech remained the same."

"Did you kill him?" Patronas asked again.

"I'm not a *palikari*, Chief Officer." A brave person. "I might spit in your food or curse you under my breath, but that is all I do."

She reached out a hand and touched his sleeve. "You have to understand: my father was a priest and he believed with all his heart in the vision our Savior held out for us, in the lessons of forgiveness in the Bible. He would recite them to me and my brothers when we were in bed, getting ready to go to sleep. *Blessed are the peacemakers, for they shall be called the children of God.* People in the village called him weak, especially after the Germans came, but I knew better. I knew it was harder to be the way he was, that he was stronger than any of them. I have nothing left of him but that, that vision. That is his legacy and I would never betray it. I would never raise my hand against another human being."

Papa Michalis was nodding. He had tears in his eyes.

"The night he died, when did you find him?" Patronas asked.

"Around six thirty, long before the gardener came."

"Where did you get the flowers and the candles?"

Perhaps someone else had been involved. She might have brought another man or woman to the house to do the actual killing, a second individual from the village.

"What are you talking about?"

"Someone burned candles and scattered petals around the body."

"It wasn't me." Maria Georgiou looked away, not meeting his eye. "No one saw me in the garden. No point in checking."

"What about the swastika?"

"It was already there."

"How long were you alone with him?"

"Not long. Maybe a quarter of an hour, no more. I arrived late that afternoon. I was supposed to stay on and help with dinner that night. They'd all come back from the beach, were inside the house by the time I got there, and I let myself in through the gate. When I didn't see him in his chair in the garden, I went looking. It's what I usually did when I came in the afternoon. I'd find him and ask what he wanted, if he needed anything. It was then that I saw him on the ground."

"Was he still alive?"

She hesitated, understanding the implication of the question. "Yes," she said. "He was breathing, but only a little, each breath taking longer than the last."

Cold, to stand by and watch somebody die. Patronas studied her. "You say you're the daughter of a priest, but you didn't call an ambulance, didn't get help for him. What were you doing all that time? Praying?" He struggled to keep the sarcasm out of his voice, thinking she must have been lying about the candles and the flowers. Killed him and then adorned the body in some unholy ritual.

"I didn't pray," she said in a low voice. "Not at first."

She went on, "I could hear the shower running inside so I knew I'd be alone for a while. They usually left the old man alone in the afternoon. The garden was his. They didn't use it much."

"Wouldn't they have noticed your absence?"

"I'm a servant, Chief Officer. As I told you before, no one notices servants, whether they are there or not."

"Why take the risk? Why didn't you call the police, dial 100 when you found him, then stand back and let us do our work?"

"Death is death. Whether you hate someone or not, it affects you. You have to acknowledge it. You can't just walk away. And so I blessed him. I would have sung a *mirologia*, a dirge for the dead, for him, too, if I'd known one. They sang them for days in my village, the people who were left. Days and days."

A bird flew down and began pecking at the seeds on the windowsill. "*Yeia sou, poulaki mou,*" Maria Georgiou called out. Hello, my little bird. She watched the bird for few moments, her face streaked with tears. "I might have hated him, but still I prayed. You see my father's goodness? It lives on in me, while that man's evil is gone, swept away and forgotten." Opening her hand, she blew across her palm like a child with a dandelion. "Chaff in the wind."

"How could you just leave him lying there?"

"For the same reason I didn't call the police," she said matter-of-factly.

"Once you heard I was from Aghios Stefanos, I knew I'd be in trouble, that you'd arrest me."

Raising her face, she looked him straight in the eye. "Besides, I was done with them. He was dead. Someone killed him and I would never find out what I wanted to know—what makes one man good and another bad, what determines what is in a person's heart. No, I was done with the Bechs, the Bechtels, whatever you want to call them. It was over for me."

Still Patronas persisted. "You didn't pick up a rock and hit him, cut up his face with a knife?"

Her gaze never faltered. "No, I swear on the memory of my family, my murdered family, and all that is holy. I did not touch him."

"Shit," Patronas said under his breath. He believed her.

CHAPTER EIGHTEEN

———◆———

Big talkers with a plentiful lack of wit.
—Greek Proverb

AFTER WARNING MARIA Georgiou to stay away from the Bechtels in the future and to report her movements to the police, Patronas and Papa Michalis left the rooming house.

Patronas called Stathis on his cellphone and told him he'd decided to hold off on the arrest, saying he needed more time. "All the evidence I have is circumstantial. We have no proof that the victim raped Maria Georgiou or killed her father. All we have is proof of his presence in the same village. We need more. We need to get this right."

"What about the assault on Gerta Bechtel?" Stathis asked.

"Again, it's the same thing. Maria Georgiou was there, but her presence is not sufficient proof of guilt. She was working the night it happened, helping with dinner, according to the family. Anyway, Gerta Bechtel didn't see who did it. There's a side entrance to the estate. The assailant might have come in through there."

"Do you have any idea who this 'assailant' might be?" Stathis' voice was heavy with sarcasm.

"At the present time, no."

"Well, find out. I'll give you another forty-eight hours."

Next, Patronas called the policeman who'd been monitoring Maria Georgiou and ordered him to step up his surveillance and keep track of her whereabouts day and night. "Get someone else to help you, but keep her in sight at all times. Also, keep track of who she talks to, especially anyone Greek. Under no circumstances is she to approach the Bechtels again or go near anyone else in that house. I'll inform them that as of this moment, she is no longer working for them."

Finally, he called the Bechtels and told them to tell the owners of the house, the Bauers, that they needed to hire another housekeeper. For a number of reasons, Maria Georgiou was now barred from the estate in Chora.

Wondering how Maria Georgiou had gotten to the house the evening of the murder, Patronas sought out the driver of the bus route between Chora and Skala and quizzed him, asking if he'd seen anything suspicious in her behavior or appearance, blood stains for instance. The only other possibility was that someone had driven her, an accomplice. She was too old to walk.

"Usually she rode to Chora in the morning and came back at night," the bus driver told him, "but I can't say for sure she was on the bus that day or if there were bloodstains on her dress when she returned home. It's not a bad stroll in the evening—no hills to climb. Could be she walked. She seemed like a nice woman. What's she done?"

"Nothing that we know of," Patronas told him. "We're just following up on that incident in Chora."

Patronas had been disturbed by the interview with Maria Georgiou. The Greek woman had as much as admitted means, motive, and opportunity, yet she'd insisted she was innocent, swearing on the memory of her murdered family. A religious woman, she would never have done that had she been guilty.

"What did you think of her?" he asked the priest as they made their way back to the station.

It was a glorious summer's night and the streets were full of people. A cluster of night-blooming flowers, *nyhtoloulouda*, was growing in someone's yard, and its scent hung heavy in the air.

"Maria Georgiou was not what I expected," the priest said. "She's a great lady, the kind one doesn't often meet these days."

"But did she do it?" Patronas insisted.

He'd already heard everything Papa Michalis could possibly have to say on the subject of the erosion of modern civilization and its influence on the Greek female, who used to be dutiful and devout, chaste—on occasion, the priest had actually used that term—and he didn't want to hear it again.

But what the priest said was this: "She could have done it, certainly, but then if what she said was true, so could any member of the family."

"In other words, I'm back where I started."

"I would say so. We need to grill the Bechtels again. Maybe one of them will spill the beans."

" 'Grill'? 'Spill the beans?' "

"Americanisms, Yiannis. The first, 'grill,' is used by law enforcement officials and means 'to forcefully interrogate.' The second, 'to spill the beans,' is a slang expression for accidentally revealing the truth. Both are used frequently on television."

Patronas grunted. When they charted the course of the western world, where it went wrong and began to fail, they should maybe start with television. 'Grill' was what you did to meat. Everybody knew that. You'd never do it to a suspect. For God's sake, policemen didn't cook people.

He vowed never to use another English expression or foreign word, to cleanse his palette, as it were, of foreign influences. Greek it would be from this day forth.

CHAPTER NINETEEN

———◆———

The ox has one thought, the man using the ox to
plow has another.
—Greek Proverb

"*CHERCHEZ LA FEMME*," Tembelos said with a laugh.
They were eating breakfast together at the hotel, taking turns
leering at Antigone Balis. She obviously enjoyed the attention and had
lingered longer than necessary while refilling their coffees, bending over them
and flashing her brassiere. To Patronas' dismay, she'd also done this with the
only other guest at the hotel, a businessman from France.

Evangelos Demos was sitting with them, working on his laptop. "I must
have read six hundred pages of testimony yesterday," he complained. "How
do the Jews do it? The ones like Simon Wiesenthal? It must be different with
them. Maybe they have more reasons than we do."

"Yeah, they do, Evangelos," Tembelos said in disgust, "six million of them."

Without a confession or compelling forensic evidence, they'd gone back to
looking for information on the massacre. Patronas was pretty sure what he'd
learned about the rapes would never make it into court. Given that the old
women hadn't wanted their pictures taken, it was unlikely they'd be willing to
testify. In addition, the trip from Aghios Stefanos to Patmos was an arduous
one, and at their age, risky. To charge Maria Georgiou and go forward, the
prosecutor would need something more—irrefutable proof that Bech and
Bech alone had been responsible for the destruction of her family.

THE AREA NEXT to the harbor was teeming with tourists. Patronas, who
was in the car with Papa Michalis, hit the brakes to avoid hitting a couple of
teenagers crossing the street.

He continued to drive along the quay, passing the Skala Hotel on the left, its entrance obscured by magenta bougainvillea, and the seaside terrace that fronted Hotel Chris.

Seeking to prove premeditation, they were on their way to interview the owner of the rooming house in Campos where Maria Georgiou had stayed.

The priest indicated a fenced square on the left. "That's where St. John baptized the first Christians. There's a spring there. Another one in the Monastery of Panagia Koumana." He pointed to a building across the harbor. "It was considered a miracle at the time, that second spring, proof that the Virgin had interceded for them and answered their prayers. You should visit it sometime. The garden is magnificent. They have all kinds of birds, even peacocks. Such a beautiful bird, the peacock, a thing of wonder."

"I've been to Panagia Koumana, Father," Patronas said. "I went there on my honeymoon."

The priest's face fell. One of the seven sacraments, marriage was a bond he took seriously. And in spite of all that Dimitra had done to Patronas and others, he mourned the end of their union. For him, divorce was a kind of death, like someone who had succumbed after a long illness.

"Ach, Yiannis," he said. "She's leaving, Giorgos said, going to Italy and resettling there."

"So?"

"So I was thinking you should call her."

At breakfast earlier that day, the priest had watched him chatting with Antigone Balis, and Patronas wondered if sin, or even anticipated sin—as in his case—gave off a scent the priest could smell the way those French pigs did truffles. Perhaps that was why he'd brought up Dimitra's departure.

"Why would I want to call Dimitra? We're divorced. We have nothing to say to each other."

The priest laid a hand on his arm. "She needs your support," he said. "She's embarking on a journey to parts unknown."

"She's going to Italy, Father, not leaving the solar system."

"I'm sure she'd welcome a word of encouragement from you. It would be an act of kindness, and acts of kindness are like pebbles in the water, Yiannis, they increase the goodness in the world. Call her and say goodbye. That's all I'm saying."

Fearing he'd overstepped his bounds, the old man went back to the peacocks, quacking and shrieking in turn to give Patronas an idea of their unholy call. "Movie stars in silent pictures became laughing stocks when the talkies came in and people heard their voices. Alas, the poor peacock is much the same. One of nature's greatest glories until it speaks."

Patronas found himself missing Evangelos Demos. Evangelos took himself seriously and wouldn't be caught dead imitating a peacock.

He turned onto the road to Campos, passing a humming generating station and walled cemetery. The latter was exactly as he remembered it, the rectangular tombs encased by white marble. *We might have lost our culture, our music, but at least the rituals of death haven't changed*, he thought. The dead were buried facing east today, exactly as they were in the time of Homer. A Greek, one day he too would be laid to rest facing the rising sun. *Who will mourn my passing?* he wondered sadly. *Who will care if I'm gone?*

He could see Panagia Koumana, the monastery the priest had spoken of, in the distance. Far smaller than St. John's in Chora, it was nearly invisible, well hidden in a cleft in the mountain.

He remembered the trip he and Dimitra had made there, how they'd lingered in the chapel, kissing the icon of the Virgin and praying for a baby that never came.

A large cross had illuminated the monastery at night then, and there'd been young people, seminarians probably, sitting outside on the hillside, chanting prayers in the darkness, a herd of goats bleating softly on the rocks below. The cross was still there, far smaller now than it had been on his honeymoon, but the goats were gone, as were the prayerful young Greeks.

Perhaps he'd revisit the monastery before returning to Chios, see if there really were peacocks. Maybe take the priest with him and make a day of it.

"Father, I need to discuss something with you."

"What is it?"

"Bechtel came by the police station before you got there, and we had a lengthy and troubling conversation. To sum it up, he wants us to drop our inquiries concerning the massacre. He must have heard what we're doing, because he said if we continue to pursue it, all the rumors and lies surrounding his father will resurface and his children will learn of them."

"The mark of Cain," the priest said. "It can cast a long shadow, the past, thrust any family into darkness. His children are innocent. Why should they be punished? And yet punished they will be. Bechtel, too, for that matter. He wasn't even born when his father was spreading terror in Epirus and yet ...."

Spreading his arms, he flapped them for emphasis. Another bird this time, a crow.

"Would *you* want to be related to Josef Mengele? This is the same."

"Bechtel was very angry," Patronas said. "He was waiting for me when I got in and informed me that he'd contacted the German embassy and filed a request seeking to put an end to our investigation. Apparently, someone told him about the leads we were pursuing, the research Tembelos and Evangelos were doing. He's claiming we planted the evidence of his father's complicity in the massacre, hoping to embarrass Germany."

The priest shook his head. "A corrosive thing, rage."

"I'm not sure it was rage. It felt more like grief to me."

"Of course, his sorrow must be profound. Flawed as his uncle was, he obviously loved him."

Patronas had called his boss in Athens after Bechtel left and relayed the German's concerns. "He doesn't want us to arrest her. He says it's all propaganda, an effort to humiliate Germany. He contacted the German ambassador in Athens."

"Ignore him. We're Greeks and this is our country, our justice system. We'll fight him on this."

"We really don't have enough evidence to charge her," he repeated for what felt like the hundredth time.

"Bring her in anyway," Stathis had ordered. "Make her sweat, keep after her until she breaks."

"She won't break, sir."

"Of course she will. She's an elderly woman. A few nights under lock and key and she'll tell you what you want to know. You just have to scare her."

"I need more time."

Stathis had reluctantly agreed to the delay, but Patronas knew he was running out of time.

He had been repelled by Stathis' words, finding them eerily familiar to what the survivors in Epirus had said of the dead man, that he liked to scare people, especially children. "Break her," his boss had said. "Do whatever's necessary." The same had been said of Bech.

Profoundly discouraged, he'd hung up the phone. If he wanted to keep his job, he would have to do as Stathis ordered. The thought made him sick.

CHAPTER TWENTY

———◆———

Now that we've found a priest, let's bury the whole
village.
—Greek Proverb

THERE WAS NOTHING on either side of the road, only great swaths of rock
intermixed with patches of brackish soil. Olive trees were planted on a
few of the terraced hillsides, but unlike the ones on Chios, these trees were
buried in brush, their branches untrimmed and brown. Patmos was like a
desert, the absence of water evident everywhere he looked. A small military
outpost occupied a stony plateau above the beach of Meloi, a huge anti-aircraft
gun set out on the sparse grass in front.

Ah, the military …. Patronas recalled his days as a soldier. *Only they would
use a cannon as a garden ornament.*

Farther up the road, signs began to appear marking the turn-offs for the
various beaches, Agriolivado and Meloi, rooms-to-let in Lampi and elsewhere.
A bus was lumbering up the hill and Patronas followed it into Ano Campos.

Like many places in rural Greece, Campos was divided into two parts:
an upper village, Ano Campos, which occupied the summit of a hill and a
lower, less populated area by the sea. There had been historical reasons
for this division. In the days of the Saracen pirates, people retreated to the
mountaintops and stayed there. The beaches and coves were only now being
repopulated with the coming of tourists.

A group of people sitting under a grape arbor at the center of the village
turned their heads and stared at the Jeep as it went by. Why, Patronas wasn't
exactly sure. Maybe their attention had been caught by the priest, who had
stuck his head out the window and was watching the road like a hunting dog
closing in on a rabbit.

Patronas smiled to himself, recognizing the look on his friend's face. It
was what Papa Michalis called his 'panoptic, all-seeing eye,' a term he'd gotten

from a book by the Chios author, Michael Plakotaris, who was an expert on Sherlock Holmes. The so-called 'eye' came upon the priest whenever he and Patronas worked together, a sign not so much of schizophrenia as of enthusiasm. But the people in the grape arbor didn't know this. They just thought he was crazy.

The windows were open and the old man's hair was sticking straight up, his long gray beard ruffling around his neck like a scarf.

The Bay of Campos was the largest on the island. A gentle breeze was blowing and *kymatakia*—little waves—made a soft, lapping sound along the shore, pleasant to the ear. Far out in the bay, windsurfers were flying through the air like human dragonflies.

Patronas wondered what had happened to the boys he'd seen windsurfing in Campos on his honeymoon, the ones he and Dimitra had spoken of. "Do you think our sons will look like them?" he'd asked her. "Better," she'd replied with that stolid, unflinching certainty of hers.

"You ever go swimming?" he asked the priest, his eyes still on the boys.

"Not anymore. I had to give it up when I took my vows. Anyway, I am old now, all knobbly and wretched. Fish would flee if they saw me, take to dry land."

After parking the car, they walked along a dusty road, checking the numbers of the buildings, trying to find the rooming house where Maria Georgiou had stayed. Rented mopeds and cars were parked in the sand, and people were lying in the shade of the feathery trees that lined the beach.

A more formal operation was set up farther down, directed by two young men sitting under a faded yellow parachute. It offered rented chaises and umbrellas, kayaks and canoes and waterskiing lessons.

Shielding his eyes, Patronas looked out at the bay with longing. The sea was absolutely clear in the shallows, darkening where the land dropped away and the water deepened. In the distance, he could see rocks on the floor of the ocean, clumps of seaweed undulating in the current.

The rooming house they sought was about fifty meters beyond the parachute, situated on an arid strip of land. A wooden sidewalk was laid across the sand leading up to it.

The owner, Antonis Pavlos, remembered Maria Georgiou well and spoke highly of her. "Sure, she stayed here," he told Patronas. "I was glad to have her. I get tired of speaking English day in and day out: 'Please, breakfast over at ten, after, no. Towels not for beach.' It grates on me. And she was a nice lady. Kept to herself and never asked a thing. She stayed on the first floor here."

"Can you show me the room she rented?"

"A couple of kids are in there now, but seeing as how you're the police ...." He shrugged. "Come on, it's this way."

Initially, he hadn't known what to make of the two of them—a priest and a detective showing up at his rooming house—but he'd made a fast recovery.

Patronas had noticed the man's discomfort. Doing something illegal on the side, Mr. Pavlos was. A fiddle with his taxes, maybe.

He didn't care. He was here to investigate a homicide. Unpaid taxes were no concern of his.

Pavlos unlocked the door and pushed it open. Sparsely furnished, the room was very clean and faced an impromptu parking lot on the sand. Two twin beds and a chest of drawers filled the space. The walls were decorated with tired botanical prints, the floor by a strip of old carpeting. The bathroom was down the hall, Pavlos informed them.

A suitcase was open on the floor, and Patronas stepped around it and opened the door of the terrace. Made of poured concrete, it held a folding rack for laundry, exactly as Maria Georgiou had described. A line of cars were parked very close to the terrace, again in keeping with what she'd said. There was a taverna on the other side of the lot and he could hear voices from where he was standing, the clatter of dishes. Perhaps the victim had been on his way to eat there with his family when she'd spotted him.

"Would you mind walking outside and standing next to that car there?" he asked the owner. "I need to check something. Once you're there, start talking in a normal tone of voice." He wanted someone besides the priest to do this, an independent observer.

"People will think I'm crazy," Pavlos complained.

"It will only take a minute. Trust me, it's important."

Disgruntled, Pavlos headed out the door and soon reappeared outside. He walked over to the car Patronas had picked out and started muttering to himself. Standing in the door of the terrace, Patronas could see and hear him clearly, every word as clear as a bell.

"*Malaka*," the owner was saying. Jerk. "*Paliogaidouri.*" Old donkey. In case Patronas hadn't realized the invective was directed at him, he opened his hand and raised it, giving the *mountzose,* in other words, 'eat shit,' the universal Greek symbol of contempt, the equivalent of 'fuck you.' He and Pavlos laughed.

When Pavlos came back inside, Patronas quizzed him about the job offer that had led Maria Georgiou to the house in Chora. "Did she hear you talking about it and volunteer? Or did you come up with the idea yourself?"

They were standing in the lobby, talking, and Patronas had his notebook out.

"It was my idea," the owner of the rooming house said. "She liked it here and said she wished she could to stay on longer, but that she couldn't afford it. We often talked about it. What's this about anyway?"

"We're investigating a murder."

"That German in Chora?"

Patronas nodded.

"Maria had nothing to do with it. Leave her alone. She's over seventy years old."

"So was the victim."

"Bah. This isn't his country. He should have stayed in Berlin."

"Stuttgart," the priest interjected. "The victim, Walter Bechtel or Bech, depending on what time frame you are referring to, was from Stuttgart. The family called themselves one thing during the war and changed their name afterward."

"Who cares?" The owner snorted. "Fucking Germans."

Patronas fought to regain control of the interview. "Who told you about the job?"

"A man who rents a room from me mentioned it. He asked me to find someone as a favor to him. Hans Müller, his name is. He's a German, too." Pavlos snorted again.

Patronas wrote the name down in his notebook. "Where can I find him?"

"He usually eats lunch across the street. He's a sociable fellow, Herr Müller. Likes to talk. If you find him, he'll tell you what you want to know."

The three of them walked across the street to the taverna. A group of Germans were sitting on the patio, their table covered with the remnants of a meal.

"Him." Pavlos pointed to a fair-haired man with a sunburned face. "That's Müller."

Dressed for the beach, he was wearing a swimsuit with seagulls on it, an unbuttoned shirt and heavy leather sandals. As Müller spoke neither Greek nor English, they had to rely on a waiter to translate, a tattooed native of Patmos named Babis.

Patronas was uncomfortable using him, but had no time to file a formal request and wait for an official translator to arrive from Athens. "Just tell us what he says," he instructed the waiter. "Nothing fancy. Keep it simple."

Müller had been coming to Patmos for years and knew the owners of the house, the Bauers, the waiter reported. They asked him to find a woman to clean and do laundry at their house in Chora, cook an occasional meal. They had specifically requested that this woman be Greek. They'd been very emphatic on this point, not wanting to trouble themselves with immigrants and their attendance problems. They'd hired one in the past, nationality unknown, and she hadn't been reliable. She'd left without giving notice, taking a trash bag full of things that didn't belong to her.

"Not the family silver, but just about everything else." The waiter snickered as he shared this. "*Hazocharoumeni*," he said under his breath. Happy idiots.

The Bauers spoke some Greek and thought it would be better if they were seen to support the natives—given the current political climate in Greece.

Hans Müller smiled nervously, watching them as the waiter translated what he'd just said. "Also, a Greek would have papers, so there'd be no problem with the authorities."

"Did you meet her?" Patronas asked. "Meet Maria Georgiou?"

"She seemed old for the job," the man admitted, "but she assured me she could do the work. Anyway, it was only for a month; summer was nearly over."

He gave them his address and phone number in Germany and his local contact information in Greece. He said his passport was back in his room, that he never risked taking it to the beach, but that he'd get it for them if they needed it.

Patronas waved him off. He'd check him out when he got back to the station house, but he was certain Müller was who he said he was. He'd played only a walk-on part in the drama of the Bechtels and Maria Georgiou and had no reason to lie.

"How do you know the Bauers?" Patronas asked him.

"I got to know them here in Campos. He and I took windsurfing lessons one summer." He shrugged. "I see them when they're here—not in Germany, never in Germany." There was anger in his voice, a sense of grievance. "I'm a plumber," he said by way of explanation.

They are rich, Müller was saying, and own a summer house while I rent a room. They might ask me to find them a maid or to fix a leaky faucet, but that is the extent of our relationship. They'd never invite me to their home back in Stuttgart or introduce me to any of their friends.

Patronas thanked Müller for his help; then he and the priest walked back to the rooming house with the owner. "She ever make any phone calls?" he asked Pavlos.

"Who? Maria? No, she never called anybody. I don't even think she had a phone. That's one of the reasons I tried to help her. She seemed so alone."

Patronas and the priest had lunch at another taverna on the beach, not wanting Müller to think they were stalking him. This place, too, was full of tourists, and they watched them without comment. Few Greeks were in evidence. The majority hailed from northern Europe.

"We're losing our country," Patronas said morosely.

"We're resilient." Papa Michalis had put on his reading glasses and was studying the menu as if it were one of the Dead Sea Scrolls. "We'll survive."

"Will we? Look around." Patronas made a broad gesture. "Do you hear anybody speaking Greek? We could be anywhere, Father—London, Heidelberg, Atlantic City. Nothing here is ours."

Even their waiter was foreign, a slight adolescent from India or Bangladesh.

They ate at a table in the corner, fish again, which Patronas, of course, paid for. His walk on the sand had given Papa Michalis an appetite, and he ate and ate, the pile of bones on his plate growing apace while the one on Patronas' dish remained relatively small.

A whale inhaling plankton didn't come close. The Greek expression, 'ilektriko piorouni' was better, electric fork, although in Papa Michalis' case, the fork might well be jet propelled.

"This murder doesn't add up," Patronas said.

Papa Michalis had pulled the head off the fish and appeared to be licking it. "You need to look elsewhere for your murderer."

"You just say that because her father was a priest. Priests get into trouble. Look at that mess they made in America."

"Those men were Catholics." Papa Michalis paused. "Priests might be sinners, Yiannis, I'll grant you that, but as a general rule, they don't kill people. Well, at least not since the Inquisition. Torquemada, the Grand Inquisitor, might have condemned thousands of so-called heretics to death, but he only signed the orders; he didn't do the actual killing. Do you know they wore special garments, the condemned, called *sanbenito*, which depicted the fires of hell, and that religious authorities hung them up on the rafters of the churches after they were executed?"

"Why?"

"As lesson to the others, I suppose. Who knows? The church has done many puzzling things over the years. Endorsing the Fourth Crusade, for example, was a mistake, and that business with Galileo and the sun .... Well, you know how *that* turned out. Far worse was affixing the blame for the death of Christ on the Jews. The suffering caused by that is unimaginable, and no amount of apologizing by the Vatican will ever make it right."

Patronas watched him eat for a moment. Wasn't gluttony a sin? He should ask him.

"Of course," the priest went on, "the Orthodox Church has also made its share of mistakes. Undoubtedly. But it lacked the power of the church in Rome, and by the Middle Ages it was in eclipse and its battles were largely external. It never went after heretics or Jews, because it was too busy fighting the Turks."

The priest fished out the eyeball and popped it in his mouth "Let's order some more. I must say, the shrimp looks tasty."

And shrimp it was, followed by a plate of feta and *kataifi* with ice cream for dessert. The total bill came to well over a hundred euros. At this rate, the priest would bankrupt him.

"Shit," Patronas muttered, counting out the money. He'd have to visit the ATM again tomorrow. He'd never get reimbursed, either. Under duress, Stathis might pay for lentils, but never, not even if you held a gun to his head, would he pay for barbounia.

"Fish was a little overcooked," Papa Michalis said on the way out. "Next time, we should eat in Skala. We might do better there."

CHAPTER TWENTY-ONE

———◆———

Second thoughts are ever wiser.
—Greek Proverb

THE ORDER TO arrest Maria Georgiou came early the next morning. Patronas was in the hotel room getting dressed when his cellphone rang. It was Stathis.

"I relayed Bechtel's concerns to the central office in Athens, and they want you to arrest Maria Georgiou immediately. They were outraged that Bechtel had contacted the German embassy, seeking to impede our investigation and withhold valuable information about the victim. They said it was a gross breach of Greek sovereignty.'"

"But what if she's innocent?" Patronas asked.

Stathis cut him off. "See to it, Patronas. Call me when you have her in custody."

Giorgos Tembelos and Papa Michalis were in the room with him and heard every word. Tembelos, who had been shaving, laid his razor down.

"Goddamn Bechtel. He's the cause of this. Government's going to posture now. Use her as an example to show how strong-minded they are, how they don't bow to foreign influence."

"They're not that venal."

"Stathis is, and you know it."

"We've got to bring her in, Giorgos. It was a direct order. We have no choice."

Tembelos went back to shaving. "Let Evangelos do it. He's the one who got us into this. Let the sin be on him."

TO MAKE MATTERS worse, there wasn't a proper jail on Patmos and they had to prepare a cell to put her in, the only space available being the holding cell the police used for drunks. Patronas sent Tembelos out to buy sheets and towels, a bar of decent soap, paying for them with his own money. A toilet seat, too, if Tembelos could find one the proper size. He would have wallpapered the space and hung curtains if he could.

Tembelos didn't question him, just took the money and headed out to do as he was told. None of them felt good about the direction the case had taken—the prospect of arresting a Greek woman in her seventies—and they were all dragging their heels. They'd summoned a cleaning crew to mop the floor of the cell with bleach and wash its rancid walls and had nailed up a handful of air fresheners shaped like Christmas trees.

It was nearly five o'clock by the time they finished. By then Stathis had called twice, furious about the delay.

MARIA GEORGIOU WAS dressed in widow's weeds this time: a black dress and stockings, a pair of black patent leather shoes.

Mourning, Patronas thought when she opened the door. *She knows why we're here.*

"Maria Georgiou," Evangelos Demos said. "You're under arrest for the murder of Gunther Bechtel and for the assault on his daughter-in-law, Gerta Bechtel."

Taking his time, he continued on in this manner, ordering her to get her things together and to come with them.

Glorying in it.

She quickly packed a little polka-dotted bag and zipped it closed, then opened a canister of birdseed and poured some out on the windowsill. Picking up the bag, she walked over and stood by the door. "I'm ready," she said.

Tembelos took the bag from her and helped her down the stairs. "*Siga, siga,*" he said. Take your time.

Hoping to forestall gossip, they placed her in the back seat of the Jeep between Evangelos Demos and the priest. If anyone saw them, they'd think there'd been a family tragedy, which in a sense this was, and that they were taking her to the boat, a common enough occurrence on the islands. The priest's presence would further the illusion.

No one would think they were transporting a murderess ... an alleged murderess, Patronas reminded himself.

She'd been very solicitous of the priest as they drove to the station, asking after his health, chatting amiably about the infirmities of old age and how best to address them.

"At our age, we must be more careful," she'd said, laying a hand on his arm. "Perhaps you should get a cane, Father—not that you need it—for stability."

Patronas listened to them talk with an aching heart. His mother had sounded much the same as she'd aged, going on at length whenever he called about the precariousness of her health—her growing list of ailments, her failing sight, her failing bowels. It had been a kind of background noise that only increased in volume as the years went by, eventually drowning out all else until she died.

Old age does not come alone, she'd often said, reciting the proverb as if it somehow explained her plight. Perhaps all old people sounded the same. What Maria Georgiou did not sound like was a killer. Patronas had known a few, one especially who'd bided his time like a scorpion, waiting to strike. She comported herself with great dignity, as she had on the two previous occasions. *I am innocent,* she seemed to be saying. *As God is my witness, I am innocent.*

After they settled her into the makeshift prison cell, she'd requested a lamp, saying she wanted to read. Then she opened a chapped leather Bible.

Patronas and the others took turns watching her through the grate in the metal door. With her head bent low over her book, she appeared utterly unaware of her surroundings, to the fact that they'd seized her passport and charged her with murder. She was totally lost in what she was doing, the verses she was murmuring.

"Praying," the priest said quietly. "Those are psalms she is reciting."

Maria Georgiou's father had taught her well. Patronas could see her at the cave after the crucifixion anointing the body of Christ. One of the myrrh-bearing women they sang about at Easter, whose faith never wavered.

Catching the light, her white hair glowed in the semi-darkness of the cell and bathed her face. A Renaissance artist might have painted her sitting there, a saint on her way to martyrdom. All that was missing were the little angels whispering in her ear.

Tembelos was distraught about the arrest. "Look at her," he told Patronas. "She's an old woman. How could she hit anyone hard enough to kill them?"

Giorgos had raised a fair point. At her age, Maria Georgiou lacked the physical strength to shatter a man's skull.

"You're the expert on murderers," Tembelos went on angrily. "How many of them invest in bird seed?"

"None," Patronas admitted. "It's an anomaly."

"An anomaly! She's innocent. Can't you see it?"

In spite of the fact that he'd been the one who'd arrested her, Evangelos concurred. Worried about possible political repercussions, for the most part, he'd let Patronas take the lead during the investigation, rarely volunteering an opinion or contradicting him. But tonight was different. Tonight, he had a lot to say.

"We should have followed up the lead on November Seventeenth," he said.

"Anything would be better than this. Arresting a woman old enough to be my grandmother …. It's a disgrace. They will destroy you in the press, Yiannis, and rightly so. The newspapers will have a field day."

You, not us, Patronas thought angrily. Evangelos was jumping ship. Idly, he wondered if that's why he'd been summoned to Patmos in the first place, so Evangelos could use him as a scapegoat. Blame him when it all came apart.

He stared at him. Oh, to be Medusa and turn your fat ass to stone.

As always, the priest had the final word. "I'd be careful if I were you, Yiannis. It's like the day they set about burning Joan of Arc. You don't want to be the one lighting a match to her pyre."

Three against one … four, if he counted Bechtel. He was on his own. And Stathis would never support him, not if the case unraveled. As if any of this had been his choice. What was he supposed to do, disobey a direct order? The police force was like the army, and Stathis was his commanding officer. He would have his head if Patronas refused, fire him on the spot.

Patronas looked through the grate again. "It's not so bad in there," he said, trying to convince himself. "She'll be all right. Anyway, the law, *aftoforo,* dictates we can only hold her twenty-four hours without a judge's decision. After that we have to let her go."

"Yiannis, she's in *jail!*" Tembelos bellowed. "We need to start over again. We got it wrong."

"All right, all right. I'll talk to the Bechtels tonight and go over my notes when I get back to the hotel. Could be I missed something."

"Could be you missed a *lot* of something."

Grabbing Patronas by the arm, Tembelos spun him around. "You need to find the killer and find them fast. Come back with a name … any name but hers."

CHAPTER TWENTY-TWO

---◆---

Making the same mistake twice does not indicate
an intelligent person.
—Greek Proverb

"I APOLOGIZE FOR THE lateness of the hour," Patronas told Gunther Bechtel when the German opened the door. "May we come in?"

Bechtel scowled. "What do you want now?"

"We need to ask you a few things."

"If you must. They phoned from Athens and said they will be releasing my father's body at the end of the week. We will be leaving then."

"What about the Bauers?"

"They'll be staying on a few more weeks."

"Are they here now?"

"Yes. They're in their bedroom. I'd prefer that you not disturb them."

He led Patronas and Papa Michalis into the kitchen and the three of them sat down at the table. "Do you need to talk to Gerta, too?" he asked. "It's late. She's getting ready for bed. Couldn't this wait until morning?"

"Let your wife be. We prefer to speak to you alone."

That caught Bechtel's attention, and he gave him a wary look. "Very well then."

Now is as good a time as any, Patronas told himself, taking a deep breath. "It's about your uncle. His wartime service."

It cost him to say 'service.' The only thing the Gestapo had been in the service of was suffering.

"Ah," the man said. He did not seem surprised.

Patronas paged through his notes. "My men and I went to Epirus earlier this week and interviewed the elderly inhabitants of Aghios Stefanos, a village near Ioannina. We spoke with a number of people there. Your uncle's division conducted an anti-guerrilla mission in that village in the fall of 1943, and as a result, many of its inhabitants were killed."

Listen to me babble, the words I'm using, Patronas told himself. An 'anti-guerrilla mission.' You'd think it was an accident that those hundred and thirty-seven people got killed, that those butchers hadn't meant to do it.

"It was war. Such things happen in wars." A guarded look had come into Bechtel's eyes and the anger was back. "Anyway, that is old history. What does it have to do with my uncle, Chief Officer?"

"Because of his distinctive scars, he was easy to identify, despite the passage of time. We think one of the survivors recognized him, hunted him down, and killed him."

"This person who recognized him ... have you arrested him?" Bechtel asked.

"*Her.* It's your housekeeper, Maria Georgiou. She lost her entire family that day. If convicted, she'll probably spend the rest of her life in prison."

"And this business about the village?" Bechtel asked heatedly. "I tried to get the embassy involved. I told you before I didn't want you pursuing this aspect of the case, those false allegations about my papa. I don't want my children to learn of them."

"I'm a policeman. I go where the evidence leads me ..." Patronas said, thinking he might as well tell him the rest, "and it led me there." He consulted his notes. "Are you aware that your uncle was a Gestapo agent?"

Bechtel's tone was dismissive. "What proof do you have of this?"

"Eye witness accounts. Photos."

"That can't be true. I knew him. I knew what kind of man he was."

"Mr. Bechtel, people picked him out; they recognized him."

"*Greeks?*" He turned it into a slur.

"Yes, Greeks. Elderly Greeks who survived the massacre. Like your uncle, they, too, have scars, only theirs are from bayonets and shrapnel. They showed them to me."

"Why are you telling me these things? It's not enough that he was killed ... now you have to slander him, too?"

"I was hoping you'd verify what we've learned."

"You bastard! Why would I do a thing like that? So you can convict him? So you can perpetuate the lie that he deserved to die, that he brought it upon himself? You masquerade as a police detective, but like everyone else in this godforsaken country, you don't know how to work, to do a proper job. Is this really the best you can offer, Chief Officer? Aren't you ashamed?"

Upon reflection, Patronas concluded it was Bechtel's use of the word 'ashamed' that set him off. He'd been willing to tiptoe around, exactly as Stathis had ordered, to pretend the victim had been a simple soldier—a good

German, one of the ones everybody talked about who'd only been obeying orders. But then Bechtel had given his little speech and all hell had broken loose.

"If your uncle, your so-called 'papa,' was indeed innocent of mass murder as you allege, why did he change his name? Gunther Bech, the Gestapo agent, assuming the name 'Walter Bechtel,' the pharmacist, while you, his nephew, the noble man in Africa, became 'Gunther Bechtel'? He didn't change them much, I'll give you that—Bech, Bechtel. Still, it's quite a coincidence."

"My uncle is the victim here," Bechtel screamed. "Need I remind you of that? What he did or did not do during the war has no bearing on his death."

"He was killed for a reason." Patronas decided to hold off and not tell Bechtel about the rapes. The German was already overwrought. It would only add to his rage.

"Nonsense," Bechtel said. "The war was a long time ago. No one would seek revenge now. Once this generation dies off, it will finally be forgotten."

"You think it will all go away, do you? If you wait long enough, no one will remember?"

"Eventually, yes. Time eliminates many things."

"Graves?" Patronas asked bitterly.

"It was wartime. My uncle did his duty. That was all."

Seeking to calm himself, Patronas lit a cigarette. He was so upset his hands were shaking and he had trouble working the lighter. He didn't care if Bechtel objected or not. "Odd word, *duty*," he said, inhaling deeply. "It can mean any number of things, depending on who you ask."

"All this is conjecture."

They were having this argument in English, Patronas pausing now and then to consult the dictionary. " 'Conjecture' means made up, right? A lie, in other words."

"A lie. That is correct."

"I believe his title in the Gestapo was *Scharführer*. That's what our witnesses told us."

Bechtel pulled Patronas out of the chair. "I want you to leave," he yelled. Turning him around, he shoved him toward the door. "Go on. Get out!"

Papa Michalis was knocked down in the ensuing melee, slamming his head against the edge of the marble countertop. Instantly, blood began to stream down his forehead and into his eyes, and his cassock was soon wet with it. It was World War II all over again, only this time the allies—at least Patronas and Papa Michalis—were losing.

Patronas helped the old man to his feet. "If I weren't on duty," he told Bechtel. "I swear I'd beat the living shit out of you."

Hearing the commotion, Bechtel's two children came running into the room, their mother close on their heels. All of them were dressed in pajamas. The Bauers followed a moment later.

Gerta Bechtel gasped when she saw the priest and pulled the children away. "Gunther, what happened?"

"He was slandering my uncle, Gerta, my dead uncle. Saying terrible things."

Gerta Bechtel became very still. "What things?"

"He said he was a Gestapo agent and that the housekeeper recognized him."

"Maria?"

"Yes. According to his theory, he was stationed in Greece and there was an incident in her village. Some people were killed." Bechtel sounded exhausted, his anger spent. "It was war, Gerta. Who knows what happened?"

"And she killed him?"

"That's what he says."

Gerta Bechtel turned to Patronas. "You arrested her?" She seemed relieved, pleased.

"It's just a theory at this point. Maria Georgiou hasn't confessed."

"A theory?" she said. "After all this time, that's the best you can do?"

And with that they were back where they'd started.

TELLING BECHTEL HE'D be back, Patronas put his arm around the priest and led him out of the house and back down to the car. He had taken off his shirt and wrapped it around the priest's head in a futile effort to staunch the flow of blood.

"Well, that was a fiasco," the priest said, settling himself into the front seat of the Jeep and buckling his seatbelt.

Starting the Jeep, Patronas drove as fast as he could to Skala. The two of them had caused quite a stir among the tourists at the bus stop in Chora. A bloody priest under the monastery's towering walls; it was the stuff of horror movies. All that was missing was Dracula cackling in the shadows.

"You showed admirable restraint, I must say," Papa Michalis said.

"I shouldn't have said anything about the Gestapo. It was a mistake."

"He provoked you."

"I know. All that crap about being ashamed. 'The best you can do,'" Patronas mimicked Bechtel's German accent.

"It came as no surprise to him, that business about the Gestapo, his uncle's participation in it. My guess is he's known for years. One thing's for sure: you didn't tell him anything new. His wife, either. He might not have known the specifics about Epirus and Maria Georgiou, but he certainly knew the rest. All that righteous indignation, the shoving and the rest, it was staged. I'd stake my life on it."

"But why?"

"Denial maybe. Who'd want that legacy? Who wants to face the fact that one's 'papa' was one of Hitler's henchmen?"

THE DOCTOR WAS very young, a recent graduate of medical school. He probed the wound tentatively with his fingers. "What happened, Father?" he asked. "You got carried away saying your prayers? Wrestling with the devil?"

Papa Michalis gave a wan smile. "In a manner of speaking."

His face was now totally covered with blood, his eyebrows and his beard encrusted with it.

"It's only a scalp wound," the doctor reassured him. "That's why it's bleeding so much. Nothing to worry about."

He shaved the hair around the cut and painted it with mercurochrome, then gave Papa Michalis a shot of Novocain and stitched him up.

Patronas had long presumed his friend had a head like a rock, but the priest had surprised him. An egg was more like it—a soft-boiled egg.

OPENING HIS CELLPHONE, Patronas stepped out of the emergency room. "What the hell," he muttered and dialed his wife's number.

Dimitra picked up on the first ring. *"Oriste?"* she said. Hello.

"It's me, Dimitra."

Dead silence.

He pictured her in the parlor of her mother's house, looking at the phone as if it had caught fire in her hand.

"Yiannis?" she said hesistantly.

"Yes. I heard you're moving to Italy."

"That's right, Bologna." She sounded relieved. "My mother and I are leaving next week."

Poor Dimitra, lugging that old walrus with her to Bologna. Her mother would sulk the whole time she was there, develop an aversion to pasta and Chianti. Cause any manner of hardship.

"Well, good luck," he said. "I hope it works out for you."

More silence.

"Thank you, Yiannis," she said after a long interval. "Good luck to you, too."

So formal they were with each another, the two old adversaries.

They spoke for a few more minutes about people they knew, how hot it was in Chios this summer and other matters, then said their goodbyes.

"Arrivederci," Patronas said. "That's Italian for 'so long.' "

"God keep you." Dimitra sounded like she was crying. "God keep you always, Yiannis, and bless you every day of your life."

"And you, Dimitra. And you."

"I DID WHAT you told me," Patronas told the priest."I called Dimitra."

"Really?"

The doctor had left and Papa Michalis was standing by the sink, dabbing his face with a towel. "How did it go?"

"Fine. We chatted and I told her *arrivederci* and she blessed me."

Papa Michalis turned and smiled at him. "Forgiveness, Yiannis, that's the ticket. Forgiveness and love. It's like the Bible says, If I speak in human and angelic tongues, but do not have love, I am a resounding gong or clashing cymbal. If I have faith so as to move mountains, but do not have love, I am nothing. You'll get there, my friend. You're just out of practice."

OUT OF PRACTICE at love?

Unable to sleep, Patronas was sitting on the edge of his bed, brooding about what the priest had said. *He* was the clashing cymbal, Papa Michalis, a damn bagpipe sometimes.

He remembered his hours practicing the piano as a child. Like his marriage, his lessons hadn't amounted to much. He'd never become adept, never mastered the art of making music. He didn't know why his mother had bothered. They didn't have the money and yet she'd insisted. Maybe love was like that, too. Some had the gift, others not. Maybe at the end of the day he was tone deaf, unable to recognize any song, save his own.

He walked over to the balcony and looked out at the street. Cars were parked under the light in front of the hotel, and a solitary man with a suitcase stood waiting for a taxi. A lonely scene, it reminded him of the paintings of Edward Hopper. Dimitra had owned a book of the artist's work.

Maybe it wasn't too late. According to the teachings of the Church, right up to the moment of death, a person could turn it around. Who knew what lay ahead? Maybe that melody, that duet he longed for with another, was still possible. The priest had warned against hope, but right now it was all he had.

CHAPTER TWENTY-THREE

---•---

Wisdom behind me …. Had I but had thee before!
—Greek Proverb

THE PRIEST TOOK a lengthy shower the next morning, shampooing his hair and beard and putting on a clean robe. He was in good spirits, joking about how the row of stitches across his forehead made him look like Frankenstein.

"I admit it was a little unsettling seeing myself in the mirror, but I'm over that now." He gave a little sniff. "Vanity is unseemly in a priest."

"I'm sorry you got hurt," Patronas told him.

"My fault entirely. Unfortunately, unsteadiness comes with age. I should have stepped aside when you and Bechtel started wrestling." His hair was still wet, freshly parted and slicked down like a little boy's.

Antigone Balis knocked on the door a few minutes later with the pot of coffee and the plate of sandwiches they'd ordered. "Let me know if you need anything else," she told them.

Patronas followed her out with his eyes. Was it his imagination or did she throw an extra something into that walk of hers, her jaunty little buttocks swinging from side to side. Not the green dress, a blue one this time.

"You told me I needed practice at love," he told the priest, nodding in her direction. "She's the one I'd like to practice on."

The priest gasped. "Oh my, no," he said, shaking his head. "Not that one, Yiannis, not her. Too brazen by half."

"I like her."

But Papa Michalis did not appear to be listening. Lifting up slices of bread, he was examining the contents of each of the sandwiches in turn. "Ham and cheese, ham and cheese, ham and cheese."

"She's shown an interest," Patronas insisted.

The priest tsk-tsked. "You don't want a woman like that, Yiannis, a loose woman. *Vromiari.*" Dirty. "You want one like they speak about in scripture: 'Who can find a virtuous woman? For her price is far above rubies. The heart of her husband doth safely trust in her, so that he shall have no need of spoil. She will do him good and not evil all the days of her life.' "

"No, I don't, Father. I want a harlot. The looser the better."

"Whatever for?" the priest asked, confused.

It had been a long night and the last thing Patronas wanted at this point was to discuss the facts of life with a priest. "If you don't know by now, Father, I'm sure as hell not going to explain it to you."

Selecting a sandwich, the priest took an exploratory bite. "Not bad," he said between mouthfuls. "Now, if we could only get her to button up, you might have something. Not that I'd bless such a union, you understand. My mother would have called a woman like her a *tsoula*." Slut. "And I must say, I concur. You might not have noticed, but that dress of hers was transparent."

Jezebel, in other words.

They debated the pros and cons of Antigone Balis a few minutes longer.

"You're a priest, Father," Patronas pointed out, "and as a priest, you appreciate chastity. Whereas, I have no use for it. I've experienced it, involuntarily I might add, for much of my married life, and found that it does not agree with me. I much prefer the sins of the flesh."

The priest pursed his lips. "You realize, of course, the key word in that phrase is 'sin.' "

"A matter of opinion, Father."

Papa Michalis ate another sandwich, looking askance at Patronas from time to time. "To welcome sin is worrisome, Yiannis. Satan, if you recall, started out as an angel, one of God's favorites. He didn't start out as a sinner. Things got away from him."

"I'll say," Patronas said with a chuckle.

Tembelos, too, had expressed doubts about Antigone Balis' character.

"*Afti i gynaika koimatai me oti kinietai,*" he'd said. That woman sleeps with whatever moves.

Difference between Tembelos and the priest was that Tembelos spoke in an admiring way, leering and rubbing his hands together. "Oh, if I wasn't married …. I envy you, Yiannis. I love my wife, but night after night, it's always the same. No surprises. You don't want to eat lentils every day; sometimes you want eggplants. I only wish I could, but you know, Eleni …."

Indeed, if Tembelos' wife caught him sampling eggplants, there'd be no plea-bargaining, no trial. No, she'd cut off his offending appendages and feed them to the dog.

Perhaps dallying with Antigone Balis wasn't such a good idea. She appeared to be a woman of passion, but passion could go either way. What was the expression, *dikopo mahairi*—a knife that cuts two ways. That might well be her. Remembering Tembelos' wife, Eleni, he touched his manly parts protectively. No telling what a passionate woman might do. Dimitra had jabbed him in the calf with a pair of scissors. If provoked, Antigone Balis might well jab him someplace worse.

He chewed contemplatively. Still, that ass of hers is a thing of wonder.

Who knew what lay ahead? *Lay* being the operative word.

He handed the priest a transcript of the first interview with Maria Georgiou. "Let's go over it again, Father. See if anything jumps out at us."

Tembelos was at the police station, looking after the prisoner, Maria Georgiou. He'd just bought her breakfast, he reported when Patronas called, and was in the process of ordering lunch for her from a taverna. In addition, he had offered to bring her books, a radio or television, even a laptop computer if she wanted—anything to break up the monotony of her confinement.

"She waved me off. Said she had her Bible and that was enough."

"How's her appetite?"

"Terrible. She didn't touch her food last night. We've got to get her out of here."

"I know, Giorgos. I'm working on it."

Patronas poured himself a cup of coffee. "What about a lawyer?"

"Evangelos is arranging it. He called around this morning, but didn't get anywhere. There are only a couple of lawyers on Patmos and they're all busy."

"Well, have him talk to Stathis," he said. "See if we can get somebody to come from Athens. She has the right to counsel."

BECHTEL TURNED UP at the hotel an hour later. He flinched when he saw Papa Michalis and started to apologize, but checked himself. He looked exhausted and hadn't changed his clothes since they'd last seen him. He seemed subdued, far less confrontational than he'd been the previous night.

"The person who killed him? You said you arrested her," he said to Patronas.

"Maria Georgiou? Yes, we have her in custody."

"What will happen to her?" he asked.

"I don't know. A long sentence, probably. "

"The motive for the killing, the massacre in Aghios Stefanos, you said it will be brought up at the trial."

"Yes. I know you objected, but it's extremely relevant. By the way, it wasn't me. It was my superiors in Athens who insisted that we charge her with murder. Your letter was what decided them." Patronas added this out of spite.

"They saw it as an 'unwarranted interference in the Greek judicial system and a breach of national sovereignty.' "

"What if I don't press charges?" Bechtel bleated.

In all his years in law enforcement, Patronas had never met the relative of a murder victim who didn't want revenge. An eye for an eye cut deep. It went to their very core. And yet here was Bechtel, pleading with him to drop the case.

"What's this really about?" he asked.

Bechtel fell back in the chair and covered his face with his hands. He stayed like that for a long time.

"It's a puzzle," he said, choking a little on the words, "how you can love someone ... love them and worship them and want to be like them ... all the time knowing they are not what they seem, that they have blood on their hands. That was my dilemma as an adolescent, reconciling the man who lived only to please me and my mother, who was a gentle and playful uncle and grandfather, with such a foul history. You asked if I knew. Yes, yes, of course I did. That's why I changed our name. It was me, not him. You got that part wrong—unfortunately not the rest. I wanted to go forward from that time, to leave it behind and start anew. My uncle was not pleased when I did it, but I told him I had no choice, that I must protect the children, and he eventually acquiesced. I did not know the specifics of what he'd done or where he had served. He never told me and I never asked. But yes, I was aware that he was in the Gestapo—my mother threw it up at him once when they were fighting— and the Gestapo was not known for its humanity."

Although Patronas struggled with the English, he understood most of what Bechtel was telling him. "Does your wife know?"

Bechtel closed his eyes, gave a slight nod. "She was cleaning out the attic of my family home in Stuttgart after my mother died and found an old uniform of his. A bunch of souvenirs from the war. I don't know why he kept them. He was very young when he enlisted. It was 1942 and they were taking everyone, young and old alike."

It had been youthful foolishness, he was saying. My uncle hadn't meant to do what he did. Some kids drive too fast; my relatives, they joined the Gestapo.

Patronas felt a touch of pity for him. To carry such a burden ....

"I don't see what good it will do to arrest her," Bechtel cried. "It won't bring my uncle back. It will only perpetuate the horror of those years."

"I'm sorry," Patronas said, and he was.

All of Bechtel's good deeds, his years of service in Africa, would soon be eclipsed by what his relative had done in the war. The trial would probably destroy his life.

And like those victims in Aghios Stefanos, Daphne Kallis and the others, he too was innocent.

"Even if it was a revenge killing, why'd she wait so long?" the priest asked, thumbing through the pages of the notebook. "We found out who Walter Bechtel was in less than a week. Surely she could have discovered his new name and where he lived years ago."

"She didn't even know he was alive until she saw him in Campos. Could be she didn't mean to kill him. He might have said something to her in the garden that provoked her."

It had gotten stuffy in the room so they'd moved their chairs out onto the balcony. Across the street, the playground was empty, the swings creaking eerily in the wind.

The priest frowned. "Yiannis, Maria Georgiou and Bech didn't speak the same language. How could he have insulted her?"

"I don't know. She implied he was an irritable, unpleasant man. Who knows what he might have said?"

"Yes, she also said he was Gerta Bechtel's problem, not hers."

"So where do we go from here?"

The priest paused for a moment. "In my opinion, the death of the cat bears further investigation. Perhaps the killing of the animal was not as random as we initially thought. We assumed it was a hostile act directed at the Bechtels or the Bauers because they were German, but maybe it wasn't. It could have been directed at the victim, at him and him alone. The cat belonged to him, after all. Someone could have been sending him a message."

Working his way through his notes, Patronas thought Tembelos might be right and that they should let Maria Georgiou go. What Daphne Kallis and the others in Aghios Stefanos had told him still haunted him. They had been hostages during the war, too afraid to fight Bech off. Afraid if they did, it would cost them their lives. He'd just re-read what Maria Georgiou had said about finding Daphne Kallis in the river after the rape and it sickened him. The image of the little girl in the pink dress, trying to clean herself in the water.

He lit a cigarette and sat there smoking. Somebody should have killed Bech a long time ago, shot him to death like a rabid dog.

"You know, pedophilia is a lifelong affliction," the priest said. "Perhaps Bech's hunger didn't abate after the war. Perhaps there have been other children."

Patronas swore under his breath. How could he have missed it?

He threw the notebook down. "That's it, Father. That's the missing piece."

He would have yelled 'Eureka!' like Archimedes, except it was late and he was outside. Unlike the ancient Greek scholar, he wasn't lolling in a bathtub.

CHAPTER TWENTY-FOUR

———— ◆ ————

The brave warrior seeks another path.
—Greek Proverb

"Just sit there in the cell with Maria Georgiou?" Papa Michalis said. "I don't know, Yiannis. It seems a little passive."

"You can read Bible verses together."

Patronas was planning to go to Chora with Giorgos Tembelos to dig up the cat—and possibly re-interview the Bechtels and make an arrest. In any of these scenarios, he didn't want the priest involved. Their last visit to the house had been a disaster. Also, the priest had a regrettable tendency to side with the accused once the handcuffs came out, to advocate for mercy and forgiveness. His being a man of the cloth inevitably trumped his role in law enforcement. In other words, too much talking.

"It's a jail and she's an inmate," Papa Michalis said. "What if she tries to escape? What would I do if that happened?"

"Yell for help. It's a police station."

The priest mulled this over. "Perhaps if you were to give me your gun."

They were standing in the corridor outside her cell, arguing.

"Although Canon Law does not expressly forbid it," the priest went on, "most of it having been written before firearms came into being, one would assume that as a member of the clergy, I am not allowed to gun people down. The Bible is very strong on this point. *Thou shalt not kill* is not exactly open to interpretation. However, I could *hold* a gun on her, I think, as long as I didn't fire it. There's no religious stricture against holding a gun on someone. If she tries to escape, I could point it at her and yell, 'Stop or I'll shoot.' I wouldn't shoot, of course, but she wouldn't know that and she'd stop dead in her tracks. Not dead-dead. 'Dead in her tracks,' in case you are unfamiliar, is just a figure of speech, Yiannis. A euphemism in English ...."

Not Sherlock Holmes or Agatha Christie, Patronas decided. No, today Papa Michalis was channeling someone new, Clint Eastwood in Dirty Harry.

He had quite a repertoire, the priest. Lots of company for the bats in his belfry.

PATRONAS BEEN WORKING hard to exclude foreign words from his speech and had referred to the batteries as *syskevi apothikefsis energeias*—energy storage devices—when he tried to purchase them at the kiosk. This had caused an unnecessary delay and Tembelos had been forced to step in.

"Batteries," he told the man, "that's what he wants."

"*Afta einai kinezika*," the man said, looking suspiciously at Patronas. This is Chinese.

"I know," Tembelos answered. "*Einai trelos.*" He's nuts.

The two of them were preparing to exhume the cat. They'd left Papa Michalis behind at the police station, and Evangelos Demos had demurred when they'd invited him along, saying he had a lot of paperwork to complete. Stathis, they hadn't told.

Opening the trunk of the Jeep, Tembelos stowed their gear inside and shut it again. "So let me get this straight. You think the victim kept going after the war, worked his way through the kids in the neighborhood ... and the cat was a witness."

"Meow," his friend added, in case Patronas had missed the point.

"Catcalls, Giorgos? Trust me, That animal is crucial to our case."

Tembelos sat for a minute before starting the car. "You said he sexually abused her. How could he do that? I just don't get it."

"Pedophiles have a different hunger than the rest of us, Giorgos. It happens sometimes."

"Whoever killed him did the world a favor. No trial, no nothing—just *bam*. Done." Tembelos thumped the steering wheel for emphasis. "End of story. If we did that with every child molester, that would put an end to it."

It very well might, Patronas thought, recalling what the priest had said about children who were abused growing up to be abusers themselves, the way such crimes perpetuated themselves.

The most tragic kind of karma.

A handful of *xelidoni* were darting through the yellow grass by the road, their forked tails like arrows. The swallows took off a moment later, coasting out over the mountain, borne by the wind.

Once, when Patronas was a little boy, swallows had nested in the rafters of his house. His mother had rejoiced, telling him the birds' presence was a great blessing. It was one of the few times he'd seen her happy.

A favorite in Greece, the birds were featured in numerous songs and poems. Usually they were depicted as messengers. In ancient times, a dead boy or girl might return to their parents in the guise of the bird.

Patronas watched the swallows. It pleased him to think of the dead as birds, that they hadn't truly left, only changed form and taken to the sky.

Maria Georgiou had been feeding birds on her windowsill. It was a sign. He was almost there; he could feel it. The Greek woman would be exonerated, and he and Tembelos could go home to Chios. Bechtel's family would be destroyed, but there was nothing he could do about it. It was almost biblical, the way the case was playing out.

"If Bechtel asks, how are you going to explain what we're doing?" Tembelos asked.

"Loose ends, Giorgos. We're tying up loose ends."

THE GARDENER WAS standing outside the entrance of the estate, waiting for them as Patronas had instructed. Ill at ease, he was wearing his work clothes. His shoes were caked with dirt. As soon as he saw them, he ran toward them and began greeting them effusively.

"Mr. Police, Mr. Police."

"We've got some things to ask you, and you must tell us the truth," Patronas told him. "You're not in trouble now, but if you lie, you will be. We'll charge you with perjury and you could get deported. Also, you must never speak about what we say to another person, not even your wife."

"I will keep the silence," the Albanian said. "I am good for trust."

They stood by the gate, talking.

"First question," Patronas said. "Did your son ever accompany you to the house where the man was killed? Spend time alone in the garden with him?"

"Mr. Bechtel?"

"Yes, the deceased."

The gardener reported that while the child had often come with him to the house, he had kept him by his side always. The little boy had helped him with his work, handing him his rake or his shovel, moving the hose when his father asked, but that was all. His son had never wandered off and had had absolutely no contact with the old man.

"Were there ever any other children around?" Tembelos asked.

The man studied the two of them, comprehension slowly dawning on his face. "Only little Walter," he said gravely. "He was there."

"Did Walter have any friends he played with? Kids from the village who visited the house?"

"Walter?" The way he said it was answer enough.

"What about Hannelore?"

"The girl, she was off at the beach most days."

He stopped, remembering something, his face troubled. "Something *did* happen there once. I don't know what it was about, but the girl and her grandfather, they had a fight out in the garden. I was in the back, pruning the roses, but I heard them."

"What were they fighting about?"

"I don't know. My German …." He lifted his shoulders and let them drop. "After that, Hannelore, she was gone."

"Was anyone else at the house then?"

"Her mother, I think. Yes, Mrs. Gerta, she was there."

Patronas nodded. "Did the cat get killed before or after the fight?"

"After," the man said. "It was after the fight that the cat died."

"Do you remember where you buried it?"

"Yes, yes. It is by the wall."

The Bechtels were packing when the three of them got to the house. Gunther Bechtel informed them that the coroner's office in Athens had called and said that the body of his uncle would be released within the next seventy-two hours. He and the rest of his family were planning to fly back to Germany beforehand to prepare for the funeral.

"I thought nothing could be worse than what I saw in Africa," he said bitterly, "but, thanks largely to you and your colleagues, this has been. My papa is murdered and instead of solving the crime, you do your best to destroy him, destroy what he meant to me, what he meant to my family. I know what you think of him, but he was my relative and I want to have a funeral and bury him. It is necessary that I do this and unconscionable that I have been denied the opportunity. Personally, I hope Merkel destroys the lot of you and bankrupts this country."

"Poor fool thinks this is the end of it, doesn't he?" Tembelos whispered to Patronas.

The gardener walked ahead of them to a clump of oleander bushes. He was standing about twenty meters from the fountain.

"Is there." The Albanian pointed to a disturbed place in the ground. "Is there where I put cat."

Tembelos quickly unpacked their gear, laid a tarp down on the ground, and began pulling on a pair of latex gloves.

The gardener watched him uneasily. "Is many weeks dead, the cat," he said. "Hot now in summer."

Lighting a cigarette, Patronas handed the pack to Tembelos, who did the same. It wouldn't help much against the smell, but it was all they had.

"Bad," the gardener warned, taking a cigarette himself. "Long time dead. Long time."

Patronas and Tembelos began digging up small amounts of soil with their trowels and laying it aside. Neither of them spoke, the only sound the steady chink of their tools against the earth. They worked very carefully, removing only a fistful at a time. When they got closer, they switched to brushes, sweeping the dirt away a half centimeter at a time.

It was the head that emerged first, whiskers and bared teeth.

Funny what happens in death … Patronas studied the animal's matted fur and milky eyes, runny now and half gone. The cat's mouth hung open, its pointed teeth exposed in a silent roar. Maggots were swarming all over it, thousands upon thousands of them, and the animal's body seemed to writhe and twitch as he watched, alive with the teeming insects.

Lifting the cat up with his gloved hands, Tembelos laid it down on the tarp. It was very small. More of a kitten than a cat, not yet full grown. Here, too, the old man had favored the young.

Patronas nudged it with his foot. Even now, in an advanced state of decay, it was easy to see that the animal's neck was broken and only partially attached to its skull, secured with little more than a few tendrils of rotting flesh.

"What do we do now?" Tembelos asked Patronas. He was sweating profusely, alternately gasping for air and holding his breath against the smell. Between the three of them, they'd already smoked the entire pack of cigarettes. It hadn't helped.

"We package it up and ship it to the lab in Athens."

"But it's a cat."

Patronas, too, was holding his breath. He felt like he was swimming underwater, and if he resurfaced even for a second, he'd die. The gardener had already vomited into the bushes, and he feared he would be next.

Don't inhale, he warned himself. Stay the course. Concentrate on the work.

"We need to find out what happened to it," he said.

"Tell me why," Tembelos said.

"Because whoever killed it, killed Gunther Bech."

Patronas had been intent on the exhumation in part because of what the priest had said about the Gestapo, how some of its agents had degenerated over time and one sadistic act often begot another. They'd unleashed the dogs of hell, according to him, and Patronas was pretty sure that was what had happened here. The cat had never been the target. It was just practice, a way of working up to the real target, the old man.

"YOU EXHUMED A dead cat?!" Stathis' tone was scathing. "What did Bechtel say when you dug up his cat?"

"He doesn't know, sir," Patronas responded in a level voice. "We proceeded without him."

This mollified his boss somewhat. "What did you do with the remains?"

"We put them in the refrigerator at our hotel." Patronas braced himself.

Stathis did not disappoint. "Jesus Christ, Patronas, what were you thinking? Some tourist will go to get a soda and have a heart attack."

"We took care to disguise it, sir. We wrapped it up in tin foil and put it in a big plastic tub with a lid—you know, the kind that people use for food. Patmos doesn't have a lab, so we had to improvise."

"I don't believe it. A dead cat!"

Patronas wasn't sure, but he could have sworn Stathis was laughing.

"And what do you plan to do with this dead cat of yours?"

"Send it to Athens."

"How? You going to mail it?"

"No, sir, we plan to send it to Leros, same as we did the dead man, and from there fly it on to the lab in Athens. It'll be all right. We bought a cooler."

No doubt now. Stathis was definitely laughing.

Patronas pushed on, "We can't let the Bechtels leave Greece. They're planning to fly out tomorrow and we need to flag their passports and stop them at the airport. Otherwise, we'll have to extradite them, and they're sure to fight it. I've posted a man at the entrance to the house, but they could slip by him, take a boat to another island—Leros or Kalymnos, someplace with an airport—and return to Germany from there."

"You're sure about this, Patronas?"

"I am, sir."

"Very well then. I'll flag their passports. But if this doesn't work out, I'm going to reassign you, send you to that rock where they used to keep lepers."

CHAPTER TWENTY-FIVE

————◆————

The wounded old horse sees the saddle and
trembles.
—Greek Proverb

PATRONAS HAD TAPED the address of the lab on the side of the cooler and
explained to the crew on the ferry that a policeman would pick it up in
Athens. He'd spoken eloquently of the cooler's importance, leading them to
believe it held a human organ, harvested and ready for transplant, and that its
safe arrival was a matter of great urgency. Although he'd gotten confused and
said at first it was a liver, switching midstream to 'an adult kidney,' no one on
the crew seemed to notice.

"Keep it in sight at all times," Patronas stressed. "It's a matter of life and
death."

After seeing the boat off, he headed back to the station, where he released
Maria Georgiou on her own recognizance. He ordered her to return to her
room in Skala and stay there, a kind of informal house arrest that he prayed
would mollify Stathis, should he learn of it. She'd cried and kissed his hands,
thanked him again and again.

Evangelos Demos said he would keep an eye on her or assign one of his
men in his place, if he were unavailable. The Bechtels were also confined to
their house and would not be leaving Patmos tomorrow as planned. The
victim's body was not going to be released from the morgue in Athens, Stathis
had informed them, or flown back to Stuttgart anytime soon. Everything was
on hold, pending the outcome of the investigation, including their departure.
If they tried to leave Greece, he'd have them arrested. His boss had made good
on his word. Gunther Bechtel had been irate, but Stathis stood his ground.

With nothing to do, Patronas, Tembelos, and Papa Michalis drove to
Lampi, a beach on the northernmost part of the island. Nearly deserted, it
extended a long way and was framed by an ancient lava flow, the movement of

the molten rock still visible on the hillside above. The beach itself was covered with pebbles. Of volcanic origin, they were vividly colored—filigreed in places with quartz and agate—and glistened like gemstones along the water's edge.

The owner of the taverna reported that Lampi had once been famous for the pebbles. Unfortunately the tourists had taken away so many that the local government, *Demos Patmou*, had been forced to post a sign forbidding their collection.

"You should have seen it before," he said.

The epitaph of modern Greece, Patronas thought sadly. There it was in that one sentence: 'You should have seen it before.'

They ate at the restaurant, sitting at a table next to the sea. Called Lampi Taverna, the interior was decorated with sea shells and fishing nets, ancient amphorae the owner said he'd found when he was snorkeling. There was a strong swell along the shore, the waves tumbling the rocks over and over, grinding them against each other. It was a soothing sound, the water rushing forward, only to pull back again a few minutes later.

After inspecting the fish on display, Patronas selected three *lavraki*—sea bass—and asked the owner to grill them and serve them with *ladolemono*, a sauce of olive oil and lemon. In addition, he ordered fried *gavros*—anchovies—and a half kilo of the tiny pink shrimp from the island of Symi. He also invested in a kilo of wine. If the priest was still hungry after the meal, he could, as the farmers said, 'go shear himself.'

"When do you think we'll hear from the coroner?" Tembelos asked when Patronas returned to the table.

"Tomorrow, maybe. Cat was small. It shouldn't take too long to cut it up."

"Which one do you think killed the old man? The boy or the girl?"

"The girl. Boy was too young for that level of violence. Whoever did it damned near broke the old man's skull in two."

"Spontaneous, you think? *Grobpapa* said something and the kid went crazy?"

"Maybe, maybe not. The cat indicates premeditation. My guess is that she was practicing, getting ready to take on the old man."

After lunch, they drove back to Chora. Papa Michalis had requested the trip, saying he wanted to visit a local shrine, Panagia Diasozoy. The church was said to possess a miraculous icon of the Virgin that answered penitents' requests, and he wanted to pray there.

The sun was low in the sky by the time the three of them had climbed up to the chapel, a terraced hillside at the center of the village. The courtyard in front was paved with red and white tiles and enclosed by a decorative wrought-iron fence. A row of palm trees towered over the church, which was very old—a dark frescoed space that smelled of incense and candles, the icons on the walls so blackened with smoke as to be barely visible. The face of the Virgin had cracked over time, and the whole of it was overlaid with silver and draped with offerings—bracelets and necklaces, even an old-fashioned wristwatch hanging from a gold chain. Patronas wandered around outside while Tembelos and the priest wrote their requests on the slips of paper provided. He couldn't think what to ask for, what his prayer should be. An end to his loneliness, maybe, or a woman. Neither seemed worth the Virgin's time.

Restless, he walked back to the parking lot to wait. Dusk was settling over the island, and he sat down on a bench and watched the lights come on. The wind continued to howl and there were birds everywhere, plummeting downward on shafts of air like aerialists in a circus only to rise up again a few minutes later.

Far out to sea he caught sight of a small triangular island. He wondered if it was inhabited or empty—if he and the island were the same, both of them passing their nights in solitude, alone in the water. The bus from Skala was making its way up the mountain toward Chora, sounding its horn as it disappeared around a curve, only to reappear again a few minutes later, its headlights playing across the darkening hillside.

Patronas heard Tembelos and Papa Michalis coming toward him, their voices loud in the stillness. Getting to his feet, he dusted himself off and unlocked the doors of the Jeep. He wasn't looking forward to spending another night at the hotel with them. Papa Michalis inevitably left his dentures in a glass of water by the sink, food particles swirling around beside them, and prayed for hours on end before getting into bed, reciting what sounded like most of the Bible. Worse was Giorgos Tembelos, who snorted and squealed in his sleep like a pig being castrated. Truth was, he was tired of their company. Tired of being driven around by Giorgos or Evangelos, tired of always feeling crowded.

He went swimming later that night after the other two turned in. The moon was full and he followed the path of light it cast as if on a road, splashing toward it through the spangled water, pretending to catch the light and pour it over himself. They said if a girl was born under a full moon, she would always be beautiful. Although it had been a long time since his birth, perhaps the moon could still work its wonders. Turn him into Adonis.

Laughing, he continued to pour water over himself. He'd read about phosphorescence and how it set the sea on fire. The Aegean was like that tonight, alive with light.

He hummed a song from his youth as he swam back to shore. A beautiful song about a woman setting her hair free and letting the wind take it. It always made him think of mermaids, that song, the way their hair floated on the waves in the storybooks, swirled around in the eddying water—a vision of loveliness just out of reach. Something he'd always assumed was imaginary, but might not be ... like love.

ANTIGONE BALIS WAS sitting outside in the dark when he returned to the hotel after his swim, and they drank a glass of ouzo together. Wrapped in a towel, he'd initially wanted to go upstairs and change, but she'd waved him off.

"*Iremise*," she said, laying a hand on his wet leg. Relax.

She lit a candle and they sat there talking while he dried himself off. She said she knew an isolated beach where they could go swimming together, just the two of them, *au naturel*. *Gymnos*—naked—in case he missed the point.

"Any time you'd like, Chief Officer," she said in a husky voice, raising a fleshy arm and smoothing her hair back. It was a practiced move and made her breasts more prominent.

Patronas watched her in the candlelight. A reflex, that hair thing was. Like one of those female baboons with the scarlet asses, who bend over every time they see a male.

She was sort of a sexual wind-up toy, Antigone Balis, far too old for the role she'd assigned herself—that of a siren, a temptress. Sitting there in the moonlight in her low-cut dress, she was in desperate need of—what was the word?—a makeover.

She was his for the asking, he'd come to understand, loneliness driving her, same as him. But he was old enough to know gifts from a woman like that were never freely given. Inevitably, there was a price tag. If he was lucky it would only be a tearful phone call. Worse would be her turning up in Chios with a suitcase. Neither of which he wanted.

Better to be like the birds he'd seen in Chora, soaring out across the sky at twilight, unencumbered, save for their need for food and rest.

"I'll let you know about the swimming," he said.

Chapter Twenty-Six

———◆———

When the wolf grows old, he becomes the clown of
dogs.
—Greek Proverb

THE CORONER CALLED early the next morning. Patronas was eating his breakfast when his cellphone rang.

"You find anything?" he asked

"I must say, you surprise me, Patronas," the coroner said. "Shipping me a cat and asking me to dissect it. Haven't done that since I was in medical school. Those specimens were in far better condition—latex in their veins, smelling pleasantly of formaldehyde instead of decomposing flesh. Still, your boss, Stathis, was very persuasive when I called police headquarters to inquire. He insisted I do an autopsy on it as soon as possible."

The coroner continued to talk, as always unwilling to be rushed. "As you well know, I have limited resources these days—I didn't see how a dead cat could possibly be relevant to a homicide—but I did as Stathis instructed."

He shifted some papers. "The cat was in a state of advanced and pronounced decay, and I had to work around a lifetime's worth of maggots— at least a a hundred per square centimeter by my estimate—but the results were revealing."

Patronas pushed his plate away. The coroner always spoke at length and in great detail about things other people found disgusting. Maggots, for example, at seven o'clock in the morning.

"I found a human fingernail lodged in its throat and I extracted it. No need to ask, I already submitted it for DNA analysis. As the nail was painted, I doubt it was left there by a vandal, who as a general rule are adolescent males, local adolescent males—Greeks, in other words. I know that was the theory at one point, that a local youth had killed the cat because the family was German, but you will have to revise that now. No, I suspect the person who left the nail was a female—probably well under forty, given the color—and she was the one who strangled it."

"What color was it?" Patronas asked, the phone pressed to his ear. "Orange? Was it orange?"

"You must be clairvoyant. Yes, as a matter fact it was." The coroner made a derisive noise. "A bright metallic orange."

Patronas ended the call and sat there thinking.

"Well, now," he said.

"YOU SURE ABOUT this, Yiannis?" Tembelos asked as he parked the car.

Patronas nodded. He and Tembelos were riding in the front seat of the Jeep, Papa Michalis and Evangelos Demos sitting in the back. The four of them had driven to Chora almost immediately after receiving the call from the coroner.

It being early morning, the streets of the village were deserted, a handful of dead leaves scuttling across the pavement. Hopefully no one would see them lead her away in handcuffs. A small mercy, that.

Patronas had called Stathis as soon as the coroner's call had come in to tell him what he was planning to do and line up the necessary paperwork to make an arrest.

"She's only sixteen years old," Stathis had said. "What possible motive could she have?"

"He sexually abused her."

"So he came to Patmos and brought his perversion with him?"

"Something like that."

An old fashioned Greek, the priest had been fighting a losing battle since the trip to Epirus to understand the facts of the case—how a human being could do such things to children.

"She was innocent, poor child," he kept saying.

"I don't know, Father," Patronas said. "She beat his brains in and carved a swastika on his forehead."

"Nonetheless, she was the victim. You need to remember that when you question her."

Patronas was sorry now he'd come to Patmos, sorry he'd ever gotten involved. The whole case had been an exercise in futility. No matter what the girl confessed to, no matter what evidence was presented, no judge in Greece would convict her, not after they learned her tragic history. In all likelihood, she would get off. It had all been for nothing. Evil had indeed existed and an adolescent girl had dealt with it. Case closed.

"What about her father?" the priest asked.

"I'm assuming he doesn't know. He spends a great deal of time in Africa, seems to have removed himself from the day to day life of the family."

"And the mother?"

"The same. I fear it will be a great shock to them."

"It's a tragedy any way you look at it. The old man is dead, and her life is ruined."

"It was ruined before. It was ruined the first time he laid a hand on her."

Today she was dressed in a lacy skirt that barely covered her ass and had painted her nails a new color, dark purple, the color of plums. She was wearing more makeup, too, her eyes rimmed with kohl and silver shadow, the same dark red lipstick on her mouth. The first time he'd seen her, Patronas had thought she'd been experimenting, using the makeup to try out different personas, but now he believed it was a much sadder thing, a mask.

He and Papa Michalis were sitting with her in the garden, not far from where the body had been found. He'd chosen the site carefully, wanting to control what happened. Gunther Bechtel had objected to the interview, saying he wanted to sit in on it, but Patronas had insisted on doing it alone, in part to spare him. Bechtel would find out eventually what had transpired between the girl and his uncle—no reason to bring such grief into his life today.

"It's only a preliminary interrogation," he'd said, "nothing formal. We can either talk to her here or take her down to the station and talk to her there. You can get a lawyer for her if you want. It's up to you."

Choking with rage, Bechtel had reluctantly agreed to let them interview his daughter, Hannelore, at the house and had left them alone with her.

Patronas positioned Tembelos at the gate and Evangelos next to the side entrance, the half door where Maria Georgiou had put out the trash, thus effectively sealing everyone inside the compound. He told both men to wrestle Hannelore Bechtel to the ground if she tried to escape and to keep the rest of the family away—the Bauers, too, should they wander out.

He'd already explained the procedure to the girl, set the tape recorder out on the table and turned it on. He'd discovered an old one at the station and brought it with him, planning to give the MP3 player back to Bechtel after they had copied what was on it.

The girl laughed when she saw the tape recorder, amused by the dated technology.

"What's that?" she asked, acting like the whole thing was a joke.

"A tape recorder."

"It looks old."

"It is." He'd installed the new batteries before coming and checked to make sure the spools were turning.

She watched them spin for a moment. "What do you need a tape recorder for?"

"To record what you say."

She studied her nails. "What if I say stupid things?"

"Then it will record you saying stupid things."

"Why do you have to do it today?" she complained. "I was going to go to the beach with Hilda. It's our last chance before I leave for Stuttgart. Now there won't be time."

Her English was better than Patronas', and she was speaking rapidly. He had to struggle to keep up with her.

"First of all, you are not going to Germany any time soon," he told her, "nor is anyone else in your family."

"But my father said—"

"Hannelore, we need to talk to you about your *Grobpapa*. Are you aware that he was in the Gestapo and served in northern Greece?"

"You want to talk to me about the *war*?" She sounded incredulous.

"Yes," Patronas said. "Did your grandfather ever speak about that time with you?"

"No, but I knew what he was. I knew all about him. He told me he knew how to hurt people, that he'd learned in the war and I better be good when he looked after me or he'd hurt me. Hurt Walter." Hannelore Bechtel reported all this in a bored monotone.

"He was also a pedophile. Do you know what that is?"

She shifted in her chair and her features hardened. Patronas could almost hear the door slamming shut. "What does that have to do with me?"

"He raped some children in Epirus during the war, worked his way through a village called Aghios Stefanos, targeting six- and seven-year-olds."

Getting up hastily, she bolted, but Patronas went after her and grabbed her by the arm. "Sit," he ordered first in English, then in German, dragging her back to the table. *"Setzen Sie."*

After she'd complied, he resumed the interrogation, speaking in a calm, steady voice. He could feel her tension. She was like a young horse, shying away from what he was about to tell her, desperate not to hear it, to be gone.

"It was a great secret in the village. People often have secrets, don't they, Hannelore? A Greek boyfriend like your friend, Hilda. Families can have secrets, too, and yours does, doesn't it?"

"No, we don't, not my family." She'd returned to her nails, chewing on them pensively.

Patronas didn't feel good about cornering her. "You were like those children in Epirus, weren't you, Hannelore? He raped you, too."

"I don't know what you're talking about," she said, her voice rising. "He was my grandfather and I loved him. It is disgusting what you say."

But her voice was unsteady and she wouldn't meet his eye.

"How old were you when it started? I'll bet it was innocent at first. He'd stroke your arm. Maybe run a hand under your clothes. Then one day he did other things to you, unexpected things that hurt."

"Shut up!" She put her hands over her ears. "Leave me alone!"

"Did he try again on Patmos? Is that why you killed him?"

"I didn't kill him."

She wasn't denying the abuse now, only the murder.

"Maybe it was Walter he was after and you tried to stop him." Papa Michalis was sitting at the table between them, playing the role of protector, as he and Patronas had discussed on their way to the house. "That would have been an honorable thing to do, Hannelore, to protect your little brother. No one would blame you if that's what you did."

She studied him for a moment. "It is true," she said, her German accent becoming more pronounced. "I saw him with Walter. The same games. *Grobpapa* was old and feeble, but he was touching him the same way he used to touch me. He said everyone did what we did. It was even in the Bible. 'Where do you think all those people came from?' he told me once. 'They all slept together.' Only he didn't say 'slept,' he said, *sie fickten einander.*" They fucked each other.

It was interesting to watch, the way the memory aged her, made her look older and coarser than her years.

"We never did it, if that's what you're thinking. He couldn't, not unless he took those pills men take, the ones that make you hard. But oh, how he wanted to. Every time we were together. You could see it in his eyes."

"When did it start?"

"When I was the same age as those kids in Epirus. My parents were away, in Africa. I don't really remember. There was a woman who came in during the day, but at night it was just the two of us. Walter wasn't born yet and I was alone with him. He took my clothes off and touched me all over. Night after night he'd come into my room and grab my hands and make me rub him, poke at me with his fingers. He was old and trembly and his hands would shake. 'Hannelore,' he'd say. 'Hannelore.' Like I was a lover, not a child. I didn't understand what he was doing. All I knew was that it hurt. Sometimes he'd unbutton his pants and make me put my mouth there. He liked that the most."

She stared off in the distance. "I'd wash myself after, but it didn't matter. I could never get clean, never get rid of the smell of him. It was like his hands were still on me, but invisible. No one could see them but me. I started cutting myself when I was older. It felt good, like I was finally getting free of him.

I would have peeled my skin off if I could. He hurt me and then I started hurting myself. Funny, huh?"

"The Japanese have a custom," the priest said with great gentleness. "When someone wrongs them, they go before that person and cut their own stomachs out."

Hannelore Bechtel contemplated this, then, nodding, made a fist and drew a circle around her stomach. "I told him to stop. But I was only six and he didn't listen to me."

"What happened then?" the priest asked.

"My parents came back and he quit for a while. Later *Grobpapa* told me it was my fault, what had happened, that I'd liked it and wanted it. I was a slut then, he said, a little slut, *eine kleine schlampe,* and I was a slut now. I would always be a slut. *Schlampe, schlampe, schlampe.*"

"Did he say this on Patmos?"

"Oh, yes." Her voice rang out. "It was after Walter went back to the house. We were in the garden and I told *Grobpapa* to leave him alone or I'd tell my parents what he'd done. He just laughed at me and told me I was imagining things. 'You're always making things up,' he said. 'You don't know what the truth is—you lie so much. I would never do anything to Walter or you.' 'But you did,' I said. 'For a long time, you did.' 'Lies,' he said. 'Lies.' *Lügen.* He was stroking the cat when he said it, rubbing its fur with his fingers."

"Is that when you decided to kill the cat?"

She nodded. "It was nothing, just a dirty stray. I don't know why he cared about it."

"How did you kill it?"

"I choked it. I wrapped my fingers around its neck and shook really hard. Back and forth, back and forth." Her eyes gleamed as she relived the moment. "It was small and it didn't take long. It kept twisting and meowing, trying to get away from me."

She dropped her head down onto her shoulder, imitating the way the cat had looked after she snapped its neck. Laughed out loud in an ugly way.

"I wanted to hurt *Grobpapa.* Hurt him the way he hurt me. I was big now, and he couldn't do anything to me anymore, but it didn't matter. He wouldn't leave me alone. All the time talking about it, using his filthy words. Whenever we were by ourselves, he'd start. 'You had such a sweet little body,' he'd say. Like it was something good we had shared, a happy memory." The girl's voice was thick with disgust.

"What did you hit him with?"

"I didn't. I know you think I did, but I didn't."

Dry eyed, she stared at him defiantly. "I'm glad he's dead, but it wasn't me. I wasn't the one who killed him." She repeated this several times.

"Who knew about the two of you?"

"Nobody, not for a long time."

"Why didn't you tell your parents?"

"I don't know. Like I said, he told me it was my fault and I believed him. 'It has to be our secret,' he said. 'Otherwise they'll send you away. Girls who do these things are bad girls. You're a bad girl, Hannelore.' I hated him," she said, almost as an afterthought. "He was always there. I couldn't get away from him. When I had a friend over, he'd sit and watch us and sometimes the front of his pants would get wet. I tried to tell my mother about him once, but she waved me off. She was in her room putting on a dress, a ruffly dress for a party. She likes to do that, my mother. Likes to make herself pretty. She isn't interested in me, in what I have to say. She never sees anybody. Only herself in the mirror."

Her anger had been growing as she spoke, had taken on a life of its own. It was a like a presence sitting with them at the table.

"Is that why you killed him, Hannelore? Because no one else would help you?"

"I didn't kill him," she said again.

"You said no one knew for a long time. Does someone know now?"

"Yes. My mother."

"When did you tell her?"

"The day I saw him with Walter. The day he died."

"So you confronted him in the garden." Patronas was seeking to establish a timeline for the murder. "What happened next, Hannelore? Did you lose your temper and hit him with something? You're a strong girl, an athlete. It would have been easy for you. Or did he lose his balance and fall and you finished the job?"

"I didn't touch him," she said. "Don't you understand? I couldn't."

Suddenly, the door of the house flew open and Gerta Bechtel came running out, screaming her daughter's name. Tembelos tried to stop her, but she pushed her way past him.

"Hannelore! What's going on? Your father said the police were talking to you! What's this about?"

"The stupid cat. The one those Greek boys killed."

Hannelore Bechtel was far more clever than he'd originally thought, Patronas suddenly realized, and possessed great presence of mind.

A wily, manipulative creature, she'd been only too willing to admit to killing the cat when it was just the three of them. She'd reveled in it even. He remembered the joyful expression on her face. But now that her mother was here, she'd quickly set about deflecting the blame. The swiftness of the change was remarkable; her face actually seemed to grow younger as Patronas watched—her voice to take on a more girlish tone as she lied—and the transformation hadn't been to spare her mother's feelings. Patronas was certain of that. It was because Hannelore was an evil, calculating little bitch. She needed her mother to keep her out of jail.

"Oh, Hannelore," Gerta Bechtel said.

"He says because I killed it, I must have killed *Grobpapa*. He's mean, Mommy. Don't listen to him."

Ignoring the outburst, Patronas continued to speak. "And then you tried to frame the maid, didn't you, Hannelore? It was you who cut the swastika on his face. As with the cat, you wanted us to think a Greek was responsible."

"Hannelore," Gerta Bechtel said, tears running down her face. "I will talk to them. Go back to the house."

The daughter dutifully got up from the chair and started toward the house, looking back at her mother once or twice. The expression on her face was unsettling. She looked triumphant.

"It wasn't Hannelore," Gerta Bechtel said after her daughter had disappeared inside. "It was me. I killed him."

Reaching for Patronas' cigarettes, she pulled one out of the pack.

"Take your time," Patronas urged, lighting the cigarette for her. "Start at the beginning and describe what happened."

"I heard them fighting. Hannelore was yelling, '*Ich hasse dich!*'" I hate you! "I reprimanded her. You mustn't speak of your grandfather that way,' I said to her. 'You must show respect.'"

Her voice was sardonic, self-mocking.

"Respect," she said bitterly. "You must show *him* respect."

"Where was your husband? Surely he must have heard, especially if your daughter was shouting."

"Gunther had just come from Africa, and he was exhausted. He was asleep maybe. I don't know. Anyway, inside the house. Walter and Maria, also."

Gerta Bechtel hesitated, as if seeking a different ending to the story. "Hannelore, she told me I must keep Walter away from *Grobpapa*. '*Schmutzig*,' she kept saying. '*Schmutzig*.' Over and over. Dirty. Dirty. My daughter, always she says ugly things when she's angry—ugly, ugly things. Gunther's uncle, he soiled himself once at dinner. And this is what I thought she meant. That he was dirty from shit."

Patronas believed her. There was nothing false in her demeanor.

"I told her she must not speak this way of him, 'He is very old,' I said. 'He cannot not help it.' It was then that she told me, told me what kind of dirty he was."

The bruises on her face were still pronounced, especially around her eyes. She looked drained, so exhausted she could barely speak. *Another victim*, Patronas thought as he listened, *another ruined life*.

"I have lived with that man almost my entire adult life. Ever since the day we got back from our honeymoon. At first it was all right. I didn't know his history and it was acceptable, but then we moved. Gunther wasn't there. He was in Africa, and I had to pack myself. We had a closet under the stairs and there I found a box. Inside were many things from that time, a uniform and some photographs, a diary from when he was in Greece. I read what he wrote. It was all about the Gestapo, full of bragging. I asked him about it later that day, thinking it must be a mistake, that the things had belonged to someone else, but he told me no, no, the things in the box were his. He said he was proud of the way he'd served Germany and kept the Jews from taking over. Proud to have been a *Scharführer* in the Gestapo."

She looked over at Patronas to see if he understood the term. "After that, whenever it was just us, he would speak about those years. He was always very crude and it got worse as he got older. I remember once he lit two paper matches and put them on top of each other, laughing at the way they writhed and twisted as they burned. '*Wie die Juden,*' he said."

"Like the Jews," Patronas said, and she nodded.

"Gunther told me to ignore him, that he was an old man and didn't know what he was saying half the time. But he did—you could sense it, see it in his expression whenever there was something about Israel on the news. He was still a Nazi; he had never changed. Blacks were *Untermenschen* because of the shape of their heads, he'd say, as if it were science. 'Racial pollution is corrupting us.' And the way he spoke about the Jews ... I was so ashamed, so ashamed to have a man like that in my life, to have him in the lives of my children. My family, we were different. My father was a school teacher, a gentle, peaceful man. He despised the Nazis."

She smoked in silence for a few minutes, watching Patronas.

"Go on," he urged.

"You cannot understand. You are not German." She shook her head. "You cannot understand the shame of those years. What we did as a people. Gunther spent his whole life making up for it. Going to Africa to work off the sin. He, too, was ashamed. All the young people of my generation were, and then to have to live with it morning, noon, and night. To have it sitting in my kitchen, talking about the war as if it had been a good thing ... but I loved Gunther and I made a kind of peace with it. 'He is my husband's uncle and I should respect him,' I told myself."

She looked back at the house, as if searching for her daughter. "We had trouble with Hannelore always—much trouble. She was not obedient. It is important, respect for parents in my country, but Hannelore, she was not respectful. Unhappy always. I didn't know what was wrong. I should have guessed, but I didn't. I overheard Gunther's uncle talking to her once in

Stuttgart. He was trying to grab her hand and she was pushing him away. 'You were friendlier when you were little,' he was saying. 'You liked to touch me.' It seemed a strange thing to say to a child, but he was like that, and I told myself I was imagining things. I should have known. The signs were there, but I didn't want to see. This is my fault. Mine, mine."

She started to cry. "Hannelore. Oh, God, Hannelore. My little Hannelore."

Patronas was watching her closely, convinced she was confessing to the murder to save her daughter, as a kind of penance.

"It wasn't so hard to kill a man, I found out. I pushed him out of his chair and hit him with a shovel, once and then again. He deserved to die. I only wish I'd killed him sooner. I only wish he was still alive so I could kill him again."

HANNELORE LATER ADMITTED she'd cut the swastika on the victim's forehead after her mother had gone back inside the house.

"It was my idea," she boasted brightly to Patronas, proud of what she'd done. "I wanted people to think a Greek had done it. I knew how they felt about us. In Athens, there are swastikas everywhere. It was no big deal. I'd cut myself before. I knew how to cut."

Pulling up her shirt, she showed him the scars, a grid of striated white lines running across her abdomen.

"I don't do it anymore, but I used to a lot. Not just there. Other places, too. He bled a little when I did it, which scared me. I mean, he was dead, so why was he bleeding? It was like he was a vampire or something."

PATRONAS HANDCUFFED BOTH Hannelore Bechtel and her mother, unsure who he should charge with the murder. He'd let the prosecutor sort it out—a jury, when the time came. He and Tembelos had found the shovel mixed in with the rest of the tools in the back, but it had been washed clean. Again, Hannelore had seen to it. It wouldn't reveal much. They were unholy collaborators, the girl and her mother, the girl carving a swastika on a dying man with a knife while the other washed his blood off her hands.

'En psychiko vrasmo,' their defense attorney would say in court, a plea acceptable in Greece. They acted while their souls were boiling.

One final question. "Your husband beat you up, didn't he?" Patronas asked Gerta Bechtel as he settled her into the back of the car.

"Yes. I told him about his uncle, what he'd done to Hannelore, and he went crazy. We are sad people, Chief Officer. Gunther, atoning for what his uncle did in the war. All those years in Africa. Never seeing what he did to us, what he did in our house."

Patronas didn't know what to do with the information, whether to charge

Bechtel with domestic assault or not. In the end, he decided to let it go. Gunther Bechtel had not emerged from the house during the interview, nor had he shown much interest when Patronas knocked on the door and told him that he was charging his wife and daughter with murder.

"You need to find someone to stay with him," Papa Michalis counseled, worried that the man would take his own life. Evangelos Demos had done what he could to safeguard against such as possibility, alerting the Bauers and finding a man on the force fluent in German to sit with him. He called a man from his office in Germany who had worked with him in Africa and summoned him, saying it was imperative that he come.

PATRONAS VISITED MARIA Georgiou in her room later that night. "It was you who burned the candles, wasn't it? Scattered the flowers over the body?"

"Yes," she said simply. "It was important to me."

"Why? You hated him."

"It wasn't for him, if that's what you think. No, never. I was grieving for *me*, for the girl I'd been. With his death, that part of my life was over. All those feelings, I could finally let go of them, bury them alongside him. After the massacre, I was always alone, always a stranger. There was no one I loved or who loved me. And I wanted to cry for that child, for the little girl who got left behind in Aghios Stefanos in 1943. Who was unlucky enough to live when everyone else had died."

"Where'd you get the candles?"

"They were on a shelf in the kitchen. The flowers, I found in the garbage. Mrs. Gerta had bought a bouquet a few days before and thrown them away. Carnations and lilacs. She said her daughter, Hannelore, always loved the carnations."

A tear ran down her face. "I didn't mind that the carnations were old and brown. It seemed right to throw dead flowers on him."

PATRONAS STILL WASN'T sure who'd actually done the killing, but he was betting it was the daughter, Hannelore Bechtel. Even at sixteen, she was an unsavory creature, had nearly torn the head off a cat. Seventy years before, she, like her *Grobpapa* before her, might have served in the Gestapo. She seemed to have the calling.

CHAPTER TWENTY-SEVEN

———◆———

Better to be envied than pitied.
—Greek Proverb

A s the boat for Piraeus wasn't leaving until after midnight and there was
nothing left to do at the station, Patronas, Tembelos, and Papa Michalis
spent the day in Grikos, a village to the south of Skala.

A nearly perfect circle of sunlit blue water, the Bay of Grikos was
breathtaking. A narrow strip of land led out to a pyramid-shaped rock on the
far side.

"Kalikatsou," the priest called the rock, saying hermits had once inhabited
it, carving out caves, chimneys, and staircases in the sandstone. "It's named
for the birds, the *kalikatsoudes*, cormorants, that nest there. Supposedly, there
was a temple dedicated to Venus on Kalikatsou in ancient times. Archeologists
think the caves might be older, might even be paleolithic. People say the place
emits a strange energy."

At first the priest had declined to accompany them to the beach, saying it
wasn't seemly, a man of the cloth sitting in a lounge chair under an umbrella,
but he'd finally agreed to join them.

On the ride to Grikos, he'd spoken of the mythological origins of Patmos,
reading from a pamphlet he'd discovered in the hotel lobby. "Supposedly the
island was once submerged, existing at the bottom of the sea, until the moon
goddess, Selene, cast her light on the ocean and revealed it."

"The moon goddess, huh?" Patronas said, remembering his nightly swims.

"Yes, she convinced the goddess Artemis to raise it from the sea, and they
enlisted Apollo, who convinced Zeus, and it was done." The priest spread out
his arms to take in the island. "*Voilà*, Patmos."

Patronas thought that if he ever had cause to leave Chios, he might take
up residence on Patmos, buy a little apartment and swim every night, keep the

moon goddess company. He had come to love the island.

The sand of Grikos was very fine, the beach lined with gray-green tamarisk trees. The old government hotel, the Xenia, was now in private hands and stood in pristine splendor at the center of the cove. A few boats were tied up at the dock in front and there was a taverna called Stamatis a little farther down.

Happy with the outcome of the case, Evangelos Demos had invited them to a celebratory dinner at his house that evening. He hadn't come to the beach with them, saying he needed to stay home and help his wife with the preparations.

Patronas had already spoken to Antigone Balis and checked out of the hotel. After the meal at Evangelos' house, he and the others planned to board the ferry and leave.

He was still working on purifying his tongue. They weren't taking a *vapori* to Piraeus, he'd told Tembelos, as the word was of foreign origin—Italian, he believed. They would instead *tha epivivastoume eis to ploion tis grammis*—experience the art of travel by boat.

These exercises gave his speech a stilted quality, Tembelos informed him, and were becoming very tedious.

"Milas san daskalos," he said. You sound like a teacher.

It was a grave insult. Maybe his language purification program wasn't such a good idea.

HE HAD DECIDED to forgo the pleasure of swimming naked with Antigone Balis. Playing Adam and Eve at his age was a perilous idea. Already rusty, his man parts might well lock up and stay that way permanently.

"I wanted to thank you for the lunch you made us," he'd told her when he paid the bill. "It was delicious, especially the *keftedakia*." He kissed his fingers like a Frenchmen. *"Magnifique!"*

He'd spent some time preparing this little speech, even going so far as to practice the hand gesture, the *magnifique* in front of the mirror. Although it was a violation of his Greek protocol, he liked the sound of it. He'd wanted to strike exactly the right note, a little show of worldly sophistication. *Cary Grant,* he was thinking. *Manly, but beguiling.*

"You're welcome, Chief Officer," she said. "Anytime."

If not her, then another, he told himself.

He was on his way. Women were fifty-two percent of the population of Greece. Sooner or later, he'd find one.

Tembelos and he had discussed it as they lounged in Grikos that day, and his friend had offered to introduce him to his cousin, a thirty-five-year-old named Calliope.

"What does she look like?" Patronas inquired. Tembelos, much as he loved him, was an exceedingly homely man. It was said on Chios that given Patronas and his friend's appearance, homeliness must be a requirement to join the force. One had to be a runt to be a cop on Chios—a runt with a big nose.

"She plays the piano well," Tembelos said of his cousin.

Greek shorthand for 'ugly as sin.'

She was newly arrived from Crete, Tembelos went on to say—another strike against her in Patronas' mind—and was looking forward to meeting people. "She's a good girl. Sturdy."

Yes, the world was full of possibilities, Patronas told himself. Him and a Cretan whale. Sure, why not?

Tembelos waded into the sea. "Come on, Yiannis!" he shouted, splashing him with water.

Patronas stumbled in after him. There were women everywhere, marvelous women swimming in the water all around him.

A woman in a red bikini was doing the breast stroke. She caught him eyeing her and smiled.

He smiled back, feeling better than he had in ages. Perhaps a woman like her would find her way into his bed someday, his heart even. Anything was possible. In the movie about his life, Stephen Hawking had said, 'Where there is life, there is hope.' Hawking knew better than Papa Michalis. He was smarter.

EVANGELOS DEMOS LIVED not far from the police station, in a large second story apartment overlooking the harbor. He opened the door when Patronas rang the bell, a brown haired boy clinging to him. The child was about eight years old and wearing a gladiator's helmet. It appeared to be historically accurate, the helmet—bronze-colored with sculpted ear flaps and a plume of feathers five centimeters high.

Patronas crouched down next to him. "What's this?" he asked the child. "Are you going to reenact the Persian War?"

"I made it." The boy rapped the side of the helmet with a knuckle. "See? it's made of papier mâché. I copied it out of a book. It took me a long time."

His name was Nikos, he said, and he had just turned nine. Patronas and Giorgos Tembelos spent most of the evening playing with him, while Papa Michalis sat in the kitchen and talked to Evangelos and his wife, Sophia.

The child had a plastic sword and they grabbed wooden spoons from the kitchen and pretended to fight with him, battling their way from room to room, shouting like musketeers, while the boy's grandmother, Stamatina, chased after them with her walker, yelling at them to stop.

Nikos' vocabulary was very childish, far too young for his age, and he kept repeating the same words over and over again in a wooden monotone. He didn't seem to understand what was being said to him and would look at Patronas blankly whenever he spoke to him.

Patronas thought he might be deaf and asked Evangelos about it when they were alone in the kitchen.

Evangelos' shoulders sagged. "No, it's something else. We took him to the doctor and he said Nikos will never grow up in his brain. No matter how old he gets, he'll always be the same, a little boy. There is nothing we can do."

Having no children, Patronas had no idea how it felt to raise a mentally challenged one. It must be hard, especially here in rural Greece, where people weren't always kind to the less fortunate, weren't always patient with those who couldn't keep up.

No wonder Evangelos was eating himself to death. He wished he'd been kinder to him.

Grabbing his spoon, Patronas stomped back into the living room. "Come on, Nikos!" he shouted, thwacking the boy's sword with his spoon.

It was the best he could do. At least tonight, he's see to it the child had fun.

AFTER HEARING EVANGELOS Demos complain about his diet, Patronas had been afraid his wife would serve them *vrasmena,* boiled crap, for dinner, but the meal she'd prepared was wonderful: a roast leg of lamb and little roasted potatoes, a savory zucchini pie with a homemade crust, and a multitude of appetizers—everything from stuffed vine leaves to artichokes in the style of Constantinople, lemony and redolent of olive oil. For dessert, there were spoon sweets, tiny nectarines and cherries, and *revani,* a cake heavy with honeyed syrup.

The four of them toasted one another, laughing and congratulating themselves on solving the case.

Patronas joined in, although his heart wasn't in it. Theirs had been a pyrrhic victory at best, like that of the king in Epirus whose victory had been tantamount to defeat. What had been gained by solving the case? Nothing. He, for one, wished they'd never gone to Aghios Stefanos, never learned what had been done to those children in the cellar.

When it came time to leave, Evangelos' son grabbed him around the waist and wouldn't let him go.

"Kneel," he kept insisting, tugging at his pants.

After Patronas got down on his knees, the child tapped him on his shoulder with the little plastic sword. "Arise, Sir Yiannis. Go forth from this day and do good."

Evangelos walked down the stairs with Patronas. "King Arthur is one of his favorites," he explained. "I read it to him every night. He knows all the words by heart."

He touched Patronas' arm. "Come back and see us sometime, Sir Yiannis. It was good having you here."

Touched in spite of himself, Patronas called Stathis after he left and asked that Evangelos Demos be reassigned to his precinct in Chios. "I need more men. There's a lot of crime now in the bars along the waterfront."

Stathis, pleased with the outcome of the case—the person of interest being a German national—readily agreed. "Sure, take him," he said. "I'll put through the paperwork. He can start immediately. I'll even kick in a little for moving expenses."

Overhearing the conversation, Tembelos raised his eyebrows. "Evangelos Demos, a burden to the earth and now, yet again, to the Chios Police Department. You're getting sentimental in your old age, my friend."

"Boy will do better on Chios," Patronas said gruffly. "There's a school for kids like him there and I know the principal. She's a good woman. She'll see that he gets the help he needs."

A GROUP OF GREEK college students were sitting on the quay waiting for the ferry. Accompanied by an older man with a bouzouki, they were passing around a bottle of wine and singing 'Strose to stroma sou gia dyo'—Make your bed for two—a song from Patronas' youth.

The ferry was delayed and the kids continued to sing, one Greek song after another. Then a pair of them got up and began to dance. The others quickly fell in, forming a line and moving in a circle across the cobblestones, singing as they danced, their feet flying.

The sight of them filled Patronas with joy. The song was by Theodorakis, and the dance they were doing was one of the most popular in Greece. Those were the steps Zorba had taught his friend on the beach at the end of Kazantzakis' novel. They were immortal in Patronas' mind. More than five thousand years ago, his people had come to inhabit this sunlit land. It was theirs then. It would always be theirs.

We tried being European, the kids seemed to be saying as they danced, and it didn't work out for us, so let us be what our parents were and their parents before them. Let us be Greek.

Patronas joined the dancers a moment later, breaking into the circle and grabbing the hands of people on either side of him. He couldn't remember the last time he'd danced, his wedding maybe, and whistled loudly as he spun around and around. Tembelos entered the circle a few minutes after him, leaping high in the air and touching the soles of his feet with a hand when his turn came to lead. On and on they danced, the crowd growing more and more frenzied as more people joined the circle. Soon there were so many, it was impossible to contain them, and they danced on into the square, pushed the chairs and tables back, and formed a ring around the blue fountain, shouting and laughing.

As inevitable as rain, trouble came. But just as inevitably, one day it departed.

Nodding, Patronas continued to dance.

His homeland would endure. These kids would see to it.

L ETA SERAFIM IS the author of the Greek Islands Mystery series, published by Coffeetown Press, as well as the historical novel, *To Look on Death No More*.

She has visited over twenty-five islands in Greece and continues to divide her time between Boston and Greece.

You can find her online at www.letaserafim.com.

Made in the USA
Middletown, DE
24 September 2015